OF HEADLESS HOLLOWS

OF HEADLESS HOLLOWS

THE VAN TASSEL WITCHES

KILLIAN WOLF

ISBN: 978-1-951140-23-6

Copyeditor: Lindsey - zeroalchemy.com
Cover design: Logan Keys - coverofdarknessdesign.com
Formatter: Michael Davie - grimhousepub.com/plans-pricing

Content warning

This book contains depictions of medieval torture and brutality, graphic sexual content, and discussions of sexual assault, and suicide. Reader discretion is advised. Read at your own risk.

"Rise, Hessian. Thou shalt rise and suffer the agonies of a thousand deaths until my bidding is fulfilled."

Chapter One

KAT

THEN

I WAKE to a thunderous gallop and pull my covers just above my nose, not daring to move an inch. The horrible moist feeling under my nightgown and the lingering smell of cigars sickens me to my stomach. But I shove the thoughts down deep inside like I always do.

A horse seems to have stopped right in front of my window.

I hold my breath as a shadow looms over my bed, its silhouette an odd shape, as if with broad shoulders...but no head attached. I squeeze my eyes shut, pulling the sheets completely over my head.

Calm down, Katalina.

This can't be the horseman. Or not the headless one, at least. He's a fib, unreal, a tale told to us to keep us safe and afraid.

I let out my deep breath slowly. It's just my eyes playing tricks on me in the dim light. It's likely the constable making his rounds. Nothing more.

The horse clops into a gallop until it continues away from my bedroom window.

Grabbing my pendant, I sit up and peek out through the glass. The mist is high above the frost-ridden yard, but there are no signs of a horseman anywhere. Whoever it was, he's gone now.

I can't remember when I fell back to sleep, but it was a shriek that woke me. And once again the trotting of a horse. At first, the rhythm of it brings me comfort to know someone is out there protecting us from whoever has been committing these murders.

The squawk of a bird followed by the rustling of leaves and heavy footfalls make my eyelids shoot open. It sounds like someone is grunting loudly. It's a man's grunts, and he's running.

Could it be Percival out there? But he would be on horseback. What would he be doing running through my wheat field? The fumes in my hearth have simmered down. No, it can't be Percival this late in the night.

Someone out there needs help, and I may be the only one to hear them.

Grabbing the candlestick on my nightstand, I plant my

feet on the cold wooden floor. Silently, I hurry outside to see what's going on. If someone's in trouble, they may need my help, but I'm careful not to wake a soul in the house. If it's just the Nightward, there won't be any use in waking up the whole manor.

Outside, the mist swirls above my ankles as the wind blows.

"Katalina... Please...help me..."

My father's voice sends cold dread down to the pit of my stomach, and I still. He's the last person I want to see right now. But what on earth is he doing outside? I squint through the darkness and find him halfway down in the wheat field.

"Katalina." He reaches a hand for me as he starts to run toward me.

I don't move.

"Come back inside." my mother's ghostly voice whispers with the wind.

"Mother?" I gape at her as she appears by the door, but just there, down the wooded road, past the house is a black steed with the figure of a man sitting on its back.

A cloak sways behind him, and in his hand, he carries an ax.

Time stops, and I forget to breathe as the man with the ax...

He's headless!

"Katalina." My mother's voice sounds eons away. "Back inside now. There's nothing you can do for him..."

The horse's eyes glow crimson as he gallops directly toward me. My knees buckle, but I can't move. The horseman rides fast, so fast that it takes everything in me to budge, but it's riding past me before I realize who he's after.

Then my legs start to work. I spin around to see my father taking aim with his musket and firing. I freeze as the shot hits the horseman right in the chest.

He seems to brush it off, and his horse surges forward.

I gasp and swallow a scream as my father takes off deeper onto the farm, away from the horseman. I don't even know what I can do, but I can't think straight. All I know is the horseman is after my father. For a brief moment, I wonder if I should let the horseman take him.

I shake away the vile thought and begin to sprint after him. I can't let him die by the horseman. Not like this.

"Father!" I call out.

My father stops and turns, fear-stricken as he spots me. He aims his musket at the horseman and shoots again. This time, the horseman falls off his horse.

"Kat!" My father starts running toward me, and I reach to grab his hands.

The horseman is still off his horse. If we can get back into the house and lock the doors, perhaps we can wait out the night. Perhaps I can give him my necklace, and it will protect him.

I reach toward him. "Come, Father! A little more!"

He stretches his arm out for me, panting hard.

Behind him, I catch a glimpse of the horseman climbing back on his horse. The relentless beat of the horse's hooves overwhelms my ears. Before my father can grasp my hands, the horseman comes up beside him and swings his ax.

I scream as my father's head flies off his neck. I fall to the ground as blood spurts in many directions, some of it landing in my mouth.

Tears stream down my cheeks, and my hands shake.

My father's head bounces off the rocky soil as the cigar comes loose from his lips, and rolls toward me. It stops at my knees. His eyes stare back at me, widened with horror, and his tongue sticks out from his mouth. The image implants in my mind forever.

The horseman comes back around, and my hands are glued to the ground. As he approaches, I dare look at the empty space above his black-on-black suit.

It's almost as if he turns in my direction and sees me. The horseman pulls out his sword. I wince when an explosion of cracking bones and a squish deafens my eardrums as he stabs my father's head, picking it up. Then he leaves me here in an empty field with my father's headless corpse.

My mother plants a cold hand on my shoulder, and I start to weep.

Chapter Two

KAT

NOW

"The Hessian mercenaries," my nana explains to Claudia, "are rumored to be hideous fiends with sharp, ragged teeth."

I drop my gaze down to Claudia, our house maid Tilly's scared eight-year-old, who is staring at the dancing shadows of candlelight on my nana's pale face.

Normally, I'd protest about scaring the young child, but perhaps this is best in order to keep her safe and tucked indoors.

Daniel barges inside the manor at the same time a thunderclap makes me jump. My hand falls over my coat pocket where I have hidden a pistol. A pistol that I stole and shoots silver bullets.

I was already on edge with Nana bringing up the Hessian mercenaries.

"Lock the doors." He grabs his chest, panting.

Nana stands, and her ashen face looks that much more ghostly in the dim lighting.

"What's all the commotion?" she asks, and it takes me a whole minute to realize she's talking to me.

I open my mouth to speak, but I have to stop myself from gagging. The metallic taste of blood still lingers on my tongue. No matter how many times I've scrubbed it with charcoal, no matter how many times I've soaked my linens, I can't get the stench of my father's blood away from me.

And Nana knows I've hardly spoken since that day.

"It's the Hessian," Daniel answers for me, his chestnut hair sticking to his forehead as he tries to wipe it dry. "The horseman has been spotted. The council has ordered everyone to stay inside."

I suck in a breath as my pulse quickens. This is enough to get my muscles moving.

The horseman has returned. This is my best chance.

I wait until Nana leads Daniel into the kitchen and offers him some tea as the rest of the housemaids bustle around to lock all of the doors. Then I tiptoe toward the front door and thrust it open.

The rain comes down in sheets, but I do my best to roll

my shoulders back and steel my nerves. Just as I'm about to step off of the front porch, a hand catches me by the shoulder and yanks me back inside.

"What are you doing?" Daniel's brown eyes bore into mine, and another burst of lightning illuminates the gold flecks dancing in them. "Didn't you hear me? The horseman has been spotted. You're going to get yourself killed."

"I have to go." I yank my arm free. "This could be my only chance."

Daniel studies me. "You're not going out there alone, Kat," he says firmly. "I won't let you."

"You can either fight me or come with me," I tell him. "You don't understand. I saw him that night."

"Yes, I know you did... We all do—"

"No, I mean before he took my father... I saw his silhouette in the window. He'd been watching me, Daniel. He'd been watching us, and he's not going to stop until he kills everyone in Sleepy Hollow. He's out there now, and to wait will be to offer up someone we care about."

Daniel's face is pale, but he knows I'm right.

"You're mad, Katalina. Why must you do it? The Nightward is out there right now, hunting the Hessian down—"

"They can't kill him. You know it has to be me. And you know why!" Rain patters down my face, but I don't care that I'm getting drenched. "Were you just appeasing me with all your talk about the wooden maiden? Or about the gun with the silver bullets?"

"I... No, of course not. But we haven't exactly planned this out well either, have we?"

I uncover the silver gun and hold it so it shines under the moonlight.

He gapes at me. "Is that my father's gun? Have you absolutely lost your mind?"

"Perhaps I have." I tuck it away again under my coat.

Daniel's father has a taste for collecting items of lore, always hoping they carry some superstitious value.

"I nicked it after you showed it to me. One silver bullet to the heart of the horseman. That's all the legend says it'll take."

"If he even has a heart, Kat. It is a legend, not fact."

I ignore his rationale. "And your father's wooden maiden?"

"In the abandoned home my father hides it in. But Kat..." He lets his words linger in the air. He knows nothing he'd say to me will change my mind.

I search his long face. Worry marks indent his forehead.

Daniel and his girlfriend, Edith, have become good friends since I moved to my parents' hometown after my mother died, and my father decided we needed to take care of the farm. To the town, I am odd—someone who talks to herself and draws dead things. But Daniel and Edith are kind to me, or perhaps they're both odd too.

"I'm sorry," I say. "I have to go. I'm doing this with or without you."

"Wait." He steps into the rain. "What kind of a friend would I be to let you go on your own?" he demands. "What if you end up like your father?"

"Then we're wasting time." I step off the stoop.

Daniel sighs but follows suit.

The wind whips around me, trying its best to push me back toward safety, but I refuse to give in to its demands.

"We must make haste," I urge him as I tack up my horse when we reach the stables. "It might be too late."

There's a crispiness to the air that makes my nose hurt. The harvest is a cold one this year. A thin layer of frost sits over the fallen leaves of the walnut trees as the rain finally, mercifully, tapers into a drizzle.

Daniel shakes his head from the stall next to mine. "No, we would have heard of a death if it were. He won't tire until he gets what he wants."

"Who do you think he's after?" I glance at Daniel.

His eyes are wide, and his face is pale. He's frightened. Of course he is. He'd be mad not to be.

My mother stands by the open stable, a disapproving scowl contorting her face. She can't stop me, so she hasn't bothered trying to reason with me anymore.

"I haven't the slightest idea what he's after, but we'll soon find out. We'll take the shortcut through the hollow grove toward town. That way, we'll be close to the Andre tree and will be able to hear his horse."

Once we're mounted on our steeds, we take off out of Van Brunt estate and down the desolate road. I lean my body forward, avoiding getting my hair caught by the ghostly fingers of twisted branches. My wet strands tap against my cheeks as Mistletoe gallops just a few paces behind Daniel.

We pass the ivy- and lichen-covered mausoleum of the cemetery and ride through the oak grove where decorative pumpkins align our path, now getting wet in the rain. We slow once we arrive at the Andre tree, and I stare up at the large, dead tulip tree with gnarled limbs.

My pulse thuds in my wrists as I glance in every direction. "Which way did he go?"

Angry hoof-falls stampede into the ground nearby, and we gallop forward. A chill runs down my spine. Why hasn't he crossed our paths? If he were meant to kill someone in town, he'd have come our way.

Unless...he's headed to Van Brunt estate.

My blood runs cold.

I squeeze Mistletoe in the flanks. She rears and whinnies but presses onward.

I crane my neck and shout to Daniel, "He's after Nana!"

"How do you know?"

"Who else lives that way? He hasn't come to town!"

We shouldn't have left.

Daniel gapes at me and urges his horse onward. We

gallop at full speed through the forest and into the manor grounds.

There, on top of the hill overlooking the Van Brunt house, is a black steed, exactly where he was before he murdered my father. Only now, I'm behind him.

Mistletoe stops abruptly and backs away with a violent shake of her head. Coward horse.

She stumbles back, and I struggle to gain control of her reins.

"Kat!" Daniel cries out, the horseman mere feet away.

Mistletoe sits on the ground, and I slide off her and land on my rear with a thud. I look up just in time to see the horseman's torso turn and appear to be glaring at us. Mistletoe speeds off into the forest.

"Kat, now!" Daniel yells.

The demonic beast upon which the headless fiend rides fixes its beady red gaze directly between my eyes. I gasp in terror.

Does he recognize me?

I push to my feet and fumble for the pistol. The horseman charges toward us.

"Daniel, go! Get away from here." My words tremble as they leave my lips.

Every minuscule muscle inside me screams to run, but although my fingers shake over the hilt of my pistol, I hold my ground. The horseman is coming, and I'm going to kill him.

I aim straight at his chest, close my eyes, and pull the trigger. The shot goes off, and my ears ring.

Daniel yells something at me, and I gasp, dropping the pistol. I open my eyes just in time to see the horseman fall off his horse. The sound of his body hitting the ground echoes through the air like a boulder.

Time slows. My hands shake.

"You did it." Daniel is now on his feet and shaking my arm. "Well done, Kat. You shot him. You shot the Headless Horseman."

My heart pulses hard in my throat. I did it. I shot him. That's truly the horseman. And he's on the ground. The horseman's steed no longer has glowing red eyes, and he's running far past us, leaving his rider in the cold frost.

"He's not dead, remember?"

"Right."

"Quickly, before he gets up." Daniel dashes forward and grabs the Hessian fiend by the shoulders.

"Wait," I say.

Daniel looks up at me, puzzled.

"Take his weapons."

"Good idea." He seizes the ax and sword and flings them aside.

I peer into the headless neck, but instead of gore or entrails, there is only darkness, as if a black shadow conceals whatever lies within.

"How long do you think he'll be out for?" I dare to ask.

He gives me a weary look. "Have your pistol ready."

He secures the horseman's body to the back of his horse with a length of rope, and then we both mount our steeds. I keep my finger poised on the trigger, prepared to shoot should he begin to stir.

Although I have only a single silver bullet, I'll continue to fire regular rounds until I am out, hoping the silver will prove as effective as the legends suggest.

His body jostles over rocks, roots, and whatever else may be hidden beneath the leaves.

Good. If he's still alive, I hope he feels every bit of that and that it causes him great pain.

We arrive at the abandoned cottage, and I dismount from Daniel's horse and make my way cautiously to the horseman. Daniel and I grasp him by the armpits and drag him inside the cottage.

"He's deadweight," I say.

"That's a good thing, isn't it?"

"Are we certain the silver bullet didn't kill him for good?"

Daniel stops and stares at me.

"Never mind. You're right. We want to be certain."

Daniel pries open the wooden maiden and then helps me prop the horseman's body inside it. His body is cold to the touch as I place my palms upon his muscular chest under his garment.

I'm trembling. I can't believe my hands are on the

horseman, and at any second, he could awaken from his immortal sleep and choke me with his fists.

With a deep breath, I press forward until I feel and hear the sharp points of the torture device piercing his torso. Letting go, I take a step back and grab the door. The horseman's torso hangs a bit low from his weight, but I shut the door before he can fall out. It slams with a satisfying thud.

"We must go," Daniel says, rising from where he has kindled a fire in the hearth.

He turns to seize the torch and lights it. We both hurry outside, but before he can turn away, I stop him.

"Wait, let me," I say.

He searches my eyes and then hands me the torch. "Katalina, you truly are different."

Out of the corner of my eye, I catch sight of my mother's ghost standing there, arms crossed but a smile gracing her face.

"I know." I lift the torch to the thatched roof above me, then dash to the opposite corner and do the same.

With a determined heave, I throw the torch as hard as I can into the house. We step back and watch as the cottage ignites and burns.

A smile threatens my lips, and I have to bite down hard to keep from letting my thrill be known.

Perhaps it's the taste of victory. Or how close I came to death tonight. But something about this night jolts me with electricity. Either way, I must contain myself. The night's not over yet.

As the fire blazes and the roof falls in, we back away and mount Daniel's horse. Just as we are about to leave, I stop him.

Firelight illuminates his face as he turns to me. "What's wrong?"

"Do you hear something?"

"Do not be frightened. I have spent much of my life working at the morgue. The sounds you hear from the corpse when it is ignited are merely the gasses escaping from the organs."

"Not gasses..." I say nothing more, but I swear it sounds as though a man is screaming in agony, as if his very soul is on fire.

But...that's preposterous, isn't it? He has no head, and moreover, how could such a monster possess a soul?

Chapter Three

KAT

I WISH everyone would just go away and leave me alone. It's been seven full days since my father's untimely death. Three days since Daniel and I killed the horseman.

My mother wraps her cold arms around me. I sit so far from the fireplace that her icy touch only makes me feel colder. Still, I don't move. I've been staring at a chipped spot on the wooden floor for what feels like hours, trying my best to ignore the chatter around me.

So much blood.

My father's wide, glossy stare.

The Hessian.

I'm still waiting to wake up from this dreadful nightmare.

"Maybe he'll turn up," my mother whispers in my ear.

I give her a slight shake of my head so no one sees me talking to myself. Not now.

This isn't the time for people to think I've finally lost my wits. Not when they're discussing who will inherit the farm and whether I'll marry, just a few feet away from me, right after everything that has happened.

I'll admit I did consider whether my father's ghost would turn up; it would be the worst kind of nightmare.

My stomach tightens into a knot, as if a sinister force has a firm grip on it. The thought of my father's ghost appearing at his own funeral awakens some sort of dark, malevolent spirit.

Henry's ghost came back to his wife, missing his head. While others talked and his wife cried over the casket, I pretended not to see him, even though I could. Later, I sketched him in my notebook before bed—it's the only way to keep him from haunting my dreams.

But that was the baker, someone I hardly knew. My father is the one person I dread seeing, and I'm over-whelmed with guilt because of it. I should be crying, especially in front of all these people, but instead, I'm just numb.

"Who found her?" A voice I don't recognize cuts through the chatter.

"Percival," another voice answers.

I barely know half the people standing in my home.

"He was badly injured when he reached the field and saw what had happened. He was brave enough to try and stop the horseman, but the demon wasn't after him. I still say Percival's lucky to be alive."

"The poor dear," someone says, and I can feel their eyes on me. "She'll be here alone, with no man to protect her. She should marry soon."

My fists clench at my sides at the thought of marrying, but I keep my head down. This is hardly the time to voice my disdain for matrimony.

We're sitting in the parlor of the Van Tassel house, and I've barely made eye contact with anyone. Poor Nana sits in the rocking chair beside me, her eyes swollen from crying, too stunned to speak.

What am I ever going to do with her now? Moving away and leaving her like this would be cruel. I have no choice but to stay in Sleepy Hollow.

"Has anyone spoken to Percival, then?"

Now my ears twitch. I do hope he's all right. Though I can't stand his womanizing stare and would never consider marrying him, I don't want the horseman to take his head.

"Stricken with grief that he couldn't catch the Hessian, but who can? The horse is a demon from hell. An immortal. There is no stopping him. All we can do is pray."

I catch my mother's gaze. There's a knowing look in her eyes but also fear. She knows what Daniel and I did the other night, but after three days with no more deaths, I'm beginning to think we're finally safe. Finally free from the constant fear that anyone could become a random victim at any moment.

"She'll have to marry Percival now," a lady remarks. "At her age, she'd be fortunate to have him, especially since she won't be able to manage the Van Brunt manor all on her own."

"Or perhaps it should go back to being the Van Tassel estate now," I say, my voice barely above a whisper.

The woman gasps, clutching her drink tightly in response.

Ignoring her sharp stares, I return my gaze to the floor. My mother's ghostly arm once again attempts to wrap itself around me.

"Ladies, could you please ensure that everyone has a nice hot cup of tea?" Daniel's warm voice comes near, but I don't look up. He drapes a blanket over my shoulders, and I grasp it as my mother's ghostly arms release me. "You looked cold."

"Thank you." I glance up at him.

"I just wanted to give you my condolences." His voice is almost a whisper.

His eyes linger on mine, and I know he's searching to make sure I haven't lost my mind since the other night. I give him a tight smile.

"Not here," I whisper. "We'll talk later."

It's a miracle that we both managed to survive what we did and live to tell the tale, though we wouldn't dare speak of it to anyone. I'd be accused of witchcraft merely for having defeated the horseman, not to mention the scandal of a woman restraining a demon.

But at least we have each other, even though we haven't spoken since that night.

Daniel's gaze shifts to Edith by the fireplace, who holds a cup of tea. Her eyes are full of sorrow as she gives me a small, hesitant wave.

"Go to her," I tell him. "I'll be fine."

He gives me a hesitant look, but I urge him to go with a nod. As much as I care for Daniel and Edith, sometimes I feel like she's jealous of my and Daniel's friendship. And now is not the time for any of that.

Love is a setup for betrayal. There's no such thing as true love—it's a fairy tale we pretend to believe, only to have our hearts broken when someone betrays us.

But I'd never voice this opinion. It pains me to think Daniel may be one of those men who uses a woman until he needs to marry someone else, but he probably would. They're all the same.

Just before Daniel leaves, Virgil, the town notary and a friend of my father's, approaches us.

"Your father was a good man," he says, resting a hand on my shoulder. "Ignore the rumors. Brom was a good man."

That sinister claw around my stomach tightens.

Rumors. The only reason I ever cared about the rumors was because they'd run us out of town. It was becoming a witch hunt. Though I knew he wasn't the horseman, I do not believe my father was ever a good man.

Not that any man is ever entirely good. I remind myself of this daily, as a way to stay focused on becoming a stately woman on my own, without marriage.

"What will they say now that your father's gone? Did this really need to happen to prove to them that he was not the horseman?"

I offer him a tight smile. "Yes, what will they say now?"

I glance to the right where everyone stands, staring at me and Nana. When my gaze falls on the closed casket, I quickly look away.

Daniel and Edith watch me with concern, their faces etched with worry. I turn my attention back to Virgil, wishing he would leave.

"My wife baked you a pie," Virgil says. "I've left it with the housemaid. She thought you might prefer some solitude and not have everyone talking over your head."

"She's right."

His forehead wrinkles, and he gives me a nod. "We understand. I'll leave you alone, but please...if you need anything at all, please let me know."

"I will. Thank you."

Not a minute after he leaves, Henry's wife, Agnes, approaches me, her face hidden beneath a black shawl. I notice Daniel and Edith stepping closer, equally surprised by her presence.

Agnes has been silently observing us since her

husband's death, without uttering a word. She clutches a kerchief in her hands. She moves closer, grabs my hands firmly, and places the covered object into my palms.

I stare at her, my mouth agape and my tongue caught in my throat.

She leans in, her eyes wide with fear, and closes my fingers around the object she gave me. With a furrowed brow, she hurries away into the cold.

I unwrap the cloth carefully and find bones, likely from a dead crow or some other small bird, half bloodied. I grimace and quickly rewrap it to keep it hidden from view.

I glance up at Daniel, whose face is pale and his mouth agape. Edith starts to approach us, but he gestures for her to stay back. Confusion crosses her face, but she retreats to her place by the fireplace.

"A witch, that one," Daniel whispers to me. "Has to be."

I stuff the bones under my seat to get rid of them later. I don't want my father's funeral to become a muck. "Yes, it was odd. But best not to speak of it to anyone. Not here. Not now, at least."

"Of course. I'll leave you to it, then." He quickly walks over to Edith, presumably to discuss the strange occurrence.

I am left alone for only five minutes before the next person approaches me.

"Do you need anything, dear?"

It's my housemaid, Jane. Behind her, Percival stands holding a drink with a girl beside him, her cheeks flushed as she blushes at something he's just said. He meets my gaze, his expression a mix of sadness and defiance, as if to say now I'm his to claim.

"Yes, actually," I tell my housemaid.

"Anything."

"For everyone to leave me alone."

Surprise flashes across Jane's face, but she quickly turns to face the parlor, where guests are still eating and drinking, deliberating over my future.

I rise and walk over to my nana, whose eyes are puffy. I reach down to help her up. "Come, Nana. Let's get you to bed."

She allows me to take her frail hands as I assist her. Her bony frame makes her seem so vulnerable, and I can't help but feel a pang of fear for her. She's the only person I have left. She's lost her only daughter, and now her son-in-law.

I guide her to the stairs and glance back. "It's been a long night. Jane will see you all out, but I must retire my nana and then get to bed."

I leave the guests to their own devices and tuck my nana in.

Then, standing at the edge of my room, I stare out the window, imagining the horseman stopping outside. Every time I close my eyes, I see it happening over and over. I just want to fall asleep and escape it all.

Hours pass as I toss and turn. The house has quieted

because everyone must have left. The housemaid came in once to check on me and bring some leftover bread, but I pretended to be asleep.

My mother sits in the corner of the room, silent and watchful. I know she's worried; now that she and my father are beyond the grave, there's little she can do to help. But securing my future has always been my responsibility. I'm not concerned about that—I'll find a way.

Pulling the sheets up to my knees, I reach for my sketchpad hidden in the bed and begin to draw by the dim candlelight. I move my fingers over the page, shading the Andre tree with its thick, twisted bark casting crooked shadows across the grove.

I recall the night I defeated the Hessian. I did it. I kept my town safe. Not Percival. Not the police. Not even my father. It was me.

So why do I still feel this unease?

Days ago, anger began to seep in. At first, it was denial —a nightmare, surely. How could a headless spirit emerge from beneath a tree and murder my father before my eyes? No, it must have been my imagination when I saw his head swing and land at my knees. It couldn't have been real.

But it was.

And despite a part of me feeling relieved to be freed from my father, I knew deep down that the horseman had to be stopped—stopped and sent back to hell.

My village, Nightward, didn't understand the threat they faced because none of them have ever dealt with the supernatural. None of them have the courage to confront the dead. They're scared, and their fear will only slow them down, make them hesitate, and put them in danger.

It had to be me to stop the horseman so that he could never kill another of my friends in Sleepy Hollow again.

The tip of my pencil breaks, and I startle awake, letting my sketchpad drop to the floor. I drift back to sleep, only to be woken by the sound of trotting.

At first, the rhythmic sound reassures me, and I think someone in town may be out there guarding us from the horseman.

I pull the sheet up to my chin, trying to fall asleep again. But as the trotting turns into a gallop, my eyes snap open.

I watched him burn. The Hessian is dead.

A horse stops right at my window, and a shadow seems to loom over my bed like it did seven nights ago. I press myself against the edge of my bed and the wall. Moonlight trickles in through the cracked window, giving off a silver ambiance over the hardwood floor.

The horse clops into a gallop until it continues away from my bedroom window.

Grabbing my pendant, I sit up and peek out through the wooden pane. The mist is high above the frost-ridden yard, but there are no signs of a horseman anywhere.

I relax back into my pillow and allow my eyes to close.

The Hessian is gone. I made sure of it.

A loud banging sound from downstairs makes me jump to the corner of my bed. I gasp, clutching the sheet. Nana! I need to get to her.

My feet hit the cold wooden floor, but just as I reach for the door handle, another loud thud echoes through the door.

I gasp and pull my hand back.

The banging resumes, this time with metal striking through the wood. I stagger backward and scramble to my bed, trying to escape through the window. The pounding grows more intense, faster, more forceful.

The cold wind whips through my hair as I cling to the windowsill, staring down at the thick mist covering the frosted ground.

Behind me, the door shatters with a loud crash as an arm bursts through. A large figure, dressed in black, forces his way in. His torso is facing me, and he's headless.

The horseman has come for me.

There's no time to consider how this is possible. I swing one leg over the windowsill, my heart pounding in my throat as I try to convince myself to jump.

The headless figure moves swiftly toward me, and with a deep breath, I let go.

A scream tears through the air as I plummet to the ground. I land on something large—with hair, and with my legs straddled on either side. Pain sears my thighs and groin. A horse grunts, and I scream, realization taking place when I see his glowing red eyes peering at me.

I jump off the horse, my legs too unsteady to support me. Terror grips me as I watch the horseman land on both feet outside my window.

I stumble backward, struggling to get to my feet, while he looms over me, his headless form towering menacingly. He grabs my neck, lifting me up. A black void inside his neckline is the last thing I see before nausea overwhelms me and unconsciousness takes hold.

The sound of the horse's trotting is the only thing I hear. I open my eyes to find myself clinging to the horse, the freezing wind numbing my nose and fingertips. I struggle to make out my surroundings—twisted, dead trees line a long path covered in dead leaves.

Rows of heads mounted on poles line the path, stretching as far as I can see. I nearly choke on my own breath as I realize the horseman is sitting close behind me, guiding his horse onward, taking us to hell.

I dare to look behind me at the headless horseman. His hand grips my neck once more, and a cold wave of dread washes over me, quickly followed by sleep.

Chapter Four

KAT

I'M jolted awake by a cold draft. The sound of drizzling rain outside stirs me, but my vision is blurry as I reach for my bedsheet. My wrists are abruptly cut by something metal and cold.

I gasp, eyes widening as I try to sit up, only to be yanked back, a metal contraption constricting around my neck. I dart my eyes around, desperately trying to see what's holding me in place, unable to move.

A pained scream escapes my lips as memories flood back—the banging on the door, the grove of heads.

I was taken in the night. By the horseman.

Goose bumps erupt along my spine, and my pulse quickens. I scan the room, my vision adjusting to the dark, greyish surroundings. I tug on the metal chain across my lap. I'm strapped and chained to a garrote!

Panic surges through my veins, making my breathing rapid and shallow. I'm here, in the horseman's...house? Dungeon? Whatever this place is, I'm a prisoner, restrained by a garrote. Tears well up at the corners of my eyes.

It appears to be an empty cabin. A dried hearth is on the opposite end to the right of the door, smoke rising from it as if it has just gone out. Cobwebs hang from the corners and crevices, and an empty table by the hearth has nothing but dust and an empty bowl at its center and a shut cupboard on top. A thick film of dust layers the entire cabin.

Then my gaze falls to what's right in front of me. I'm not sure why I missed it at first. Sometimes I miss large things that are in front of me. It's another table, but on top of it are various torture devices—an ax, a whip, chains, different knives and blades, and a pike.

My breathing picks up, and my gaze lingers along the shadows now, looking for him. The Hessian. He brought me here. It's a matter of time until he turns up.

A shadow of what looks like a large wheel casts across the floor to my bottom left. A sinking feeling in my gut tells me it's not from a horse-drawn carriage. If I'm strapped to a garrote, then that shadow is likely from a breaking wheel behind me.

My throat dries.

There's a dampness in the air that smells of death. I am going to die today.

I absentmindedly go to pick up my necklace, but I only yank on the chains. I stifle a gasp, and dread overtakes me.

Desperate, I start yelling for help, pulling at the chains, my neck aching from the strain. I call out for anyone—Daniel, Percival, anyone who may come to my rescue.

Heavy footsteps echo from behind me, intensifying my fear since I can't turn around to see who approaches.

A deep Irish accent drifts through the air. "Admiring my collection, then?"

An Irishman? I wish I could move my neck, but I'm stuck like this, completely vulnerable to him.

"Who are you?" I manage to choke out. "Where's the Hessian?"

"Shouting won't do you any good, love. No one'll hear a whisper from down here. Not a soul." He walks over to the hearth, and now I can see him, though only his back as he bends down to light a fire.

As he stands, he walks slowly over to the table in front of me with all the torture devices. He wears suspenders over a white shirt rolled to his elbows, showcasing Celtic knot tattoos of ravens on both arms.

I swallow a gasp as he traces a finger over each one of his tools, as if trying to select one to use on me.

"Where's the Hessian?" I manage to ask again, my voice trembling.

This makes him cringe, and he glances at me. A cruel smile lifts the corner of his lips, and he walks over. I yank on my chains.

"Who do you think the Hessian is, Katalina?"

I gasp. "H-how do you know me?"

He's standing a foot in front of me now, the dim flickering flames of the hearth backlighting him. He has dark, chestnut-colored hair pulled neatly back and striking pale-blue eyes that catch me off guard.

My heart begins to race as he unfastens a few shirt buttons, showing his muscular pecs.

He lifts his chin and pulls his shirt to the side, to show me a hauntingly deep slash reaching around his neck. The look in his eyes speaks of an unworldly terror, like he knows hell and cannot wait to share it with me.

"I know everyone," he says, his eyes lingering on me. "I've been watchin' Sleepy Hollow for a tiring long time."

He begins to refasten his buttons. My lips part.

"I don't understand... Are you one of the horseman's victims?"

A cold chuckle. "No."

The blood drains from my face. "No, you can't be... You're not..."

He tilts his head to the side, and a bored look crosses his face, as if he's waiting for me to hurry up and come out with it already. But I don't miss how his eyes trace me up and down.

"You have a head." I yank on my chains.

"Fascinating observation." His gaze dips to my chains. "You can keep tugging at those, but it won't do you any good, love. Not a bit."

"No...no...you're dead. Does that head even belong to you?" I've heard stories of demons changing their guise, but...

"Does it belong—" He grits his teeth and turns back to his table of horrors.

"They said the Hessians were deformed monsters with shaven teeth."

He grimaces, and the disgusted look deepens his features.

It *is* him, isn't it? Somehow his head has grown back like magic.

"I suppose it shouldn't surprise me that you can grow your head back, given that you're a demonic headless horseman from hell who can roam around without a head."

He ignores me as he walks around his table, his back still facing me.

"You killed my father," I spit out.

He continues to methodically pick up each weapon, inspecting it with a detached precision before setting it back down.

"What are you going to do with me now that you have me, Hessian?" I demand, trying to steady my voice.

He doesn't answer. Instead, he takes his time selecting

his weapon from the table. Finally, he chooses one and holds it up, examining the blade.

He moves his gaze to mine, and he touches the tip of the blade on the metal table, then drags it across as he slowly walks over to me. He has a grim expression on his face. Serious and unwavering.

"Answer me!" I cry out, my neck aching from being attached to this horrible thing.

Of course he would have something like this.

"Being rude won't do you any favors, witch."

My lips twist at him calling me a witch. Why would he call me a witch?

"I'm planning to kill you, but unlike me other victims, I don't intend to make it swift."

I dare open my mouth to ask him another question, even though I'm entirely at his mercy, but this question is burning inside of me. I will not show fear.

Carefully, I drag my cuffed arms up. "Why did you take me? Why not cut off my head like all the others?"

"Why not indeed..." His gaze falls to my throat, and I swallow, realizing he must be staring at the symbol on my necklace.

Perhaps it's why he thinks I'm a witch.

He lowers his head, a glint in his icy-blue eyes boring into me. "The last man who took my life met my blade right after. You're the first woman to do so again. Alas, witch, I cannot die."

I lift my chin. "I'm not a witch."

"Then you'll find my methods even more tantalizing."

My eyes widen. "I would have preferred a clean death..."

Whatever he has in store for me, I fear it is going to be cruel punishment.

A sinister chuckle leaves his lips as he places a hand behind my head on the garotte.

He leans in closer, his cold breath on my ear. "I've brought you here to show you true suffering. The torment your people have heaped upon me has been cruel and unusual for nigh on a century. Now, you'll be the one to endure the agony they've caused me. And I'll be savoring every bit of it."

He pulls the lever, and the metal around my neck tightens, constricting with a cold, unyielding grip.

Chapter Five

KAT

My esophagus closes, and my chin is forced up. My heart goes wild in my chest, and spots start circling my vision as tears fall down my cheeks. I brace myself for death.

I think of my mother, and cling to that thought. She'll be there on the other side. Waiting for me.

He lets the lever go, and the metal releases only slightly. My chest pants as I try to catch my breath.

There's a crazed look in his eyes. The bluish-gray color cannot mask the many different shades of insanity he has inside them.

He selects constraints made from metal and leather from the table and hangs them off his broad shoulder. He strides over and reaches his arms around me, but I can't do anything with my hands cuffed in front of me.

I do kick at him, though, but all he does is smile to himself, like he's enjoying this. With one fierce whip of the constraint, an alarming pain sears through both my legs, and I let out a scream. Unable to lift my legs away from the pain, I watch in terror as he ties my hips and legs.

"What are you going to do to me?" I ask as he walks back over to his table of horrors. "Choke me to death? Tie me up bit by bit?"

He selects a scythe and walks callously back over to me, every bit of his demeanor carrying the torment he intends to inflict.

"Yes," he simply states.

Raising the scythe up to my cheek, he carefully roams over my skin with the curve of the blade. I try to move my face away from him, my heart beating so loudly in my ears. I'm desperate to keep myself calm, to not show him fear.

But my eyes betray me and well up with tears. I close them, breathing hard.

The blade touches my necklace. So much for my silly necklace protecting me. I suppose it's time I make my peace with it. I don't regret trying to kill the Hessian.

A clatter makes my eyes snap open. A loud yelp escapes me as he drops the weapon to the floor, somehow changing his mind.

He strides over to me with fierce speed and leans in

nose to nose. "No one'll ever hear your screams from here." A curl of his lip, and he sucks in a gasp, his eyes meeting mine. "Don't you get it yet, witch? This is an ungodly place—me prison within the dimensions of the Andre tree."

Memories of the legends permeate my mind. How a headless horseman came out from the roots of the Andre tree to bring death to Sleepy Hollow.

I like to draw the Andre tree in my sketch pad. I like its twisted branches and the wicked shadows it casts on the ashen ground.

Now I'm being held prisoner in a place I only ever dreamed about. The memory of the long grove lined with heads resurfaces. Was that before or after he took me down the tree roots?

He reaches for my neck, his eyes roaming over me with a curious intensity that seems both inquisitive and passionate, yet tormented. He lifts his fingers as if to touch me but then lets them fall.

My heart skips a beat as I feel the weight of his gaze, studying me with an intensity that is almost unbearable.

How is he here, standing in front of me with his head intact?

Is he an immortal god of some kind?

His eyes snap to mine, and I gasp.

His breathing is deep and hard as he fixates on my throat, his fingers brushing under my chin as I swallow hard. I try to kick again, but his restraints make it impossible for me to move.

He sticks his fingers under the metal clasp of the garrote, drawing goose bumps on my skin. His fingers tighten underneath it, and when I think he's going to tighten his grip, he stops.

He sucks in a breath and takes a step back. He's about to speak when a ghostly gallop fills the air. The Hessian's eyes widen.

To my left, a rider on his horse breaks time and space as he charges out of thin air. The sound of a musket cocking right before a gunshot makes me scream.

The Hessian's head comes clean off. The smell of gunfire lingers in my nose.

The Hessian's body wavers a bit before dropping cold to the ground. The blood drains from my face as I turn to face the rider who saved me, but I gasp as the horse takes off toward the opposite end of the cabin, only to shimmer out into ghostly dust.

Another gallop has me twisting and turning in my constraints. The door to the cabin bangs open, and a large black steed with glowing red eyes appears at the entrance.

The Hessian's body stands, his clothes now fully changed into his black-on-black cloak. He turns, collects his ax from the table, and mounts his steed. He takes one turn toward me before taking off through the open door.

Good God!

What on earth was that?

The fire has gone out, and now my bones shiver, my skin rippling with gooseflesh.

Fog escapes my lips, and I wrestle with my restraints, trying to kick. I scream. Someone has to hear me. The Hessian said no one ever could, but what about the dead?

The ghost who just came and saved me disappeared shortly after. But would my mother be able to hear me down here? Or any other spirit? Or am I stuck in some corner of hell no innocent spirit can enter?

Dread overtakes me as the realization that he left me here to die, tied to this garrote, without warmth, and unable to move hits me. I scream and scream until my throat aches, and dizziness forces my eyes to close as I'm dragged out of consciousness.

I'm six years old and sitting at the top of the stairs with my arms wrapped around my knees and my head down. My parents are shouting at each other, and tears stream down my face.

"It isn't true," my mother begs. "Please, Brom, it isn't true."

"You're a despicable whore, Katrina. How dare you accuse me of infidelity when all this time you've been the one to—"

"No!"

My mother's screams shatter my eardrums, and I catch the house maiden sneak out the front door.

Fear constricts me as my father grabs my mother's arms and shoves her toward the lit fireplace. She screams and begs.

I gasp, but a hand grabs my shoulder. I stare up at my nana, who scowls at me for eavesdropping.

I fight her as she forces me up and into my room.

It's all so confusing. At first, my mother was mad about something my father did. But then he was the one mad at her, and she was scared.

Nana pushes me inside my room and slams the door shut.

My mother's screams die down into sobs. Minutes later, the door slams, and I know my father has left because my mother starts talking to someone.

"I know he's been unfaithful." Her voice cracks. "I know it."

"Yes, ma'am, but you know how men are. Hold still. Let me clean you off."

Footsteps come walking toward the door, and I run to my bed to pretend I was under the sheets the whole time. My mother walks in, a weary smile on her face.

Her gentle hand rests on my back. "Awake, are you?"

I peek from under the covers, and she takes a seat.

"Oh, Kat, promise me you'll only ever follow your dreams."

"Yes, Mama," I say, peering at her puffy cheeks. I check for burn marks, but there aren't any.

A smile tugs at her mouth. "Oh, don't listen to me, bug. Come now. Let's get you into bed."

The door hits the wall with a crashing thud. The Hessian stands at the entrance, headless, and holding a new head.

I've only just opened my eyes, my arms and legs unable to move. My body aches, and I'm cold. So very cold.

Fear constricts my throat at his presence. I thought—I hoped—he was gone for good.

But he's back. Why is he back? And holding a... I swallow a gasp. Whose head is that?

He walks over to me slowly, his heavy footsteps sending shivers down my spine. I don't even know where to look, as he doesn't have a face. Then he drops the head at my feet. I peer down at it, and then I scream.

Daniel's cold, dead eyes gape up at me. My heart rips from my chest, and I wish I could curl up into a ball and cry.

Tears stream down my face, and my screams turn to sobs as I call out for Daniel.

Even though he's gone.

The horseman took him, and now he's here to rub it in my face.

"Why?" I rasp. "Why him? Why? What did Daniel ever do to you?"

The headless horseman staggers backward, his knees buckling beneath him as he collapses to the ground.

Chapter Six

FALLON

SHE's different from all the others. But what makes her so different?

I rise from the floor, my usual neck pain aching something fierce. I give it a rub, letting out a pained groan.

Her eyes are bloodshot, and she has a horrified expression on her face as she stares at me.

I nearly kick the head I dropped at her feet and step around it to get close to her.

She shivers uncontrollably as I draw nearer. I can't blame her. To her, I am death. Worse than death, even. I am the torturer and executioner come to wreak havoc in her life and all she cares about. And she's not wrong.

"W-why kill Daniel?" she stammers out as my head grows back. "What has he ever done to you?"

I pay her question no mind and stand before her, brushing my fingers against her cheek. She winces with those pretty green eyes, but I don't care. She's a mystery I need to solve.

The truth is, I didn't want to kill this man. I've no control over who the curse chooses for me. Only after I've done its bidding can I kill of my own free will.

My gaze falls to her constraints, and I can't help the smirk appearing on my lips as she struggles to look at me.

"Uncomfortable?" I ask.

What did she think would happen to her after attempting to murder me in such a heinous manner? Death by burning, trapped in a sorry excuse for a maiden —a wooden one. I scoff, and she stares at me, unblinking.

I lift my fingers to her chest and trace the skin under her reddening neck. Such soft skin. Such a pretty thing, come to harm me.

I'd be lying if I said I wasn't the least bit turned on by her wit. Even when terrified, she still holds her ground. Like the way she thought she could save everyone on her own.

After all, I did murder her father. She probably thought she was doing something noble.

But I can't let it go unpunished. And it isn't for me to decide.

I reach behind her, ignoring her useless plea for me to let her go, and turn the lever on the garrote once. She screams, and her body convulses. Drool fills her mouth, and her chest pumps out.

I lick my lips and turn away from her, searching for my next tool to use. She sobs behind me while I grab what I need.

"What is that? What are you going to do now?"

A sigh leaves my chest. "Must you keep asking me the same question? It won't do you any good to know what's coming."

"Please," she begs.

"Keep begging me, witch. See how far that gets you."

"Please, I—" She breaks off with a sob.

I walk over to her and bend down so she can read my lips loud and clear. "You're no innocent princess, so begging me will do absolutely nothing. You're a monster, just like the countless cruel witches who have enslaved me. Your kind likes to enslave others. Now you'll be mine to toy with."

Her eyes widen, and I think she's trying to shake her head. It's kind of cute how she keeps forgetting she can't move.

"You belong in hell for being a Hessian."

I cringe at her words.

"For killing hundreds or thousands of innocents," she snaps. "How is it even that you're Irish? You joined the Germans and—"

"I was forced!" My shouts make her shake. "I was

enslaved and forced! My free will taken from me, tortured and cursed to live out this dreadful life of eternity, witch!"

She falls silent, her eyes wide and stricken with fear.

My chest heaves. I shouldn't have lost it. I don't need her to know anything about me. Only that I mean to kill her.

"You killed my father." She spits at my face, and I grimace, wiping her saliva away from my sleeve. "Whatever curse you carry, you deserve it."

I chuckle then force the leather band I have in my hand into her mouth to keep her from talking. I tie it behind her head, and her eyes bulge as she tries to fight me. With another slow turn of the lever, the garrote tightens around her throat. Tears fall freely from her eyes as she pleads in silence.

I'm unable to take it too far. Not because I don't want to, but because I am physically unable to kill her. I don't know why that is. But the urge to kill her is strong and painful, a compulsion brought to me by this stupid curse.

But I cannot complete the act. It is because she is a witch, and the only thing I can do is torture her until she dies on her own, lest I suffer in the pain this compulsion brings me.

It never goes away until I make sure my victims are dead.

Chapter Seven

KAT

HOURS HAVE CRAWLED BY, and I'm still bound to the garrote.

My neck throbs with a dull, relentless pain, while the rest of my body feels numb. I can't tell if it's the cold or the tight leather straps cutting off my circulation. Every slight movement sends a wave of pins and needles through my limbs, and my mouth aches from the leather strap biting into my skin.

I can't tell where the horseman is. He left me here to see what would "kill me first—pain or starvation," as he'd put it.

He left enough room in the metal choker around my neck to breathe because he wants to keep me alive long enough to endure this torture before I die.

Daniel's head sits on the table where the horseman has his weapons displayed, facing me with a blank, horrifying stare.

It's vile. I try my best to keep my eyes closed, hoping to escape into sleep so I don't have to look at him, but each time I drift off, a creak jolts me awake. My heart races as I brace myself, fearing it's the horseman returning to torment me again.

Poor Daniel. This is all my fault for wanting to kill the horseman and letting him help me.

A roar echoes in the pit of my stomach, and a wave of nausea rolls over me. The hunger gnaws at my insides, and I think I may throw up.

"What in hell's name is that dreadful sound?" The horseman's dark voice comes from behind me, and I startle.

My eyes struggle to focus as he moves to stand before me. His white shirt is no longer buttoned, his muscles on display. His coat is no longer on either.

I'm not surprised he can't feel the cold. He is dead, or at least I think he is.

I stare at the ink on his skin... I've never seen anyone with tattoos before. He follows my gaze to his arm.

He steps up and removes the leather strap from my mouth, and I inhale sharply and then let out a fit of coughs. I lick my dry lips and pant. My throat burns with each swallow.

"I can't sleep with these strange noises coming from this room."

"Strange noises?" I ask weakly, my head bobbing, even though it's being held up by the metal choker. "Please...I need water."

"Like a wet gurgling sound. It's revolting. Where is it coming from?" He looks around.

"My stomach?" I stretch my jaw.

A repulsed look forms on his face. "That disgusting sound is coming from you?"

"Haven't you ever heard a stomach rumble?"

His gaze narrows, his brows drawing together. "Yes. Yes, I faintly remember it."

"You've left me here for hours without food or water. Naturally, my stomach is making noises... And..." I swallow hard. "I may vomit. I am in dire need of sustenance."

The horseman's lip curls in disgust. "Fine."

He turns and grabs his coat hanging from the chair.

I blink rapidly. Is he...? Is he really going to get me something to eat? I guess since he's an immortal, food isn't a concern for him, but maybe my hungry stomach and the thought of me possibly vomiting have convinced him that I need something to eat.

"I'll sleep outside, then." He walks out and lets the door slam behind him.

I gape at the door. Of course he wasn't going to feed me. How stupid of me to have any hope that I won't starve to death here. I will die here, one way or another, whether it's from starvation or when he finally gets bored of torturing me and just kills me.

It's complete darkness now, and I'm left to go mad, not able to move or see. At least now I don't have to stare at Daniel.

I'm thankful the horseman didn't stuff the leather strap back in my mouth.

Now that I'm the only one here, the tears fall freely down my cheeks. My body shakes as I cry. From hunger. From pain. From thirst. For Daniel. For myself and my failures.

And for knowing I'm going to die. Nana will have no idea what happened to me. Perhaps Edith will assume Daniel and I ran off together.

No. They'll have found his headless corpse by now. What will they think happened to me?

Exhaustion hits me, and this time I let it drift me off to sleep.

I wake up gasping for air, my eyes flying open to find the horseman standing over me, two fingers pinching my nose.

"There she is,' he says with an insidious smirk. "I thought I'd finally killed you. But no, you had only passed out, and we can't have that, now can we?"

I catch my breath, wishing I could quench this horrid thirst.

"Why not?" I rasp. "Why wouldn't you want me passed out?"

"Because if you're not conscious, witchy, you're not being tortured."

I huff, struggling to find words, but I fall short. I'm too exhausted and weak to come up with anything.

Light trickles in through the half-covered window. Has a full day passed? The town will likely be in a frenzy, organizing a search party for me—or perhaps they're holding a funeral for Daniel first. Most likely the latter.

The horseman walks to the hearth and calls over his shoulder, "I've given it some thought and decided if I wouldn't like the sounds of your hunger, I likely wouldn't fancy the smell of your vomit on my floor either."

My pulse quickens.

"So, I have brought you something to eat."

A short gasp comes from the back of my throat, a bit of excitement pulsing through me. I'm ravenous. And I hate that I'm at his mercy and will have to accept it, even though I wish I could refuse it. Possibly throw it at his face, even though he'd punish me for it.

He comes back around, holding a plate in his hand. Some moldy-looking bread sits on top, and I can't help the tears forming in my eyes.

"What's the matter? All living souls eat bread."

"It's bad. Don't you see the mold? It'll just make me sick. I thought you didn't want me vomiting."

He scoffs. "Such a princess, aren't you? It's still good. Do you think there's a grocer beneath the Andre tree?"

"Where did you get it from, then?"

"People toss all sorts along their route, and it ends up falling down here. You won't find anything fresh down here, and I don't feel hunger. Haven't for a long time." He breaks off a piece of it and steps toward me, pushing it toward my lips.

My stomach rumbles at the notion of food, and I take a bite of it anyway.

"There now, that's a good lass." He takes a cup from the table and brings it up to my mouth.

Water soothes my dry lips, and I happily drink it all, some of it spilling down my chin. I let him feed me the rest of the bread, but I manage to stop at the green moldy bit. Luckily, he doesn't force it down my throat.

"Thank you," I say.

I thought perhaps the moldy bread was just another form of torture.

He quirks a brow, shock flickering across his features.

"I didn't know you could sleep," I say, now aware of the fact I managed to wake him by my rumbling stomach.

"Aye, it's the one thing I look forward to. Sleep."

"Do you dream?" I ask, pushing the fact that he's actually talking to me.

"No."

Keep asking him questions, Kat. Maybe he can find the humanity in me, if there's any in him to recognize it. Maybe he can untie me and let me go. Or I can escape.

He stands there, staring at me, still holding the plate and cup in his hands. His eyes are intense as he looks me up and down, his gaze searing into every inch of me.

"Something on your mind?"

His upper lip curls. "I'm enjoying studying your body. My mind hasn't drifted this far in a very long while."

My cheeks heat.

He leans in. His voice darkens with that sinister chuckle of his. "I'm having fun coming up with all the creative ways I'm going to torture you. It won't be hard to break you."

He sets the plate and cup down and grabs the leather gag from the table.

My eyes widen, and my heart starts to race. "No, please. You don't have to do this."

"Oh yes. I can't have you talking my ear off and asking so many irrelevant questions."

"Please...won't you just please...untie me?"

He guffaws. "Look who's finally remembered her manners." He walks over and taps the leather gag over my lips. "But no. I do not trust your pretty little fingers to not try and escape."

I turn my neck sharply, ignoring the pain from the

garrote constricting me as I jerk away from the gag. "I'm too weak to escape. Ple—"

The gag goes in, and he ties it behind my head.

I scream into it, violently kicking at the restraints.

Chapter Eight

KAT

MADAM CHATTAWAY'S *sneers cut through the air, her gaze fixed on me, almost as if I've somehow offended her, even though I barely know her.*

Maybe she's heard of my sketches of fantasies, such as stories of the undead. I enjoy sketching what makes us despair, to conjure our mind's most twisted desires. They call them fantasies. But they're no fantasies of mine. They're as real as the headless corpse inside that casket.

"What do you think she's staring at?" my mother whispers into my left ear, a hint of amusement in her voice.

My eyes widen, and I hold my breath for just a second before answering.

"I don't know. Perhaps it's that I'm new to this town, and there's been a murder," I mutter back. "Either way, I

wish I could leave. I didn't even know the baker Henry. This feels...awkward."

I shift in my seat.

"It would be odd if you weren't here," my mother says. "No, it looks as if she's peering right through you."

This time she says it loud enough for anyone to hear. The old woman widens her eyes, and I gape at her.

"Oh, calm yourself, Katalina. She can't hear me," my mother says.

I gulp.

"Good thing you have me here to keep you company," she says. "Especially with the horseman back."

Ignoring her fishing for a compliment, I whisper, "Do you really think the horseman is back and that he murdered the baker?"

I make the mistake of turning toward her and getting captured by her once beautiful blue eyes before her sickness took her.

She gives me a wary smile, one I'll never forget. "Do you still have the pendant I gave you?"

I touch it under my shirt, a star inside a circle, with a blue eye at the center of it. "I never take it off."

"Then you'll always be safe from the horseman." She smiles.

I frown and clear my throat, forcing myself to stare forward at the old woman.

The old hag stares at me in silent accusation from across

the parlor; she hasn't so much as glanced in the direction of the casket for the entirety of the evening.

I've forced myself to peel my gaze away from her prying eyes, no mocking smile twitching my lips in retaliation, even though it might have once been expected of me.

"Tell me, what would you sketch right now if given the chance?" My mother's voice soothes the stubborn air of argument and tension.

She always had a way of making me feel calmer, accepting me for who I am. She always told me that to find my center, I first have to accept who I am so that I can conquer with confidence.

"I do wish I had my sketchpad with me, but it would be improper."

She nudges my elbow, and I gape down at it. She normally doesn't push so much.

"I, um..." I clear my throat again. "I'm finding the lighting here mesmerizing."

Flickering candlelight illustrates mercilessly dancing demons across her face, spanning out to the parlor walls as my neighbors mutter solemnly about the deceased baker.

"I wonder if no one else notices how the shadows twist into sinister bodies over his closed casket. It's probably just me."

She smiles, this time showing her teeth. "Tell me more."

"If I were to draw this room... Let's see... Everyone will be exactly in the same position—Henry's widowed wife tight-lipped with her arms crossed, all dressed in black by the

coffin, the demons dancing over his coffin, and my father speaking to the councilmen and constable in the far corner.

"The group of people in front of the food. And Henry's ghost standing over by the grandfather clock, which has time stopped at exactly 10:03, his time of death. Only, I'd draw him with his head as I remember it. Not with his guts pouring out."

I don't know why his ghost doesn't have a head. How is it that the head of his spirit was severed as well?

My mother's eyes are beaming at me. I should feel lucky I was raised by someone who encouraged this sort of talk. All the other mothers at school would have been appalled and sent me away to live in a nunnery.

Instead, when I was eighteen years of age, my mother encouraged me to pursue my dreams instead of finding a husband. Three years later, I'm still unmarried, but I'm not sad about it.

"Oh, Kat, I am so very proud of your imagination. I do think you'll like it here in Sleepy Hollow."

Her enthusiasm makes my lips tug into a smile. "I promise to draw it when I get home, then."

"Who are you talking to?"

Dread lands in my stomach. I swallow and turn my head slowly to my father, who is walking over to me.

"And who are you smiling at?" He looks over to the side as if to expect a man standing over by the wall flirting with me.

"Um." I dart a glance back to where my mother sits, but she vanishes before he approaches.

She never stays long enough to see Father. Even though he can't see her, I guess she can't bear to look at him.

"No one," I lie. "I was just muttering to myself about the old woman who keeps staring at me."

Truth be told, I haven't smiled much since my mother passed away last month from typhoid. I'm not finding much to smile about these days. Even with her ghost popping up every once in a while, it isn't consistent enough to know she'll always be here, and I never know if and when she'll stop turning up.

But I admit it is nice to have her here speaking with me, her hair a shiny gold, her eyes a bright blue, and her skin almost glowing as if she were alive and well. Before she fell ill.

"Everyone's on edge," my father mutters as he takes a seat to my right.

Bile rises up my throat, but I suppress it down, turning my head away from him.

"Madam Chattaway is probably just overhearing the conversation between the council. There's been a murder, and I take it she most likely doesn't believe in ghosts," he says matter-of-factly. "And we just moved here. It's only natural she'd be staring at me."

"At you?" I snap him a side look. "I thought she was staring at me. It'll do her no good staring at me with those accusing eyes. It's not like I killed Henry."

Her gaze moves from me to my father.

"Looks like she's staring at both of us."

"Ignore her, Kat. She's old."

I barely knew Henry Corbett, and I'm certain I'm doomed to dream with the image of his headless corpse. So here I sit, arms crossed, avoiding the unwelcome hard stares of the mute old Madam Chattaway, waiting until it's polite to leave.

I lean closer to the edge of my seat to try and catch more of any word about the horseman, and if I'm honest, away from Father. I wish he'd leave.

A hush falls over the group as Bernice, the constable's wife, leans in closer, her voice dropping to a conspiratorial whisper. "His wife swore she saw an owl during the day—a sign of death, you know. And wouldn't you believe it, death followed soon after. His death."

One of the ladies gasps, clutching her shawl tighter around her shoulders.

"Do you really think he's headless in there?" she asks, her voice trembling.

She looks toward Henry's widow, Agnes, who stands a distance away, oblivious to the gossip.

I glance over at the gossipers as they pause, their eyes fixed on the closed coffin. A shiver runs through me. Then his wife's gaze locks onto mine—cold and unblinking. She's not crying, but I can tell she's been through enough.

When she finally looks away, I let out a sigh of relief.

Despite my parents' attempts to keep me sheltered from hearing about the headless horseman, I've always been fascinated by the legends and have sought them out myself.

I suppose I've always been drawn to the dark and unnatural, though that doesn't mean I don't want him stopped. He's taken three innocent lives, and the thought of a headless supernatural being out there killing chills me to the bone.

"Brom Bones!" An old, frail voice breaks my concentration as an elderly man walks toward us, his eyes on me.

I sneer.

My father stands. "It's just Brom now. Amos Wright, how nice to see you. I'm sorry for it to be in such unfortunate circumstances."

"Yes, unfortunate." Amos turns back to me. "I dare say, is this your lovely daughter, Katalina? You look just like your mother did. Katrina was a sight."

I offer him a tight smile and a curtsy of only my head.

"I'd like for you to meet my grandson, Percival," he says, gesturing toward a lean, brown-haired man with a perfect smile.

He's surrounded by a group of women near the food, all of them giggling at something he's said. When he notices his grandfather looking his way, Percival raises his cup in acknowledgment, but his eyes soon settle on me.

I quickly turn my gaze back to the wall, pretending not to notice.

I have no time for boys. Not when I want to make a

name for myself in the art world. My mother would be saddened if I left all that behind to get married and bear children. Not that it's something I want anyway.

Besides, is he flirting at a wake?

"She's a serious one, isn't she?" Amos remarks, his gaze fixed on me.

"Well, her mother just died," my father says grimly, passing me a scrutinizing glare before taking Amos by the arm and walking away toward the councilmen.

I shift in my seat.

"Yes, I suppose this is true," he responds, giving me a pitying look over his shoulder.

I scan the parlor for sights of my mother's return but to no avail. My gaze falls back to Madam Chattaway, her eyes not having moved a muscle. I let my shoulders drop, a soft sigh escaping my lips. Will this night ever end?

"Don't mind my grandmother." The soft voice interrupts my daydream.

I glance up at a young woman around my age, with dark-brown hair and blue eyes, lifting Madam Chattaway by the arm.

"She's senile," she whispers. "I hope she hasn't put you off."

"Oh no, no...it's fine," I say, forcing a thin smile that quickly fades back into a frown.

"I'm Edith. You must be Katalina. We haven't met yet."

Her grandmother starts walking over to the food, but Edith stays behind.

I tilt my head with polite courtesy. "I've kept to myself these days. I haven't had the chance to meet everyone in the town yet."

"How are you finding it?"

"Sleepy Hollow?" A breathy chuckle escapes me. "It's..." I swallow and glance out into the darkness. Rain has started pattering against the window frame. "Quite charming."

The corner of her lip twists upward, and she lowers her voice. "It can be sort of quirky, can't it?"

She cants her head to an argument that just started to blossom over by the food.

"What's with the stopped time on the grandfather clock?" I blurt.

I've never been one for small talk.

She darts a glance at the clock behind her. "They say it's bad luck not to stop it once someone dies. Superstitions." She rolls her eyes.

"Yes, superstitions. Seems to be a theme here."

"I don't care much for them either." She giggles. "Well, I must look after my gran. She seems to have found the pudding. It was nice talking with you, Katalina."

"Kat is fine."

"Kat, then. I work at the flower shop in the square. Do stop by sometime. Perhaps I can give you a tour of the town."

"That would be nice," I say.

She smiles sweetly and follows her grandmother.

A chair scrapes the floor, and I look over to where the constable is standing, speaking to the city gatekeeper.

"Don't start that bloody nonsense, Benjamin. Not today, especially not now."

"So we're just going to do nothing, then?"

"Do what? Hang garlic over our windowsills to ward off ghosts of legends? Hogwash."

I bite my lip and glance at my father standing behind the constable, but he isn't finding this funny.

The gatekeeper points his finger at my father and shouts, "Don't think I haven't forgotten you all those years ago. It was you. You're the horseman!"

My mouth drops open.

My father squares his jaw and takes a deep breath. "I admit in my youth I pulled some foolish pranks, but I did not kill Ichabod Crane."

My father's voice rings with authority, calm yet direct.

"Lies!"

"The horseman may not be a ghost, Constable, but we know who he is."

"Enough," Constable Felix says. "Get Benjamin out of here. This impropriety at Henry's wake? Really? Let his wife mourn in peace."

"You won't get away with this!" Benjamin shouts at my father as two men grab him by the arm and waist.

"Right, we only just moved here, so how do you explain the two murders last month?" my father calls out to him.

"From Connecticut! Some coincidence that is!"

My father has a fist up to his lips, and I know he's biting down his words.

Muttering breaks out in the room as two men escort Benjamin out of the house.

I glance over at Henry's ghost standing beside his wife.

I stand, mouth agape, as everyone's eyes shift from my father to me. I catch Madame Chattaway's gaze, her stare piercing and full of accusation.

It makes me wonder if she knows something about my family, something my father has kept hidden from me.

The strangest sensation of my throat constricting makes my eyes fling open.

The horseman is standing in front of me, his hand on the lever behind me, and a sadistic look on his face. He has something crumpled in his left hand.

"Good morning, lass. How'd you sleep?"

I scream from the back of my throat, but it comes out muffled from the leather strap inside my mouth. His smile widens, and he removes the gag. I lick my dry, chapped lips.

"Please...no," I beg.

The pain is unbearable. My entire body has been in this tight position for a day. Perhaps more. And if he constricts the metal once more, I fear my head will fall clean off.

"But we've only just begun." He turns the lever tighter, and a strained cry rips from my throat.

My voice is as ragged as a beggar's cloak.

"Had enough? Where's the book?"

I blink up at him, trying to process his words. "The what?"

"Don't give me that dumb look, witch,' he snaps. "I know you have it. Where is it?"

"Please. I don't know what you're talking about."

"The spell book," he says impatiently. "You're going to tell me where it is, and then you're going to use it."

I try to shake my head, even though I know the garrote makes it impossible to move.

He turns the lever once more, and a pained scream escapes my lips. I close my eyes, struggling to endure it.

He slaps me, making my cheek sting, and my eyes open to find him inches from my face.

"I know you're a witch. You can't lie to me because I know it to be true." He holds up a crumbled paper for me to see.

I can tell it's a ripped page from an old book because of how the edge is torn. At the center is a large familiar symbol. My eyes widen at it, and he smiles, showing his teeth.

"Ah, there. See? I knew it." He stands, smoothing the page. "Unfortunately, the history book I've found does not come with any more of an explanation except that this symbol is used by witches."

He huffs to himself then looks at me. "Whoever the unknown author of this book is doesn't want to be helpful, does he? Would you know why that is?"

He quirks an expectant brow.

My chest heaves. I haven't a clue what he's talking about. It's curious that someone would write a history book and not put their name on it

And why mention a symbol at all without any further explanation?

His gaze moves down to my necklace, and I manage to swallow the dry lump in my throat.

He bends toward my face. "If you don't tell me where you have the book that binds my curse, I will make sure you will live out your entire life in this garrote, eating moldy bread and suffering from thirst. I will decide when you die and how you die. So it's either a clean, quick death. Or excruciatingly long and painful. The choice is yours, love."

Despite the calmness in his voice, his eyes remain fierce, unhinged.

"I don't know about any book," I tell him, my voice just above a whisper.

He stands, biting out a sharp tsk behind his teeth and startling me. Then, with one swift move, he turns back to me. His hand goes to the lever, and this time he pulls it fast, all the way.

I squeeze my eyes shut, knowing this is it. I'm about to die.

A deafening clank bursts my eardrums.

A yell rips from his lips, and I open my eyes, my chest heaving and tears blurring my vision. He holds the broken lever in his hands, and his eyes are wide. Shock plasters his features. His eyes slowly narrow at me.

"Witch," he hisses.

He drops the lever on the wooden floor with a loud thud, and it bounces toward my tied feet.

The horseman rushes at me, and I gasp. I want to plead that I'm not a witch, but only a whimper leaves my lips.

The cocking of a musket makes his eyes widen, and the sound is followed by gunfire. My mouth hangs open as once again my life's been spared by the ghostly rider, gunning for the horseman's head.

His head disappears the moment it lands on the floor, and the last thing I see of it is his fear-stricken eyes.

But I don't have time to be relieved as the horseman's headless body moves toward the door, awaiting his steed. I watch in horror since I know what he's about to do, and there's nothing I can do to stop it.

Someone else from Sleepy Hollow is going to be killed tonight, and I won't know who until the horseman brings back his head.

He climbs his steed and leaves once again, and the smell of gunfire lingers in my nose.

My head drops slightly as once again tears fill my eyes,

and I'm left with a sense of hopelessness. I inhale deeply, and my neck cracks, causing me to wince in pain. But then I do it again. I can stretch my neck a little. That's odd.

I drop my gaze to the lever by my feet. It somehow broke when he pulled it all at once to kill me. I try pushing my neck forward, and the metal gives an inch. A spark of hope rushes through my blood. I try again, then again.

The lever breaking must have loosened the chain that it pulls in the back. Now that I have a little more neck room, perhaps I can move my body down enough to reach the lever with my feet. If I can bring that up to my hands, I can try and cut the rope with it.

My heart thuds loudly in my ears for fear that the horseman will come back and catch me doing this. He just left. How long will he take to kill an innocent from my village?

I don't even want to think about it.

The metal chokehold is up to my chin as I reach with both tied feet for the lever. Just a little more...

I touch it with my toes and let out an exasperated hiss. I bring it in slowly, careful not to kick it too far. Once I have it close enough, I try picking it up with the tips of both my feet.

This takes me a few tries, but I finally grab it with my hands and begin to work on the rope, wedging it in through the middle and slowly prying it apart.

Despite the cold, I'm beginning to sweat from nerves. I don't know how long it's taking me to do this. It feels like an eternity, but I don't think it has taken that long based on the burning wick of the candle.

The rope finally gives, and I almost scream for joy. But I keep silent. I grab the metal choker and pull on it, releasing my head completely.

I take in a deep breath and let the choker clank to the floor. My neck cracks, and I grimace at the pain as I rub and stretch it. Mustering the little energy I have, I pull the rope free from my feet and then bolt out the door.

Don't think. Run, is all I tell myself. *Get as far away from the horseman's house as possible.*

Gray skies shadow the silvery grassland of whatever this place is.

My stiff body aches as I plant one foot in front of the other, trying not to look back. I almost trip over the length of my nightgown, realizing only now how exposed I am. I'd nearly forgotten he took me in the middle of the night.

Hours on that awful wooden garrote, unable to move my head, blur in my memory. The horseman's eyes flash in my mind, spurring me to run faster.

The idea that the horseman is out there, looking to kill his next victim lodges my heart in my throat. There's no method to his madness; Daniel did nothing wrong.

He was killed because of me.

The horseman killed Daniel because we tried to burn him together. He did it to punish me. If he wanted to punish and torture Daniel, he would have been taken by the horseman and made to suffer along with me. He killed him because I put him in this mess.

My body heaves, and my legs grow tired of running. Everywhere looks exactly the same. Rolling hills.

How far away from home am I? Am I even running in the right direction of the Andre tree? I don't even know what it looks like or what I'm looking for. I was unconscious for most of the ride.

The grove of heads. Look for the grove of heads.

Thunder roars above, and I spin around, searching for cover. I didn't expect it to rain down here—wherever this is. When I first woke up, there was a light drizzle, but now the rain has intensified into a storm. I thought we went down a tree...

My eyes widen at the gray clouds and the ripples of purple lightning dancing in the same spot ahead. Below it stands another tree, similar to the Andre tree.

"There you are!" A voice comes from behind me, and I yelp, spinning around.

My mother's ghost appears before me, her eyes wide with fear, and she touches my shoulders with her spectral grip.

I pant rapidly. My heart feels like it wants to jump out of my chest.

"Mother," I rasp. "How are you here? Where have you been?"

Even though it was a woman's voice I heard, my nerves are so frayed that I still thought it could be the horseman who found me. But he wouldn't know where I am now. He'd get home soon enough and find me gone.

My mother's eyes grow solemn, but she doesn't answer my question. "I'm here now, Kat. I'm sorry I left you alone."

Not that she could have done anything against the horseman. My mother's ghost has been following me around ever since she died, but when I needed her the most, she disappeared. What happens after I go back up? Will she leave me again?

"You left me. I thought I'd never see you again." I can't keep my voice from shaking.

"Kat...I... I was ashamed."

My cheeks heat. She saw what happened. The hollow pit in my gut I've had for months returns. Or maybe it's always been there, replaced by the recent terrors.

"You were ashamed of me." Tears well in my eyes, and my voice cracks, humiliation crashing into me.

"No, not of you, honey." She reaches for me even though she can't feel me, and I can't feel her.

"What are you talking about?"

She shakes her head. "Not here. Let us talk when you get back, when you're safe. He'll search for you."

I'm reluctant to leave her like this. What was she ashamed of, then?

"You must leave now," she says. "I cannot enter the horseman's house. It's imbued with dark magic to keep out the dead, but I followed you here."

She points to the purple lightning in the sky. "Those ripples are the roots of the Andre tree above ground. This is an undead dimension. You'll have to climb the tree, and you'll be taken above. We'll be able to talk then. I promise."

"You won't leave me again?"

"I promise, Kat."

The world spins around me. I don't know what to do with what she just told me, but I turn to face the direction of the tree. I know I'm running out of time.

I hurry toward the tree, and my mother follows.

The echoing thuds of hooves make me freeze. His steed emerges from the lightning—one moment, there's nothing but darkness between the flashes, and the next, the horseman is descending from them.

The horseman directs his steed to face me and charges fast. The impending doom muffles my mother's screams next to me.

He's now blocking my only way out of this place, and he's coming straight for me. He lifts his ax, and my knees buckle. He wants to chop my head off.

Maybe this is a good thing. If I can't escape him, maybe it'll be quick and painless instead of slow torture, like he promised.

There's no other place to run, but I turn anyway, summoning any strength I have left.

The horse's hooves gain on me, and I wince, preparing at any second for the blade to end my life.

Instead, the cloth on my back yanks, and nails dig into my skin. I pull down hard, tearing part of my nightgown and managing to escape momentarily.

He grabs me by the neck, and this time he pulls me up, kicking and screaming. He throws me onto the horse in front of him.

My breath leaves me, and I can do nothing but lie on my belly and stare down at the moving ground.

Chapter Nine

FALLON

I WAKE on my bed when my head has come back.

After swinging my legs from the mattress, I plant my boots firmly on the ground, my memories coming to me in feelings. The type of memories you get after sleepwalking.

When the curse overcomes me, I can't actually see what I'm doing, but I have memories of doing the things as if they were a dream.

I pulled her by the hair off my horse, kicking and screaming. She clawed at my arm like a feral cat.

I bring up my sleeve and see her scratches along my skin. A smirk curls my lip, and I stand, making my way over to where I placed her last night.

She's hanging by both her wrists, tied together in a rope off a large hook on my ceiling, undoubtedly the cause for the leak just above it. If it rains in Sleepy Hollow—and it is—then it rains down here too. Her hanging here wouldn't let her dry.

Her feet dangle, only just touching the floor with her toes, and her chin touches her chest. Her eyes are shut. Probably tired herself out and passed out.

She's soaking wet, and I can see right through her white nightdress. The morning sun illuminates her from the window behind her, making her look like some kind of angel.

The cloth sticks to her body, outlining her every curve, exposing the shape of her breasts and hard nipples. My cock strains against my pants.

Christ.

How can something so gorgeous be so wicked?

I have to remind myself that she's dangerous. That she's a witch from a long line of witches who cursed me. Did this to me so that I could live out eternity reliving my head being blasted off, my free will taken from me to be under the command of some witch.

She may not be the one who is commanding me now, but she is still one of them. She either knows who is, or she knows where the book is. Either way, now that I have her, I'm going to make her release me from my ethereal binds one way or another.

Her eyes flutter open, and she starts to whimper, trying to pull herself down from the rope.

"Good mornin', witchy. Did you get plenty of exercise

last night? If you were tired of the garotte, all you had to do was ask me to change your position." I widen my grin.

"Please. I don't know anything about a symbol." Her teeth chatter from the cold. "Or about any book. You're wasting your time with me."

"Well, if that's the case, I'll kill you now, then." I walk over to my table and pick up a blade, bringing it up to inspect it.

Then I set it down and pick up a dagger. I eye her from the side. This got her quiet. I set the dagger down, turn to my collection of whips, and select the riding crop.

She gasps when she sees what's in my hand. A whimper leaves her mouth, but I don't hit her with it. Not yet anyway.

Instead, I start from her thigh, trace it slowly up her left arm, , and turn at her shoulder to her neck.

She shuts her eyes, breathing hard.

"Where'd you think you could run? Were you going to try and climb your way out of the sky?" A dark chuckle leaves my cold lips. "I suppose you could do that, but you wouldn't make it very far."

I bring the leather down her clavicle, and my gaze lingers on the planes of her neck. Her chest rises with each breath, and I drop the leather on the floor.

She startles, opening her eyes just a second to look at me, then closes them again. Like she can't stand the sight of me.

I lift my hand and wrap it around that pretty little

neck of hers, but I don't squeeze. I caress her soft, wet skin with my thumb, and she lets out a scared whimper.

I step into her, and now her breasts are right in front of my face. I try to ignore them, keeping my eyes trained on her neck. "You know, witchy, from this position, I can do a whole lot to you, and you couldn't do anything about it."

I would never go farther than what would torture her. I've killed men for forcing themselves on those who can't defend themselves. But it doesn't mean I won't try and scare her.

When she was seated in the garrote, I would tower over her, but I quite like having her in this position.

I squeeze her neck, and she lets out a strained cry, her eyes finally settling on me.

"Please," she says, and I laugh.

"Listen very carefully, you wicked thing."

She tries to breathe as I linger my hand on her neck.

"For every lie you tell, I am going to hit you with this leather strap, and I will make it hurt." On the last word, I squeeze her neck tighter.

She pants hard.

"The first question. Which other witch lives in Sleepy Hollow, then?" I release her neck so she can answer.

Her eyes well up immediately, and she stares down at me with glossy eyes. "I-I don't know any witches..."

"Wrong answer." I pick up the leather on the floor and

then spin her from the rope so she swings around, her back to me.

With one quick flick, I release the strap toward her ass, and she cries out. I do it again harder, and her scream fills the space. I'm not satisfied with the way the cloth protects her skin, so despite the fight I'm having with myself to look at her body, I lift her nightgown and hitch it over her ass.

Christ. It's perfectly round and taut.

She starts to cry, and I ignore it, hitting her one more time, admiring the red mark left by my leather strap. Then I let the cloth fall over her and spin her back around.

She quivers, tears streaming down her cheeks.

"You must like pain, witch. But I am enjoying this, so you better answer the question truthfully because I'm just getting started."

And I am enjoying this too much. Having her here, practically naked, is a torment of its own—a torment I rather enjoy.

But I can't let myself get distracted by her. She'll only use it against me, and I'll never be free. I can't let her convince me she's anything other than a wicked thing that will continue to enslave me.

"I—"

"Careful with your words now." I twist the leather in my hand.

"P-perhaps I know of someone." She squeezes her eyes shut.

I smile, knowing she's got someone in mind and she's about to give 'em up. It's cute how she wants to protect her townsfolk. Perhaps in another life, I may have found that quality admirable. Too bad I'm about to take it all from her, just like me own freedom was taken from me.

"Who?" I ask.

"I don't know for sure."

A sigh leaves my throat. I grab her leg and start to spin her around again.

"You can't expect me to tell you someone is evil...without..." Her breath shakes as I spin her around faster, my leather strap touching her waist as I go. "Knowing for certain."

"I need a name. Unless you'd prefer it if I just kill everyone there to search for the book myself. After all, I already have a witch who could break the curse." I smirk.

Truth is, moments after my curse subsides, I start to come to. I have been killing those I know are bad people to help with my process of elimination. Whoever is commanding the curse is meticulously selecting people for me to kill for their benefit, but the ones I take out don't see me coming. They've got no spell book, nor incantations near them.

And I only kill those who don't deserve to breathe. Despite what this pretty little witch thinks of me, and what I'm allowing her to know.

"Please."

I grit my teeth, growing tired of hearing her beg for the

same thing—to let her go. "It's not going to happen, witch."

"No. Please—"

"Please what?" I growl.

"Tell me...who was it?"

My brow quirks. She wants to know who I killed. Of course she does, still caring about her traitorous friends. I contemplate not answering her, but if I let this linger, she won't focus on my questions.

"Samuel," I tell her, watching her expression closely.

A tiny gasp leaves her lips, and her eyes grow distant. She looks away from me. Samuel is her uncle, her father's brother.

She swallows. Her hand makes a fist, and I squint at the action.

"What's that, witchy? How does that make you feel?"

She doesn't answer me, but her eyes meet mine.

Samuel wasn't a good man. He was my charge, but I would have killed him anyway.

"Will you miss him?" I ask.

She sniffs but doesn't speak.

"Perhaps you'll miss his late-night visits." As disgusting as it was to say that, even for me, I'm trying to get her to give up her friends. None of these people are good people. Not one. "Or has it been years since you saw him last? I suppose now you're too old for him."

She lets out a sob and shuts her eyes.

"Perhaps for this one, you should be thanking me."

She opens her eyes and stares at me with disdain. I scoff.

She was more upset over the head I brought back yesterday.

"What of the man you worked with? What was his name? Daniel?"

Now her eyes are on mine, hatred seething inside them.

I smile. "Ah, there she is. Was he a friend of yours? Or possibly your betrothed, the way you cried for him."

She grimaces, showing her teeth. Feral like the feral witch she is.

Good thing I killed him, then. They don't deserve love.

My breathing picks up, feeling the curse rising, but not because I'm being summoned. Because she's still my charge.

My urge to kill her is strong, but I fight it.

It didn't work last time, but if I could just try... I wrap my hand around her cold neck, and this time I squeeze hard.

Her eyes bug from her head, and her lips open. Her chest heaves under my wrist, her breasts moving up and down with each rapid breath. I squeeze harder, her pulse racing. It will eventually stop.

Then I can rest, if only for a moment until the next summoning.

The impulse grows stronger, and I squeeze even

harder. Her eyes bulge, her tongue sticks out, her whimpers are lessening, and her pulse slows.

Burning sears into my bones, and I let her go with a loud scream, hunching over and clutching my hand as I stumble backward.

"Fucking witch!" My hand is bright red, browning to a crisp.

I stare up at her, anger coursing through me. She has a spell on her to keep me from killing her.

This is why I can't kill her.

She gasps for breath, the sounds of pained coughs coming from her in tiny whimpers. Her body droops as she struggles with her wrists tied above her head.

Chapter Ten

KAT

I COULDN'T JUST MAKE someone up. He knows everyone in Sleepy Hollow, so he'd know I was lying.

He's been sitting with his back against the door, his knees drawn up to his chest, simply watching me. We've been like this for what feels like an hour, maybe two. I can't tell.

My hands and arms are numb.

When he had his hand around my neck, I was terrified. Knowing I was going to die just then... Having the air cut off from me was painful...

But I'm ashamed to admit I almost enjoyed the thrill of it. After he let go, I found myself needing more.

Not that I want to be dead. I'm not saying I want him to kill me. But perhaps the fact that he didn't, the fact that it brought me so close, made me realize how much I value being alive. It made me feel a pleasure beyond my comprehension. One that would challenge me beyond anything I've ever felt.

Like a need for a release I never thought could be possible.

When he let me go, I was relieved to still be alive. I don't know how I burned the horseman's hand, but he's been mad ever since, sitting in the same position, a look of disdain on his face.

I'm glad I hurt him. I don't understand how I did, but I'm glad I did it.

The question of how I burned him has been coursing through my head. None of this makes any sense to me. But he's been calling me a witch all along. Could there be something about me that I never knew?

Could it be my necklace, or could it be something more about me? Whatever it is, I bet my mother knows. She's been hiding secrets from me.

I have to find out what they are.

I need to get myself loose again and find my mother's ghost. I need to get out of this hellish place and back to Sleepy Hollow.

Clearly, the horseman cannot kill me, but he can hurt me, and he's already made himself clear that his intention is to torture me for as long as I live.

A cold draft passes through my gown, and I shiver.

It's only just occurred to me that he can see through

my gown. I've never felt so vulnerable before in my life. My cheeks heat.

His eyes narrow at me, and I wonder what he's thinking.

"Does it hurt?" I ask, not recognizing my own voice. It's weak and hoarse from screaming.

"My hand?"

"No, I mean...your head when..." I lick my cracked lips. "When..."

"Are you asking me if it hurts when my head gets blown off each time?"

I breathe sharply at my stupid question.

"Only for a moment. Why would you care anyway?"

"I was only curious."

He nods once, his eyes still trained on me.

"I didn't put this curse on you, you know," I finally say.

"I know that, but you're still a witch who can undo it. You're wicked just like all the rest."

"All the rest of who? Who put this curse on you?"

He guffaws. "If I knew that, love, I would be going after them instead. Usually, I would know. But this time, they have kept their identity a secret. Why am I telling you any of this anyway?"

They've kept their identity a secret? Now my eyes narrow down to the floor. I don't know anything about spells, but he's known who has commanded the curse in the past. Whoever is doing this now is either using a different curse altogether or two different ones.

Not that I care about any of that, but it attests to the knowledge of whoever's behind this curse. The fact that this person is someone in Sleepy Hollow boggles my mind. Clearly, it's happened before, but who among those I know could be capable of such a thing?

"What's on your mind, witch? Thinking about the hellion who's responsible for everyone that's dead?"

I manage to swallow the dry lump in my throat at his words. This is something that hasn't occurred to me yet. I mean, I know someone is commanding him, but I guess I haven't stopped to think that he...

"Have you ever tried resisting the curse?"

"Yes. Every single time it happens." His voice sounds pained. Strained. "I try to resist it, but it drives me like a force I can do nothing about. Imagine being puppeteered without a head to commit a tragic crime."

The look on his face tells me he isn't lying. He's had to go through this over and over. And the way he said it tells me...he doesn't want to?

"That must be awful," I say.

He blinks up at me, and his face softens for a moment before he hardens it again.

"And this book you speak of..."

"The spell book."

"It will stop the curse? You've seen it?"

He scoffs at me and glances away. "It's a big leather-bound book, with the same symbol that hangs around your neck. My previous master," he says with a look of disgust, "used it rather flauntingly."

My brows furrow. The same symbol on my pendant? "What happened to it?"

"I don't know."

"Who held it last?"

He fixes his eyes on me. "Your mother."

A gasp leaves my lips as I stare at him. My blood must be draining quickly from my tied-up arms because the room starts to spin.

I shake my head. "No..."

"She wasn't my master."

I let out a slow breath. That explains why he thinks I'm a witch and how he knows so much about the symbol around my neck. I suspect he couldn't rip it off me if he tried, considering how his hand burned when he had it wrapped around my neck.

"What did she use it for?" I ask, wishing even more that I could speak to her.

His eyes search mine, seeming surprised as to why I don't know these answers already. "Why don't you tell me?"

"I really don't know," I answer truthfully. "I swear if I did, I would help you."

He laughs. "You? Help me willingly? None of you witches have ever cared to help me. Your mother was only looking out for herself. She knew who commanded me, and instead of punishing her and burning the book, she sent me to hell and kept the nefarious pages for her own. So tell me, daughter of Katrina Van Tassel, why should I trust *you*?"

My chest heaves. There's so much he's told me just now that it's running wild in my mind. Things I cannot make sense of.

We sit in silence, and he watches, studying me carefully.

I need to ask my mother these questions. But perhaps the answer to stopping these killings is to find the person in command of the horseman. Maybe he's been right all along. And perhaps I am the key to finding them.

But he's not right about me being a witch.

The fact that my mother had the spell book last, though... Who could have found it? Where would she have left it?

They moved to Connecticut before I was born, so why would she have left it here for someone to find?

And what would she have wanted it for to begin with?

I needed to find the spell book and break the union of the spell of whoever is commanding him. Like my mother did, I will send him back to hell, where he belongs. He's a sadistic demon, and I don't believe a word he says about not wanting to kill.

He *wants* to kill. He enjoys it, just like he's admitted to enjoying torturing me.

If he had his way, he'd kill whoever he wants, whenever he wants. He just doesn't like being commanded.

I break the silence, hoping to start on my plan. "Maybe I can help you."

"And what would you have in mind?" He crosses his leg over the other.

"Let me down first."

He chuckles. "So you can try to escape again?"

He gets up and picks up the leather strap. I gulp.

"No," he says. "In fact, I'm enjoying having a little toy to play with. Who knew torture would be so much fun?"

I hold my breath as I watch him slowly come nearer, playing with the leather strap in his hand, confirming my earlier thoughts about him being a demon who enjoys doing this.

His blue eyes drift down to my breasts and linger on them before drifting lower. My breathing picks up, and I'm once again acutely aware of how exposed I am. If I ever get out of this alive, I am going to go to bed fully clothed for as long as I live.

He stands in front of me, wisps of his hair falling over his eyes as he takes the leather and wraps it around me, moving it up to cover my breasts. I gasp and squeeze my eyes shut as he tightens it as much as he can.

Pain sears through my back and my nipples. The leather strap is so tight I can hardly breathe, and a soft moan comes from my mouth. I open my eyes and see him standing in front of me, rubbing his chin as he admires his work.

A smirk dances on his face, then he turns to his table of many devices, trailing his fingers over all of them as he makes his selection. Before he chooses, I speak.

"Let me go with you on your horse next time."

He doesn't look up. "Why in hell's name would you want to do that?"

Because someone will see me as his prisoner and shoot him down, giving me a chance to escape. This time, I'll ask my mother to help me find the book, and maybe she can put an end to this.

He chooses a thin blade and turns with a sadistic look on his face.

"I can be your eyes!" I quickly state.

He pauses, holding the blade in his hand. "How do you mean?"

"If you're under the spell's control and really can't choose who you're meant to kill...then maybe I can be your eyes."

His eyes narrow on me. "Keep talking."

"I know everyone in town. I can help you look for clues."

"I too know everyone."

"But you don't know what they're doing behind closed doors. If you did, you'd know who was controlling you."

He strides over to me and holds the blade under my

chin. I try my hardest to keep my breathing steady, keeping my eyes on him below me.

"And you know what they're doing behind closed doors, do you?"

"I know enough to piece things together."

In fact, I can think of a few odd women in my village. Madame Chattaway for one, and Henry's wife, the way she dropped that dead bird on my lap at my father's funeral. That's most definitely witchcraft.

But I won't just give any of them up to the horseman. I need proof. If they really are an evil witch commanding the Hessian, then they deserve what will come to them, and we will put an end to the murders.

Stealing the book is also a good option. End the murders and put the witch on trial.

"I can search someone's house while you take your... charge." I gulp, not wanting to think of that.

Hesitation flickers on his face as his eyes remain narrowed on me. He trails the blade down my neck and my arm, goose bumps trailing in its wake.

"If you so much as think about running, I will know. And then, considering you're a useless witch, and by then a useless spy, I will kill you."

I swallow. "Understood."

"Then we have ourselves a deal, witchy. Find me the book and release my curse, and I'll let you go."

Chapter Eleven

KAT

EVEN AFTER OUR DEAL, he still hasn't untied me.

I'm supposed to wait until the spell starts, but I'm afraid that once it does, he won't remember to let me go so I can get on his horse.

He hasn't been out of his room. I couldn't see where it was when I was tied to the garrote, but it's just in the corner of this cottage. I also have a dreadful view of the breaking wheel and a real iron maiden that's covered in sigils of some kind. They stay in view like a promise to what else could happen to me if I try to run away again.

"Horseman!" My voice is raspy.

He doesn't answer, so I try again.

To my surprise, he comes out. He doesn't say

anything, just stands at the doorway, squinting at me expectantly.

"How do you know you'll be able to take me once the curse is enacted?" I ask.

"I don't."

I gape at him. "Then let me down."

"You are in no position to be making commands of me, witch." He tilts his head. "I thought you were savvy enough to let yourself down. After all, you already did once with the garrote."

"Please," I say. "That was sheer luck. I've got no feeling in my fingers. I can't..." I sigh. "Let me down."

"So you could escape?"

"I won't. Where would I go? You've already proven your point that you'd catch me in a moment's beat."

A wicked smile lights his face, and he crosses his arms, leaning on the frame of the door. "Truthfully, I quite enjoy you in this position. Gives me a good view."

My lips part, and my cheeks heat.

He chuckles to himself and walks back into his room.

An exasperated sigh leaves my throat, and I close my eyes, trying to think of anything that can take away the pain in my arms. My mind drifts back to school notes, things I had to memorize.

There was a poem I found in my father's study. He said it belonged to my mother, which I didn't find surprising, considering my father didn't read. But my mother very much enjoyed books.

"Till death's cold touch her chiffon wheel-affail,
And vain regret and vain defire fall fail;
Tho' now where eft the gray-clad peasant fray'd—"

"What are you doing?" he snaps.

I startle and look at him. "Sorry?"

"Why are you rehearsing a poem? And most particularly, *that one?*"

I gasp. I didn't even realize I was saying it out loud. "I was just trying to keep my mind occupied."

His eyes narrow, and I swallow. Is he going to punish me for disturbing him?

He walks over to me slowly, his eyes trained on me. My nightgown is damp from the drips that keep falling on me, and I still wish I were wearing something else. I hate being this vulnerable to him. To anyone, frankly.

He walks to his table of weapons, and I hold my breath, expecting him to select something new to torture me with. Instead, he leans against the table, facing me with his arms crossed in front of him.

"Go on, then," he says. "Finish your poem."

Did I just hear him correctly?

We lock eyes for a brief, tense moment, neither of us moving or speaking.

"Have you something better to do?" he demands.

I stare at his features. Does he really intend for me to recite the poem to him?

His eyebrows rise as he waits for me to start, so I take a

deep breath, disbelieving I'm about to finish reciting this poem to the headless horseman...

Here goes.

"To break the quiet of the village fade." I pause. "I, um... I was getting to a part I couldn't remember. It's quite a long poem."

"It isn't so long. Try memorizing *The Iliad*. Now that's a long poem."

I can't help but widen my eyes. *Literature?* The horseman is interested in *literature?* This is what gets him to come out of his room to talk?

"I believe the next line is..." He clears his throat, and my mouth falls open. "Gleam war's *difcordant* habits thro' the trees," he says with his deep voice. "And the red banner mock the fallen breeze..."

He keeps going, reciting the entire poem without stopping, his eyes not leaving mine. I feel a cold draft and an odd tingling sensation in my core as his gaze sears through me as he speaks. Like he's looking at me with new interest.

And then he reaches the last line, "Beyond the cottage hearth, the cottage door."

I stare at him. I want to tell him that was brilliantly spoken. He recited it in one breath, his gaze never faltering.

We stare at each other in silence for a few seconds until he pulls himself up and walks back to his room.

It's the oddest interaction I've ever had with the horseman. Yet he still left me up here, tied to this rope.

Seconds later, he walks back out, holding an old, small,

leather-bound book in his hand. "If you like William Wordsworth, you should try Robert Burns." He flips through the pages and stands before me. "To be honest, witch, I'm quite surprised you knew Wordsworth at all. But I am also surprised a witch like you wouldn't have been able to recite it without problem."

I roll my eyes. "Are you always so condescending? And I've already told you, I'm not a witch."

"So you say."

"I'm not," I huff.

He smirks.

"What if you were to find out I wasn't one? What then? Would you let me go?"

He guffaws then steps into me. "What could possibly make you think I would ever let you go?"

A chill runs down my spine.

"The living are all vile and hateful creatures. Getting rid of each of you one by one brings me solace."

I suck in a breath. "Y-you can't truly believe all the living are...hateful?"

"This coming from the woman who trapped me in a wooden maiden and caught me on fire."

The air escapes me. I had almost forgotten I had done that to him. The sounds of his screams... I tortured him. It wasn't my imagination. He feels pain as much as I do.

"You were killing my friends and loved ones," I say.

He frowns. "Yes."

"You killed my father."

"Brom was not your father," he says quietly.

My blood grows cold. My mother was keeping something from me, and she wouldn't say what it was. It must have been this. She was ashamed because she knew what had happened and never told me he was not my father.

"How do you know this?"

"I have been watching everyone closely for a very long time, Katalina."

This is the first time he calls me by my name rather than witch or witchy. His lips part, and shock reflects on his features, as if realizing he called me by my name. Somehow, it feels intimate.

"I am quite fond of Sleepy Hollow," he finally says, breaking the awkward silence. "It's the inhabitants I despise."

The inhabitants who have enslaved him. Ones who commit crimes and use him to cover them up.

I despise him, this demon sent to destroy us all. He took my father's life, and the lives of those I held dear, yet deep down, I know the true guilt lies elsewhere. Someone else pulled the strings.

But I also know he likes torturing me. He hates us. He just admitted it, and if he had any control, he wouldn't stop until all of us are dead. I cannot forget that.

I manage to fight down the fear of asking this next question. "Why do you think the witch who commands you wanted my father dead?"

He steps back, his gaze drifting to the book, dismissing

my question without a word. He sets it down on the table and picks up a knife.

My heart starts racing as he turns and swiftly walks over to me. I swallow and shut my eyes, not wanting to beg him this time. It doesn't help, and it makes me feel even more pathetic than I already look.

I gasp and open my eyes when I feel him getting close, his body pressing up against mine. He reaches up over my wrists. I get a whiff of the gunpowder on his clothes. Probably from when he's shot dead each time.

"I don't have to tell you what will happen to you if you try to run," he states.

I stare up at him, my mouth agape. I nod in understanding.

I fall to the ground as he lets me loose.

Chapter Twelve

FALLON

"Thank you."

My lip curls upward in acknowledgement of her thanking me, but I don't look her way. I can't look at her.

I hope I don't regret letting her loose. I'm a fool for letting her think she connected with me.

Even though I know she's a witch and about her past. And how much torture she has already endured—not all from me entirely. Perhaps a little bit of false security will show her just how much freedom she truly does not possess.

After walking to the table, I set the knife down, but I leave the book of poems on the table for her. I bring myself to face her.

She keeps picking up her garment and placing it over

her shoulder. It's torn open at the collar, so she fusses with it to keep herself covered. There's ash and soot all over the once cream fabric of her nightgown.

She stares up at me with wide green eyes, and she bites her bottom lip, so unsure of what to do with herself now that I've untied her. Scared of what I'll do to her if she tries to escape. I leave her there on the floor and walk back into my study.

Hopefully she'll make use of her time, read the poetry book, and keep quiet so that I can look up the stupid symbol on her necklace and figure out where I'm headed to next.

I shut the door, but I can hear her fumbling outside it.

Christ.

I hope I don't regret this.

After opening a book of occultism, I flip through its pages, finding where I last left off. There's nothing in this library of books that I have that speaks about that symbol. That symbol that keeps me from killing her.

That's what I've come to realize —the symbol protects her. I can get close to her. I can touch her, so long as my skin does not come in contact with her pendant. I can nearly kill her, but I can't complete the action.

If I'm honest, it was stupid of me to let her loose.

Once the magic of the charge on her overcomes me once again, she'll run.

I killed Brom of my own free will after completing my charge. But she cannot know this. It is something I was punished for. Something my last master could not do to me.

Whoever this person is, who has such command and control over me, is the strongest I've ever had. The only saving grace I have is Katalina. And perhaps she really is not a witch. Although she has the power inside her. That I know, and perhaps she just doesn't know it yet.

I pinch the bridge of my nose. She will have to learn to be a witch in order to save me, then, won't she?

Am I the one to train her in witchcraft? Seems to me like a double-edged sword.

When it comes down to it, will she be strong enough to release me from these hellish binds? In that case, perhaps letting her loose will conserve some of her energy. And perhaps she should be training her power.

Though I despise witches, it may be the only chance I have. But I need to find how to break this blasted curse, and I didn't figure it out last time. It was Katrina Van Tassel who broke the curse. But then the bitch sent me to hell.

I will not let Katalina do the same to me.

A soft tap comes at the door.

I grimace. "What is it?"

She doesn't respond. She's probably too frightened of me to open the door.

I sigh and get up off my seat. I open the door, and there she is, her hair mussed, and her garment nearly see-through, showing off her curves.

God, she's gorgeous. "What do you want?"

"I was wondering if you had any more of that bread."

Right, the bread. She must be hungry. When was the last time I fed her? A day ago? Maybe two? Time blurs under the curse.

"In the pantry," I say. "Make it last. Once it's gone, there won't be any more. Don't forget you're my captive here."

She nods and walks toward the kitchen.

I watch her walk away, my eyes narrowing on her. These days will be long. I'm not always summoned, and there isn't anything here for her to do.

I liked it better when I had her hung up for me to torture as my plaything.

A day has gone by, and I've barely left my room. I've been deep in thought about who will be my next victim after I get summoned.

I've read through a pack of books, over and over, scrutinizing every word in case I missed something.

She's been quiet outside my door. I get up to make sure she hasn't escaped or died of starvation to find her sitting by the now open window, staring out at the gray trees.

I walk over and stand in front of her, but she doesn't look my way. Part of me is almost disappointed she didn't try to run. It would have given me something to do.

"Not much to look at in this domain."

She jumps about a foot in the air, a cry ripping from her lips. She grabs her chest as it heaves, and she glares up at me.

A wide smirk crosses my lips.

"You startled me!"

A dark chuckle leaves me. "I suppose I did."

My smile stays plastered on my face. That was fun. Maybe I should scare her again later.

Turning on my heel, I walk over to my kitchen. I don't eat, so I'm not sure what I'll find, probably nothing but empty jars and rat skeletons. I start opening the cabinets.

"There's nothing there," she says from behind, now getting up. "I've already looked."

"Hm." If I let her starve, she'll be useless for what I need her for, but there is nothing for a human in this domain.

"Have you ever gone up to Sleepy Hollow with your head—as in your curse not enacted?"

"No, they would recognize my horse. I have an unmistakable stature. They would shoot me down and kill me on the spot."

"But you can't die, can you?"

I scoff and briefly close my eyes. "How would you like to be shot down, feel the pain of dying, then be taken and trapped in a wooden box and then burned to death?"

She remains silent, realizing what she asked me, knowing precisely what I'm talking about and what she did to me.

"And then to likely be brought back to life while still caught on fire just for the sake of the curse."

She swallows and looks away.

After shutting a cabinet, I grab my coat. "I'll be back."

"Where are you going?"

"To find you food." I stare at her. "Do not—"

"Leave," she finishes for me. "I won't."

I stare at her a bit longer, searching her face for any signs of trickery.

She looks down, my gaze seeming to make her feel uncomfortable, and I smirk, walking out the door.

I step out to the dusky horizon and find Vengeance eating straw on the side of the cottage. I give him a few pats on his muzzle and quickly mount him to head toward the Andre tree portal.

Despite what I told her, I can't actually leave this domain without my curse enacted. It is the only way I can rise to Sleepy Hollow.

It's not a bad idea to take Vengeance out for a ride without the curse having been enacted. If I'm honest, that's the only time I ever take him out, and it's not of my own volition.

He deserves better than this.

The fields of my domain are familiar to me, a distant memory frozen in time. If I keep going in any direction, I'll reach vacant homes from fifty years ago. The rolling hills come into view, and it makes me homesick.

Ireland.

I'm forever trapped in a semblance of my life before my wife and I were promised freedom after indentured servitude in America. Until everything exploded. And I lost the only love I will ever have.

For this is the reason I have no pity for the residents of Sleepy Hollow. Their ancestors took me as a slave, with no promise for freedom, and sold me to the Hessians. To kill for *them*. Only to then raise me from my eternal rest to continue murdering. I lost everything and everyone I ever loved.

Vengeance snorts and snaps me out of my daydream. He goes off trail, spotting a half-eaten apple, thrown at the Andre tree, no doubt. I let him eat it and climb down to collect some uneaten apples and a few walnuts.

A cool breeze passes through me, and my brows furrow. It is not the typical breeze that sweeps Sleepy Hollow before a storm and affects this plane. No, it's... something else I can't put my finger on.

I turn around, inspecting the rolling hills. The dead grass is as still as the stale air.

I take a good amount of apples and walnuts and open a bag slung over Vengeance's back. Holding it open, I stare inside. This is where I store the heads. Grunting, I toss the fruit and nuts inside and climb on top of Vengeance.

She can clean them in the sink if she cares about a little blood.

I nudge Vengeance to head home, and we take off down the rolling hill. My body vibrates as a vicious wave of my curse sweeps down my head.

Kill her.

Katalina Van Tassel must die.

Red bathes my vision, and Vengeance takes off at full speed.

Chapter Thirteen

KAT

I'VE BEEN STARING at the running water for nearly twenty minutes, waiting for it to clear. It's improved but still not drinkable.

He's given me water before, so where did he get it? Could there be a stream nearby?

And how does this water work if the only food I can eat is what gets thrown at the Andre tree?

The door slams open, causing me to jump. The horseman stands there, his ax in hand. Despite still having his head, there's a crazed look in his dilated eyes as he stares at me.

A scream tears from my throat as he lifts his ax and marches toward me. Tripping over my own feet, I fall to the ground and scurry across the floorboards until I hit the wall behind me.

He towers over me, blocking any escape.

He swings his arm back, and I cover my face.

A gunshot makes me lower my arm, and I'm shaking. My ghostly savior has once again blown off his head. The horseman lowers his ax and stands there for a moment before turning back to the door.

He's been called to kill someone else.

I'm shaken. Why did he return to kill me after seemingly deciding to fetch me food? He appeared to be under the curse, yet he still had his head.

It seemed as though he could not control the urge to come after me...

I've absolutely lost my mind, but...I stand and head for the horseman. He seems to be ignoring me as he begins to mount his horse. He most definitely does not have control.

Still shaking, I grab him, his arm like steel as I lift my leg up and over the horse. He doesn't seem to mind me being here, and if he tries to kill me, I'll die knowing I've taken the only chance I have to try and leave this hell and save Sleepy Hollow.

I never wanted to be this close to the headless horseman, but I have to squeeze him hard as his horse runs up the Andre tree, defying the laws of physics.

The familiar smells of forest and moss greet me as we emerge into Sleepy Hollow. This time with me willingly on the horseman's back.

It's the dead of night, and most will be asleep. I can't help the emptiness in the pit of my stomach, not knowing who he's about to kill.

His horse runs until we enter the thick of the village. My father's farm is behind me, and while that makes my nerves ease knowing my nana is safe from the horseman tonight, I have the biggest yearning to go home. To see Nana, to sleep in my bed. Then the memory of my father interrupts those thoughts, and my stomach curls.

We pass by Edith's house, and I hold my breath. Is the horseman going to finish her too? First take Daniel then Edith?

When we pass her house, I let out a tiny sigh of relief. Where is he taking us?

We turn right at the corner of Chapel Road, passing Madame Chattaway's cottage and a few others. The horse slows down at the end of the dirt road, and my brows furrow. There's nothing down here except...

The blood drains from my face as we make a sharp right toward the long, wooded driveway of the Wright estate.

No... Not Percival.

I grip the horseman's coat hard. Wait. Percival would be with the Nightward right about now. He always takes the night shifts.

"His father?" I scream, even though I know it's no use.

It's not like he can hear me, or if my protests would matter.

The horseman unsheathes his double-edged ax, and the horse kicks at the ground. A small gasp escapes my throat, and I clutch his coat tighter. He's getting ready to charge right for the estate.

I gape at the ground. If I'm meant to go off and look for clues to find the witch who has the spell book, I'm about to lose my only chance.

But I can't let him kill Percival's father. I may not have romantic feelings for Percival, but I definitely don't want his father to die! He's a God-fearing man, a good Christian. I know it!

The horse rears, and I scream, gripping tightly to the horseman. I've lost my chance to get off the horse. My heart pounds in my chest as he lands and begins to gallop toward the front door of the estate.

I should have jumped off. What could I even do?

The manor comes closer as it starts to rain. I hold my breath in anticipation of us breaking through the walls, but instead, he makes a turn. The horse slows to a trot.

That's when I remember the sounds of death coming to awaken you from your sleep. Letting you know the horseman has come for you. Almost like a warning, except there's no escape. There's nothing anyone can do to prepare for him coming to take your head.

We reach the front of the manor, and the horseman jumps off. I catch myself on the reins as he dismisses the fact that I'm still here. Either too consumed in the curse, or he's forgotten about me.

He kicks through the door, the heavy hinges coming undone from his impossible brute strength, and he swings the rest of it open.

A gunshot fires from inside and hits the horseman right in the chest. His shoulder jerks back, but he keeps walking inside as if it were rocks hitting him instead of bullets.

The only gunfire that will bring him down is a silver bullet like the one I used to shoot him with. Maybe with enough shots of regular bullets, they will eventually bring him down.

"Keep shooting at him!" I yell, not wanting to walk in after him for fear of getting shot.

My gaze falls to the lit torch beside the window. Fire will kill him. Not permanently, but long enough to save Percival's father and for me to get away.

How long did it take last time? Three days. That's three days for me to pack up my and Nana's things and leave Sleepy Hollow for good. We can go up to Connecticut and start a new life.

The horseman doesn't leave Sleepy Hollow. He never has. He can't with the curse binding him here.

I grab the torch, and just as the gunshots cease, I run inside. He's weak, wounded. That much I know. It'll only make this easier.

Blood splatters on my face. I swallow a scream as Mr. Wright's head rolls on the ground. His body lands hard on the wooden floorboards, the sound echoing like a sack of potatoes. Images of my father's head rolling to my legs crashes into my thoughts.

The cocking of a gun snaps me back to the present. Percival's grandfather stands on the top of the stairs, the barrel pointed down at the horseman.

"Shoot him!" My scream hurts my throat.

The sound of gunfire fills the air.

With the torch in my hand, I plunge the fire into the horseman's back.

Ignoring me, he pulls out his sword and stabs the head to collect it. Turning around, he grabs my throat and pushes me hard, rushing me outside.

I still hold the torch, but it sputters out in the rain. Smoke sizzles off the horseman's shoulders.

Another gunshot hits his back, but he remains steadfast, unmoved.

I let the torch drop and start punching and kicking him with all my strength, pounding my fists and feet against his arms, chest, and knees. He remains unyielding, unaffected by my efforts.

The sound of the musket cocking again makes the horseman push me to the ground, and I land in the mud. The horseman takes a dagger and throws it toward Percival's grandfather.

"No!" I croak.

The dagger hits him square in the shoulder. He grabs at it as he falls to the ground.

He didn't kill him. Had he wanted to kill him, he would have done it already. He wasn't his charge.

I scramble to my feet, slipping over my now wet and muddy nightgown. This stupid nightgown!

He towers over me and grabs me by the hair. I scream, grabbing at his wrists. He wraps an arm around my torso and lifts me over the horse. This time, I leap off and land heavily in the mud.

I scramble to my feet, the cold earth squelching beneath me, and run. As he comes up behind me, I turn around and kick him hard in the groin.

Surprisingly, this makes him pause. He didn't react to the gunshots, but he notices a kick to the groin?

His hands are suddenly on both my arms, and he picks me up with supernatural strength. I push against him with my entire weight. I can't let him take me back. Not when I'm finally away from that horrid place. Not when I could have gotten away.

I'm such a fool. Why didn't I jump off before?

To my horror, he takes out a rope from the bag he dropped the head in, and he swings it over my back. I try squirming free, but it only yanks me against him. How is he doing this? How can he even see what he's doing?

He ties the rope into a tight knot around me and my wrists. Tears stream down my face as all hope evaporates from me.

He picks me up and sits me on his steed to take me

away, back under the Andre tree, where I'll live out the rest of my life as his toy to torture.

115

Chapter Fourteen

FALLON

I HOLD my throbbing head and squint through the offensive daylight intruding my bedroom window. My body aches as I sit up off the floor. I didn't even make it to my bed last night.

I open my button-down shirt and take it off to inspect my wounds from last night's gunfire. Closed, but not fully healed.

I groan as I stand. The fact that it's too quiet makes me recall what else happened. My mind floods with the memory of that witch trying to catch me on fire *again*, and my fist hurts from gripping the door handle so tight.

I swing it open, letting it hit the wall, and step out into the living room. I find her lying on her side, hogtied and wet on the hardwood floor. This fun fact should make me smirk, but the mere sight of her angers me. My boots echo on the hardwood floor as I approach her.

Her gown clings to her like a second skin. I say nothing, allowing my presence to loom over her dreams. Soon, her eyes flutter open, and she gasps.

I smile. "Hello, witchy. Sleep comfortably?"

Her eyes narrow, and I sense her hatred for me seething out of her.

"Feeling's mutual," I tell her. "You were supposed to get down off my horse and look for clues."

"And you weren't supposed to try and kill me again, Hessian!"

Her scream rattles my already throbbing headache. I pinch at my temples and turn to pick up a knife from my table.

"I should really leave you hogtied on the floor." I bend down, and she winces as I run the knife under her arms and cut the rope loose. I leave her ankles and wrists tied, though.

She kicks back all the way to the wall, but I follow after her, bend down, and pull her up by her neck. She lets out a rasped grunt as she tries to fight me, but my hold is too strong for her. Her nipples poke out of her soft linen, and I have to force my gaze to her face.

"You tried to burn me alive *again*." I tsk.

"How could you expect me not to try?" Her voice shakes. "I thought you were going to look for food, and you barged in trying to kill me. Then you k-killed…" She swallows. "What did Mr. Wright ever do to you?"

"What part of I cannot control this curse do you not understand?" I strain to keep my voice calm.

She struggles against my grasp, trying to stretch her neck. "Or maybe you're just a demon Hessian."

Her voice muffles as I press my hand over her face and push her against the wall.

Leaning into her, I whisper, "Call me that one more time. I dare you."

Her hot breath wets my palm as she forces her mouth open to speak.

"*Hessian.*" She stares at me daringly.

My lip curls upward, and I release my belt with one hand while keeping her pinned to the wall with my other. Her eyes grow big, and she starts to beg as I bring the belt up and stuff it into her mouth. I tighten it around her head to the last hole until she gags.

"That's not my name," I tell her.

She coughs, her eyes pleading.

I never told her my name, but it doesn't matter. I've asked her not to call me a Hessian, and she does it out of spite.

I lift her by her waist and carry her over to the breaking wheel I keep in the dark corner of the cottage in front of the iron maiden. Her muffled cries grow louder when she sees it, and she starts to kick.

Her hair is still damp from the rain last night, and it

whips me in the face as she fights me. I lie her down on the wheel, and her legs slip off the bars as she tries to get away.

"Don't make me knock the wind out of you. If I have to tie you up unconscious, I will."

A tear runs down her cheek as she realizes there's nowhere for her to run. And she doesn't want to be unconscious.

I lift her up and mount her on the vertical post, her back against the thick, wooden spoke. I use the rope to hogtie her again, this time spreading her arms out and tying them to the spokes on either side. I don't bother with her legs but keep them tied at her ankles.

Once I have her secured, I walk toward the back of the wheel, where her head is. She whimpers, unable to see what I'm doing. I pull down on the lever beneath the wheel, causing it to stand as upright as it can go so that she's facing me.

"Well, then, now that I have your attention, maybe we can start over." I keep my voice steady as I stare her in the eyes.

Another tear runs down her cheek as she bites down on my belt. I take my knife and slowly start touching her skin with the tip of the blade. Softly. Gooseflesh rises in its wake.

"I realize I never told you my name."

She whimpers, looking away from me.

"It's Fallon," I say, drawing the blade down her gown. "Fallon Callaghan." Even though the fabric is almost dry, it still clings to her, accentuating her figure. "You know, they used to tie witches to breaking wheels and hit them with iron rods until they died."

This makes her snap her attention to me. Drool drips down from the side of her mouth, and her chest heaves.

"Tell me, Katalina. Do you know the story of Saint Catherine of Alexandria?"

She shakes her head.

"Catherine was placed upon a wheel just like this one. I believe they were going to catch her on fire, right after some rather brutal beatings."

Her throat works as she starts to sweat, her eyes pleading, but I keep going.

"The wheel miraculously broke, setting her free. Do you know what they said to that?"

Her eyes are wide as she stares at me.

"Some say it was a miraculous act of God, suggesting to let her go free. Others said she was a witch. They beheaded her right after." I lean in and bring my knife up to her neck, slowly drawing out the lining of her throat with the tip of my blade.

She winces and tries to pull out of my reach, but I chuckle at the act. There's nowhere for her to go.

My right leg is on top of the wheel now, my body close to hers as I lean in.

"What do you think would happen to you right now, witchy? If I were to set you on fire right upon this wheel, as you did to me? Would your magic cause the wheel to break?"

Her heart beats hard, so loud I can hear it. Her ragged breaths cause her chest to rise up and down.

I lick my lips. "Or would it be an act of God?"

I now have both hands on the bars on either side of her, my body hovering over hers.

"Answer me." I reach to the back of her head and untie the belt so she can speak. "Tell me about your magic. Could it save you if I put it to the test right now?"

Her voice is hoarse as she cries out, "I'm not a witch."

I sigh. "Then I suppose your heartless God will save you. Although, he hasn't saved any of your townsfolk, has he?"

She swallows. "And what would have happened if you would have stopped yourself from killing Mr. Wright? Like you haven't killed me?"

"Nothing would have stopped me from killing him."

"Then why haven't you killed me?"

I bang my fist against the wooden bar next to her head. "Trust me, witchy. I'm trying."

Pain flashes through my head, and I wince, a groan escaping from the back of my throat.

Her eyes widen, clearly now seeing I didn't mean to just bring her here to torture her out of spite. That there is something keeping me from succeeding in killing her.

The curse's need for me to end her life rushes into me. My hand finds her throat, and I start to squeeze. Red swarms my periphery, the veins in my eyes throbbing, making my vision pulse as I stare into her pretty blue eyes. She quivers and shakes, begging for air with tiny gasps.

The sharp pain in my head increases, blinding me momentarily. Hard and heavy breaths escape my mouth as I squeeze her neck tighter. With my other hand, I clutch the knife and raise it.

Why is my curse telling me to kill her so soon after the last time?

It's happening more frequently.

My urge to kill her increases with every breath I take. And every rise of her chest. Now.

I'm acutely aware of my arm touching her through her wet, translucent clothes. I have to do it now, before her powers break my hand like it broke the lever of the garrote.

Tears stream down her cheeks, and her plump lips open as she tries to breathe.

I dip my gaze to her lips and slam my knife down hard. She winces as the blade digs deep into the wooden bar an inch next to her ear.

The next thing I know, my lips are crashing against hers, but my grip doesn't weaken around her neck.

At first, she gasps against my mouth, but then her back arches into me, giving me her soft lips. The pain at my temples subsides, and I have no idea why that's happening. My grip loosens as the compulsory need to end her eases away.

My chest heaves as I trail my hand from her neck down to her waist and clench the side of her damp gown until I feel her slender hips. A groan catches in my throat, and I pull away from her, stepping off the wheel.

Katalina's eyes burn into me, shock on her face, her cheeks a rosy blush.

Why the fuck did I do that?

I take a step away from her, running my gaze down her body. My groin strains uncomfortably against my trousers. I grab the knife from the wood and pull it out, startling her by my sudden action.

I walk away from her toward my room and slam the door shut behind me, resting my head against it.

I can still taste her on my lips. I cannot begin to process why the pain from my curse subsided when I kissed her when it's been searing into my skull all this time.

Fuck. I can't let this witch cast her spell over me.

If I manage to kill her, I won't get the spell book and have her break my curse.

That's why I kissed her. It has to be the only reason why I did it.

The only explanation for my curse easing its hold on me must have been due to me squeezing her throat tightly. I was still torturing her, giving her pain. Scaring her. The more pain I give her, the less the curse has its hold over me. If only momentarily.

The only good witch is a dead one. Even though she

has something to protect her from me killing her, torturing her will have to do for now to suffice my curse, until she helps me find the spell book.

Until then, I must be careful not to look at her. I can't let myself get tempted to let her go. The people of Sleepy Hollow care only for themselves. And she's one of them.

Running my hand down my face, I lift myself off the door and walk over to my dresser. I select a few articles of clothing and then head out of my room.

The witch is just where I left her, tied to the breaking wheel, her translucent dress now flat against her body at this angle, showing me everything.

I walk over to her, the sound of my boots echoing off the hardwood floor. I toss her a pair of trousers and a black shirt. They fall in front of her, but she can't see them from the position I have her in.

Quickly, I cut her loose, my narrowed eyes inches from hers. She swallows, understanding my silence as a threat. If she runs, I will catch her, and she won't like the outcome.

"Put those on." I don't wait for her before spinning on my heel and walking out of my cottage.

I'm not about to stand there and watch her get undressed. I'll give her some privacy while I try to reconcile what the fuck I just did.

Chapter Fifteen

KAT

I kissed him back.

I absently run my fingers through the clothes he threw down in front of me.

He kissed me. But I kissed him back.

Why in heaven's name would I do that? He had me tied to a torture wheel and was trying to kill me. How could I be so foolish?

Confusion swarms my mind as I sort through the garments. A black long-sleeved shirt and a pair of trousers, both too large for me to wear, but it's better than the damp, muddy, see-through gown I've been wearing for the last week. I better put them on quickly before he returns.

The look he gave me before he told me to change my

clothes told me everything I needed to know. Run, and he'll punish me for it.

I almost want to try.

Don't be stupid, Kat. You don't have a death wish.

He forgot to untie my ankles, though, or perhaps he left them tied on purpose to make it difficult for me to dress. I lift the gown over my head, the cold air of the cottage chilling my skin as it drifts over my wet body. Outside, it's drizzling.

I lift his shirt over my head and pull it down. It covers my hips, which makes it suitable for me to crawl over to his table and pick up the knife to untie the rope around my ankles. I didn't want to do that naked, and I was itching to get out of my wet clothes.

I select the knife he dropped earlier and begin to cut at the rope. When I get it loose, I use my hands to unfasten it quicker, then I pull the trousers on. I'm dressed all in black, but despite feeling strange about wearing the horseman's clothes, the warmth makes me feel better.

I rub my arms and legs, my hair falling over my face. My gaze lands back on the knife I used to cut my ankles free, and I grab it and tuck it inside one of my trouser pockets.

He can come back at any minute with his curse steering him to kill me again. This time, I can slice his throat open.

His lips were on mine.

And then he stopped trying to kill me. He said he was *trying* to kill me.

I bring my hand up to touch my necklace. Perhaps he really physically cannot. The question is...if he says he can't control it, why could he control it just then? Why kiss me instead of killing me?

The way he looked at me before that... My core heats as I think about the way his eyes roamed over my body. I suppose that's why he gave me something else to wear.

Could his desires have stopped his yearning to hurt me?

My breathing picks up. If that's true, perhaps there is a way I can survive this after all.

My thoughts drift to last night. The horseman killed Percival's father. Poor Percival. He doesn't deserve any of this... To find his father's body headless, his grandfather surely traumatized.

And now, he'll know I'm alive, trapped by the horseman. He'll likely try to find me, but it will be in vain.

I'll die here. At the hands of the horseman, eventually. Or of starvation or old age if he keeps feeding me bread and water.

Unless we do find that spell book. But even if we do get it, what am I to do with it? I'm not a witch, no matter how many times I keep telling him...

Fallon. The Hessian has a name, and it's Fallon.

Every time I close my eyes, I hear gunshots and see them firing at the horseman, but he doesn't go down. Why did he become so consumed with taking me? And not trying to kill me on the spot?

Somehow his curse is selective. As if it cycles and runs its course. But in that instance, he had already killed his charge. He could have just climbed on his steed and rode away, except he remembered to take me back with him.

He also chose not to kill Amos. He only wounded him.

I blink down at the floor. Before that, he didn't even gesture my way. It was like he became a marionette before his charge. How long does it take him to regain consciousness?

The door swings open, and I startle. Fallon walks in carrying a bag. He glances at my nightgown on the floor then back at me.

Isn't that what he told me to do? Change into his clothing?

"Is something the matter?" I ask.

"No." He drops the bag on the floor in front of me, and a few apples roll out.

My stomach roars, and I move to take one.

"I washed them," he mutters, then pulls a chair from his table of weapons and takes a seat.

His gaze doesn't leave me as I take a bite of the apple.

"Thank you," I whisper.

A mixture of sweet and tart juices explodes on my taste buds as I devour the fruit.

"I can't leave you for dead yet, witchy," he says with a hint of amusement in his voice.

Swallowing a bite, I suddenly feel once again on display as Fallon watches me eat. He's silent, and I wish I knew what he's thinking. The memory of his lips on mine makes me stop eating, and I stare back at him.

He tilts his head.

"Your curse caused you pain just then. You fought with yourself whether to hurt me or..." My cheeks heat, and I stare down at my apple. I can't believe I'm bringing this up to him. "Does it hurt you...that you cannot kill me?"

His eyes flash with anger, but his features remain calm. "Aye."

"I'm sorry."

He quirks a brow. "You are sorry that my inability to kill you causes me pain?"

"I know it's not your fault—"

"Whatever it is you think you're doing, stop it now."

My brows furrow. "Stop what?" I look around me. "I'm not doing anything."

"You can stop your tricks, witchy. I know what you're up to, and I won't fall for it again."

"I don't know what you're talk..." I gasp. "I did not make you want to kiss me if that's what you're thinking."

He stays quiet, but his eyes narrow on me.

Unbelievable. "That's what you think, don't you?"

His eyes spark with rage, and he lifts his chin at the rise in my voice.

I stand, no longer wanting him to tower over me. He notices my feet are untied and flicks his gaze to the table. Instead of growing angrier, though, a smirk flashes across his face, and he sneaks a look at my pocket where I stuck the knife.

"Typical man, thinking it's my fault he desired to put his hands on me," I tell him.

He stands and takes a step toward me. I swallow.

"Are you a masochist interested in the thrill of testing me, witchy?" His voice is calm. Collected. But I can sense the edge to it, a sign that he's willing to get creative with torturing me again.

I take a step back.

"Would a typical man kill willingly to honor a woman he doesn't know?"

I squint at him. "I don't know what that means."

"Never mind." He turns away from me and starts clearing the rope from the floor. "Keep the knife if it makes you feel safe. It'll do you no good against me anyway."

This man is unhinged. He means to torture me. He wants to kill me because it literally hurts him not to. And then he acts...nice to me. He could just leave me tied up here since it would make no difference to him, so why not just do it?

"What would happen if you would withstand the

curse?" I ask.

He faces me. "Which one? The main charges, or the one that cycles with you?"

I swallow.

"If I withstand the curse, I fail my mission and go back to hell. But that is never an option, for I can never withstand the curse. Except with you."

I grab at my necklace. "It's because of this, isn't it? It has the symbol you showed me in that book."

"I believe the moment you take it off, I'll be able to kill you. And I can't touch it. You better never take it off, love, or you will die."

I lick my dry lips as he disappears into his bedroom. He shuts the door and leaves me alone with my thoughts.

I stand in the middle of his living room, twirling my necklace. If anyone would consider this a living room with all the torture devices and weapons.

I've had this necklace for as long as I can remember. My mother gave it to me when I was a baby. She'd hang it right above my crib, and I grew up with her telling me to always keep it nearby.

It'll protect you, she'd say.

When I was old enough to wear it around my neck, she'd get angry at me if I ever took it off.

I always thought she was just superstitious, until, of

course, the horseman came to Sleepy Hollow, and I learned the stories were true.

After she died, I swore to always wear it.

Not that her ghost wouldn't berate me if I didn't. I miss my mother.

I stare at the horseman's bedroom door. I wonder if he'd mind if I walked out of the cottage. I'd knock on the door to ask, but I've had enough of him.

I decide to step out without asking. I'll beg for forgiveness later. Though he knows I can't go anywhere. I pick up two apples on my way out and stick one in my pocket.

Outside, the sky is gray, and the winds are cold. The black steed is standing by a nearby dead walnut tree, grazing on dead grass.

I scan the rolling hills around me, and for the first time, I realize I'm not in Sleepy Hollow. I'm not sure what this place is, or if it even exists in the real world.

How did my mother's ghost get here last time? I think of calling out her name, but I don't want to alert the horseman. I'd prefer some alone time.

Walking over to his horse, I roll the apple in my hand and take out the knife in my pocket. He doesn't seem bothered by me nearing him, so I start slicing the apple into thick slivers.

"Hello there," I say softly.

His ear flicks, but he doesn't look up. Gently, I stroke his hair. This gets his attention, and he moves his head over to me, pressing his muzzle to my stomach. I bring up the apple to his mouth, and he immediately eats it.

I blink at him, and a soft giggle escapes me. "I wasn't sure if you could eat."

I mean, he is a dead horse, isn't he? Or some sort of magical, immortal horse. At least his eyes aren't glowing red at the moment. They're black.

I give him more of the apple and pet his muzzle. "You're not so scary, are you?"

He eats the rest of the apple and walks closer to me, searching my hand for more. I laugh and reach into my pocket for the other one. My stomach grumbles, but I start slicing the apple for him anyway. The poor beast probably hasn't had a real bite to eat in...well, I couldn't say how long.

"Do you ever eat while you're up in Sleepy Hollow?" I ask him, as if expecting him to answer back.

Could the horseman eat if he wanted to?

"He does manage a bite to eat here and there." The horseman's voice comes from behind me, and I spin around, dropping the apple to the ground.

The top of his shirt is unbuttoned, and his sleeves are rolled up to his elbows, showcasing his black crow tattoos with thick Celtic knots. His suspenders hang lazily down his trousers, and his hair is ruffled.

"A horse will do what a horse will do out of habit. He has no agenda other than to eat."

"Sorry, I..." Had he been asleep?

He walks over, eyeing me. "It's all right. Vengeance is a hungry beast. If you don't mind sharing the only food you'll get, I won't stop you."

I swallow a dry lump in my throat. "I don't like seeing animals hungry."

"We're dead, witchy. It matters not for us." He takes Vengeance by his reins and pulls his head toward him.

"Just because you won't eat doesn't mean Vengeance doesn't feel hunger pains."

He passes me an odd look. "Perhaps."

I take a bite of an apple slice.

He starts to walk Vengeance out to the stable. "What are you doing out here anyway? Thinking of riding my horse out to the portal?"

My eyes widen. "No!" I hadn't considered that. "I was after some fresh air."

I'm not going to tell him I was out here hoping to find my mother's ghost. He already thinks I'm a witch.

"Vengeance can only leave when the curse is enacted," he says over his shoulder.

"Right." I follow him to the stable. It's either that or go back inside that dreadful cottage.

The stable is a few feet away from the cottage, along a woodless path with what appears to be a blackberry bush, but no fruits are visible.

I stop at the entrance and study the horseman as he leads Vengeance to his stall. He takes the brush on the open windowsill and begins to brush his coat. Vengeance closes his eyes at the horseman's gentle touch. Who would have thought the horseman would be so kind to his horse?

"It's been some time since I brushed his coat," he says after a few minutes of silence. "He deserves some attention."

"I suppose you don't have time with all your murdering."

His frown deepens, but he doesn't respond.

I can't help myself from poking the bear sometimes. I walk over to Vengeance and start stroking his muzzle. He pushes his nose into me, and I can't help but smile at the horse.

"You mentioned the curse cycling back to me."

He quirks a brow.

"How come you don't lose your head when that happens? I mean, I'm glad your head stays on... I was just wondering."

He licks his lips and continues brushing Vengeance's coat. "It's because you are still alive, hence my charge being left unfinished. The curse cycles, rather than starting anew." He flicks his gaze at me. "And it will keep happening."

I press my lips together, already knowing it will keep happening. "So what's next?"

"I don't care," he responds, his voice deep.

I knit my brows together and flick my gaze at him.

"Just stay away from me. But be ready. When it's time to go, I won't be able to wait, so you'll have to jump on

Vengeance. I cannot control what happens next, not until I take my first charge."

I swallow. Not until he takes his first charge.

"No tampering with my charge next time. Understood?"

"Yes."

"I mean it." His voice is demanding and his eyes dark. "The only way out of this, Katalina, is releasing me from these ghostly chains. If you won't help me, I'll lock you up in the iron maiden and just wait for you to die."

My heart hammers in my chest, my hand pausing on Vengeance's muzzle. This is why he's given me freedom to roam around and hasn't stopped me. He's giving me a taste of freedom so that he can take it away indefinitely if I mess it up.

I give him a brisk nod. "I understand."

"Good. Now leave me. I'd like to be left alone with my thoughts."

I turn away, creating enough distance from the stable so that I can scream out to the world. Hopefully, he won't hear me.

Chapter Sixteen

FALLON

I watch her as she walks away and smirk to myself when she begins to run.

I know she isn't planning to escape. Not that it would do her any good. But the sooner she understands how important my mission is, the sooner her family and friends will stop dying, and I can be released from the earth.

And finally be put to rest.

Vengeance takes a step toward her direction to follow, but I place my hand on his chest.

"Let her be," I say. "Don't get used to her either, Vengeance. She's not a friend."

He grunts at me, and I shake my head. Brute horse.

"What do you know? You're just a horse, aren't you?"

A horse who didn't deserve to die with me and become

a casualty of this brutal curse. If there's one thing I do know, the witch who cast this curse should burn in hell for what she did to a defenseless animal. Vengeance has nothing to do with wars of men.

Katalina's warm mouth forces itself into my memory, and I lick my lips.

Christ.

What was I thinking giving her my clothes to wear? The way she looks in them... It's almost worse than when she wore that translucent gown. Like she somehow has ownership of my clothes. Of my things.

The way my trousers fit around her perfect arse... It makes me wish I could show her off to the world, as if she belongs with me.

She does not. And I won't touch her again.

I toss the brush back onto the windowsill.

It's for the best I sent her away until it's time to go. When she's near, I feel as though there's a burning beneath my skin I'll never be able to soothe.

Although... I should be having her learn from the books on magic I do possess. That way I can study her and see if she is telling the truth about not knowing witchcraft, or if she's been lying.

I leave Vengeance alone in the stall. He has complete freedom to roam wherever he pleases. As soon as the curse becomes enacted, he'll be compelled to retrieve me, so there's no point in bringing him along with me.

Back at my cottage, I'm surprised to see Katalina

inside. I gave her free range, and she chooses to come back here?

I stand at the entrance, allowing a sliver of light to spill through the door as she bangs walnuts on the floor to get to the nut. Her messy blonde hair sprawls over my black shirt, falling to her waist.

Why she couldn't have grabbed the bag of fruit and taken it elsewhere is beyond me.

I let the door shut behind me as I make my way directly to my bedroom, but it doesn't make her turn to acknowledge me. Maybe what I told her earlier got to her.

Good. Maybe this time she'll behave.

After rummaging through my books, I select the ones I need and return to the living room, where I shift my various blades and weapons aside to make space. Then I carefully lay the books down.

She glances at me.

"You can sit at the table to eat instead of like some heathen on the floor."

Her eyes narrow at me, and I fight myself not to smile.

"That's rich coming from a demon."

I glance down at her. "Calling you a heathen offends you?"

"Do you really expect me to sit at a table full of weapons you mean to torture me with? I'd rather sit on the floor to eat, thank you."

"Fair enough, witchy. Come here. There's something I'd like to show you."

Her brows furrow, and she stills.

"I'm not going to hurt you." I spin the book around, opened to a page with sigils on it. "We don't know how long it'll be till I'm summoned again, so you might as well get to learning something useful that's going to speed up the process of breaking my curse."

She climbs to her feet and walks over to the table, glancing down at the book. "Won't it be repeating some words on a page?"

I scoff. "Is that it, then? Anyone can be a witch by just repeating some words on a page?"

She stares at me blankly.

I cross my arms. "Right, then. Would you know what to look for when we have the book?"

She shakes her head. "I suppose it would say something about breaking curses."

I guffaw and take a seat, leaning back in my chair. "Christ. This whole time I've thought you were lyin' to me, but you really don't know the first thing about spells, do you?"

Her eyes narrow as she crosses her arms in front of her. "I've told you that about a hundred times. I'm. Not. A. Witch."

"Well, then, I have no use for you." I stand and snatch the book away from her. "If you won't take this seriously, there's no point in doing this. Come with me."

"No, wait!"

I stare at her, my annoyance rising.

She reaches for the book in my hands. "I am taking it seriously. I don't know what to do, but I'll...figure it out."

"Right, then, that's a good lass. Study these books and see if there's anything you can practice. Pay close attention to the sigils and symbols. Try and remember if you've seen any of them in anyone's home."

"Like what?"

"Like perhaps a protection charm, a warding of some kind. I don't know. Anything. A good Christian wouldn't have symbols like the one around your neck lying around, now will they?"

She shoots me a hard glare but takes a seat in the chair and buries herself in the pages. I take the seat in front of her and start flipping through another leather-bound book called *The Discoverie of Witchcraft.*

"My mother gave me this necklace to keep me safe from you."

I huff as I flip another page. "I don't doubt it."

Katrina Van Tassel was a closeted witch. This is how I know Katalina has some kind of power.

I lift my head. "And you never thought to question it?"

She shrugs a slender shoulder. "Everyone in Sleepy Hollow is superstitious over you. Why would I have questioned it? No one else did."

That's a point.

She flips the pages slowly, mesmerized by the symbols inscribed in red on the pages. Her eyes are wide as her fingers delicately trace one of them before flipping to the next page.

"Finding anything of interest, witchy?" I ask her.

She darts me a sardonic look then goes back to studying the pages.

Truth is, I've read all of these books fifty times over, and all I've gathered is without the spell book that governs me specifically, none of the incantations scribbled in these pages will ever be of use.

This is the first time I have someone reading over these pages, too, though. Perhaps the introduction to this world —magic, this domain, all of it—is enough to either scare her away or distract her from the problem at hand and release me from the curse.

However, it doesn't look like she's getting scared. More like captivated by the notions of spell work. I'm not the least bit surprised.

She gasps and moves the book closer to her.

I narrow my eyes and lean in. "What did you find?"

Her lips part, and she flicks her gaze to me then back down. "There's a spell to ensure your harvest will never falter."

I lean back in my chair. Of course there is.

Running her index finger down the page, she begins to mutter the words to herself.

I resist the urge to roll my eyes. Instead, I lean over and snatch the book away from her.

"Hey, I was reading that."

"You're getting distracted." I slam the book shut and set it aside. "Growing crops isn't going to help me, witch."

"Well, I don't know the first thing about magic. Shouldn't I be practicing in small steps?"

I smile. She isn't exactly crying heathenry and trying to run out the door after reading about spells that would benefit her farm.

"Your little manipulations aren't going to work on me. Try again."

She blinks at me. "I—"

"Try telling me something useful instead, then. Tell me about your neighbors."

Her hands ball into fists, and she stares off to the side. I can tell she's getting nervous about wanting to reveal anything incriminating about the townsfolk.

"What do you want to know?" She glances up at me.

"Let's start with something easy. Tell me about the lady of your house, your grandmother."

Her eyes flare, that fist of hers digging nails into her skin. "Nana has nothing to do with any of this."

"Just like your mother didn't?"

Shock crosses her features.

"It's better we rule out the innocent. So, beg her case for me, and we'll move on to the next good Christian of Sleepy Hollow." I smirk.

"Fine." She swallows. "Nana hardly ever leaves the house, except to go to church and take walks around Winter Garden. She's been devastated since my..."

She takes another swallow, harder this time.

"Your father's untimely death?"

Her eyes burn into me, and her lips thin.

Gods, she's beautiful when she's crossed with me. I'm starting to think I enjoy winding her up just to get this reaction from her.

"Nana spends most of her time at night reading her bible by the fire. I've never seen any other book in her belongings, nor anything suspicious at home."

I offer her a plain smile. "Good. And your housemaid?"

Katalina gapes at me. "She's just the housemaid..."

"I don't trust anyone close to your family. What's her name? Tilly, was it? What does Tilly do in her spare time?"

Crossing her arms, she leans back in her chair. "She takes care of her child and makes wreaths and decorations for town festivals."

I'll have to keep a close eye on that one. In my experience, anyone close to the Van Tassel family has had sticky fingers with things they shouldn't, like spell books and the like.

"What about your friend I killed?" I ask. "Can you think of any reason why someone would want him dead?"

Her bottom lip quivers, and she squeezes her eyes shut. When she opens them again, her eyes are bloodshot. "Daniel was good. I can't imagine why anyone would want him dead."

"Did you have naughty thoughts about this Daniel?"

Her cheeks flush, and she gives me her death stare. Adorable.

"Relax, witchy. I'm only asking because of the way you get so bent up about him. I'll tell you what." I lean in. "Anyone who has had the shit luck to meet me blade has been a poor excuse for a human being. So maybe stop holding people you know to such high standards."

"I won't believe that. Not Daniel. He was good."

"Says the woman who had his help in burning a man alive."

"Not a man," she hisses. "A demon."

"Right, that again." I lean back and cross one leg over the other. "Tell me, then, witchy, do my looks match your expectations of a demon?"

Her cheeks turn an even deeper rosy color. She nervously moves a loose strand of blonde hair behind her ear.

My gaze catches on the contrast of her light hair against the black fabric of my shirt, and it reminds me of how much I wish I could tear it off her.

I stand. "We're not finished talking about your town yet." I pick up the book I took away from her and put it back in front of her. "For now, keep reading. You may read as many of my books as you like, but keep your mind focused on the task at hand. There's no time to waste."

She nods and flips the book open. I start to walk to my bedroom when she speaks again.

"Why do you have so many torture devices?"

I pause. "Each of these was once used on me. I've reclaimed them and made them my own so no one can ever control me with them again."

She takes in a deep breath. "And the torturer?"

I don't respond to her question and slam my door behind me.

Chapter Seventeen

FALLON

It has been twenty-four hours since the curse was enacted. And my last compulsion to kill her.

The rest of the day passes quietly. I sit close to the windowsill in my bedroom and stare out at the trickling rain.

Rise, Hessian. Thou shalt rise and suffer the agonies of a thousand deaths until my bidding is fulfilled.

Those were the words I heard before I rose again. After that, I found myself and Vengeance alone in the field in front of my old cottage.

I normally hate it when the curse enacts. I loathe being made to act against my will. But now I'm itching for it to happen.

Whoever has control over me won't be doing it

forever. They're bound to get what they want soon, and then what? Will they keep me alive until their next desire for me to kill? Or are they after something specific, and once they get it, they'll be finished with me?

What will they do to me after they've gotten what they want?

That's the part that unsettles me the most. I hate living knowing someone out there controls my fate, and there's nothing I can do to stop it.

But now I have a plan, and the sooner the curse enacts again, the sooner Katalina can find me that spell book.

The house sounds eerily quiet, so I go see what the witchy is up to. Half expecting for my living area to be converted to a ritual space, with symbols drawn on the floor and an altar in the middle, I'm surprised to find her gone again.

She seemed so interested in the spell book she was reading and the spells to keep famine away. I was sure she'd try something.

A strange, sweet, yet spicy smell engulfs my nostrils. Something simmers in a cast-iron pot on my stove, and I go to it.

What is this?

The hot fumes bring a memory of long ago. Back when…I was a child waiting for my mother to finish baking an apple pie while I sat playing with a wooden toy.

Something scratches at my throat, and I take a step back, my memory disappearing as fast as it came. I haven't thought of my childhood in… It's been so long that the last time I had a memory such as that one, I was still alive.

What is this witch doing to me?

Grimacing, I turn to go find her.

Outside, night has fallen, and there's a chill in the air. I skim the fields for the blonde little minx, a bit surprised she's out here in the cold. I thought she'd be warming up by the fire she made in my stove.

I sense no movement by the Andre tree portal, so I start toward the stable. Sure enough, there she is, seated next to Vengeance. Something about her caring for my horse enough to be out here alone tending to him stirs something inside me.

I shove it back down.

Ruthless witch.

"What are you doing out here?"

She jumps at my sudden appearance. Vengeance only looks at me, unimpressed by my tone, no doubt.

I walk over to him and take his reins from her when I see the pile of nuts, berries, and seeds in her hand. "Are you still giving your food away to my undead horse?"

"Just because he's undead doesn't mean he's not hungry."

I narrow my eyes at her. I'm not having this argument again.

"Besides, there's plenty by the Andre tree."

"You went to the Andre tree?" And she didn't try to escape? Not that she could, but had she not believed me, she'd be scuffed up from trying and then being thrown back down.

"Yes." She takes the reins back from me, and Vengeance nibbles away at the food she's offering in her hand. "It's cold out. I thought he'd be uncomfortable. I hope you don't mind. I found a blanket inside that chest by the table."

I bring my gaze to Vengeance and notice the knitted pattern of a blanket I haven't seen in years. My throat dries, and I clear it.

"I'm sorry... I can put it back..."

I dart a look to her. She must've caught me looking miserably at it.

"No. It's fine," I say.

I watch her closely as she finishes giving the rest of what's in her hand to my horse. She then gives Vengeance a few pats and kisses him on the muzzle.

I start walking back to the cottage, leaving her there, unsure of what to do with her oddness.

Her footsteps come up behind me, and I flick my gaze to her. I didn't expect her to follow me back so soon.

"What kind of potion are you cooking up in my kitchen?" I ask her.

"It's not a potion. It's hot cider."

"Are you sure you didn't learn it from one of my books?"

"Wouldn't you recognize something you've supposedly read dozens of times?"

I can't help the smirk cross my face at her wit.

I pull the door open for her. "Fine. Get inside."

She swallows and glances at the door I'm holding for her, and my breath catches. I'm not usually a gentleman around her. I don't barge in first, though. I stare at the ground and let her walk past me. She strides directly to the pot and breathes in the fumes.

"Would you like some?" she asks.

"No."

She starts rummaging through my cupboards, looking for something. I walk over to where I keep my tankards, pull one out for her, and set it down on the counter. She takes it and starts pouring in cider with the ladle.

"That was clever of you," I tell her.

She gives me an inquisitive look.

"Finding something to sustain you out of nothing."

"Not nothing. This land isn't barren."

I scoff. "It is barren. The only things in it are dropped in from the Andre portal."

"But there's grass. And some trees. Shrubbery."

"None of it has sprouted any fruits. It is all frozen in time, the way it was when I was alive."

She pauses to stare at me, as if I just gave her some information about me and my past. About what this place is, what it could mean to me.

She walks quietly toward me, and my eyes widen. She strides past me to the cupboard I took the tankard from, and she pulls out another. I squint at her as she begins to ladle in the cider.

She hands it to me, but I step back.

"I said no."

"Won't you just take a sip? Try it."

"I don't need sustenance."

"Yes, I know. Just like your horse." She walks over to me and takes my hand.

I still. Her touching me willingly awakens a feeling I didn't think existed in me anymore. Tingling skitters up my arms, and my grip tightens around the tankard. I quickly turn away from her and bring the drink to my lips.

The warmth of it scorches my tongue, but I take it in, allowing the beverage to soothe the lining of my throat. The sweet apple aroma grips my chest with so many strange sensations. Things buried deep in my past come to the surface.

My childhood. Parties. My mother. Noreen...

I set the tankard down on the table.

"Well? What do you think?"

Without meeting her gaze, I tell her, "Just make sure you don't burn the place down," and then I leave to my bedroom.

The next day, I wake, unsettled by the fact I fell asleep. I don't need to sleep. Not that I mind it, but it isn't like me to let my guard down with her here.

Today, I need her to learn something from those books. I can't have her staring at the pages of the spell book when we find it, not knowing what to do, and wasting more time.

I swing the door open to find her gone again. This time I'm not surprised, since I know where she probably is. What I do find surprising is... I sniff the air.

The place is clean. The floor is still wet from her mopping. I walk over to my table and drag my finger over the wood. No dust. The sweet aroma from her apple beverage still hangs in the air.

I grimace and bolt out the door. My first instinct is to go to Vengeance since that seems to be her favorite place to dwell, but when I get there, I pause. Vengeance isn't in his stall. I furrow my brows. That good for nothing, apple-eating beast betrayed me for some minx.

Laughter carries on the wind, and I turn to spot the witch under a tree with my horse standing beside her.

I walk over to her, my eyes narrowing as I try to gauge what she's doing. She pops a piece of apple into her mouth and flips the page of a book she's reading. Her chin lifts when I step closer, and she sits up.

"Just what do you think you're playing at?"

Her eyes widen. "I don't know what you mean."

"Why is my cottage clean?"

Her bottom lip trembles, and she starts to twirl her hair with her fingers. "I just thought—"

"And you making potions."

"Cider," she corrects me.

"Whatever it is. Why are you doing it? If you think you're going to soften me up so that I let you go, you are poorly mistaken." I look over to my horse, who's nibbling on some grass. "Traitor."

"That's not why I'm doing it." She closes the book with her finger still inside it.

I notice the cover doesn't match any of the research books I've given her and scoff to myself. "Then why?"

She squares her gaze on me. "Because if I'm going to live out the rest of my days here, I might as well make it have a semblance of a home."

I regard her face. "I'd rather you learn to break my curse. That's what you should be doing."

A tear rolls down her cheek. "But what if I can't do it?"

"You must try. You'd rather just give up and die? Let me torture you?"

She sniffles, her eyes red. She drops the book on her lap, now losing her place, and starts to shake.

I deepen my frown. "Why are you shaking like that? I'm not even touching you."

"I'm sorry." She sniffles again, rubbing her eyes. "I'm exhausted. I haven't slept in days."

"Did you not rest last night?"

Her eyelids fly open, and she gapes at me. "Who could sleep on that hard floor?"

"Your discomfort should be enough motivation to get moving with your lessons. Instead of reading... What is this?" I lean in and rip the book out of her hands. "Shakespeare?"

She winces at my rush of movement. "I was, but I got tired of reading those books. They're just filled with spells. I don't see how any of them can help me with breaking your curse. At least Shakespeare offers me some sort of reprieve from you."

"Shakespeare won't help you when you're the last person of Sleepy Hollow alive, with me as your only companion."

"If you're to kill everyone I know, then perhaps Shakespeare will help me escape the prison of *you*." Her words seethe out of her lips like venom, letting me know how much she hates me.

The feeling, my dear, is mutual.

"What would you know about it anyway?" she asks. "I bet you only knew the Wordsworth I recited because it had to do with war. These are all just books you've stolen in your quest to break a curse. You probably stumbled upon it by accident."

My breath shallows, and I lean into her. "You want Shakespeare?" I whisper.

She blinks up at me, confusion scrawled on her face.

"Coral is far more red than her lips' red," I begin.

"If snow be white, why then her breasts are dun;

If hairs be wires, black wires grow on her head.

I have seen roses damask'd, red and white,

But no such roses see I in *her cheeks*." I let the *S* of the last word linger on my tongue.

Her cheeks flush.

"Shall I keep going?"

Her lips press together in a thin line. "I get your point. Good thing I'm not your mistress."

My lip curls. "So you know the sonnet. Good. Then, you have enough Shakespeare to last you your life."

She frowns. I lock her in place with my gaze, the both of us staring at each other, not moving.

"I may have given you free range, but don't get complacent, witchy. It's only because I know you can't leave and don't want you disturbing my peace with your perpetual sobbing and hunger. The kiss we shared was a desperate act to ease my compulsion to kill you. Nothing more. You will do as I say when I say it, or you'll be studying while seated in the garrote. Now, get up."

Her throat works as she stumbles for words.

"I said stand."

She climbs to her knees. Her lips press tightly together, but something in her has changed. Her eyes narrow, and she keeps her chin held high.

I push at her arm toward the cottage, and she begins to move toward it. She keeps her head straight to our destination, quiet all the way.

Her silence makes my chest tighten. Honest to God, I don't know why I care how I made her feel.

"What are you going to do to me?" she asks once we're back at the cottage.

"Nothing," I mutter, almost inaudibly.

She stares at me blankly.

"Sit at the table and study the books I lent you."

Perhaps I'm too tired for torture. Too tired to argue. It's a useless task anyway. She's not here to get comfortable. She's here because I can't kill her, and the only way out of this hell is to use her to break my curse. That's it.

The curse to kill her hasn't come again... Not since... I dip my gaze to her lips and then immediately look away.

She buries herself in a history book.

I lock the Shakespearean novel away in my bedroom before leaving the cottage to tend to Vengeance. A good ride will help me clear my head.

Outside, the wind hits my face as Vengeance and I speed down the path between the rolling hills. There's nowhere to go, since this domain eventually loops me back to where I started, but we can go as fast as we want.

I had to get out of there before the memories hit me like a flash flood.

My hands are shaking, covered in firearm grease. I had

been cleaning my guns before I heard my wife's screams coming from the lord's bedroom.

Before I even know what's happening, fury instantly blinds me, and I see red. I cock one of the guns and barge through the bedroom door.

She's cornered by the window curtains, her eye makeup running down her face. Her auburn hair is sweaty and stuck to her neck.

Our master shouts something at me. His pants are down, yet he still reaches for his gun on the table. I cock the musket and shoot.

Noreen screams and runs toward me. "What did you do!?"

I knew this was a risk, us coming here. I knew this would happen. We'd hear the tales of it happening to women indentured servants all the time. Being here was the only bargain we could make to keep me out of prison, and my wife with me. We were called lucky for being kept together. Normally, we'd be separated.

"We have nowhere to go!" Noreen whispers desperately.

I touch her cheeks and look into her eyes, ignoring the pool of blood making its way beneath my shoes.

"Did he touch you?"

Her lip quivers, and that tells me all I need to know.

"God, Noreen. How long?" I wasn't angry with her. I knew she wasn't willing with anyone but me. "I'll kill them all."

"N-no. Fallon...we—"

"Yes," I whisper. "We must go now." I kiss her forehead. "It'll be okay."

She nods.

The only chance we have of surviving this now is to escape without being seen.

"Leave everything behind. We'll find new clothes wherever we go."

"And where are we going to go, Fallon?"

"Let me worry about that later. For now...just stay close behind."

The front door swings open from the first floor, and I grab my wife's hand and make a sharp right toward the back. There's another stairway leading down to the kitchen of the two-story manor. Shouts come from downstairs as one of the staff tells someone else they heard gunfire.

Noreen squeezes my hand.

We get to the end of the hall, and someone is already coming up the stairs.

Fuck.

"Fallon." Noreen whimpers.

I rush her to the window and pry it open. I let her out first onto the balcony. I have one leg over the windowsill when someone grabs me and violently pulls me back inside.

I swing my fist and clock whoever has me square in the jaw. We struggle as I shout at Noreen to run. To leave me. And then there's the familiar feeling of a gun's barrel shoved against my back. I still.

"Try it again, and I'll shoot you here and now," a voice says.

I look over my shoulder to see the master's brother, George, holding the musket.

He sneers. "I believe you've overstayed your welcome, Paddy boy."

"George!" Another voice comes from down below, and my chest tightens. "I've got the bog-trotter whore."

"Hold her tight. I'm bringing the Mick down now," George calls.

"No!" I shout. "Leave her alone!"

George kicks me in the kneecap, and I fall. He kicks me again then grabs at my torn shirt and lifts me against the wall. His breath stinks, and he has blood on his hands. His brother's blood.

"Listen to me, you piece of shit," he growls. "We let you into our home. We had a contract. And you thank us by killing my brother."

Blood rises in my throat, and I cough it up, spraying him in the face with some of it.

"He had my wife..." I can't bring myself to finish the sentence.

The look in his eyes tells me he knew what was going on. Bile threatens to surge up my throat. Rage boils in my blood, and I ready my strength to take this motherfucker down too.

A smile spreads on his face, and he leans in close. "You think that's bad? Wait till you see what we're all going to do to her. We'll tie you up and make you watch. Then we'll kill her."

Chapter Eighteen

KAT

SINCE HE DISAPPEARED out the door, I've read the same sentence over and over. I'm glad he's gone.

For the past two days, I've been trying to keep my distance. It's bad enough I have to live here, reading these stupid books while I wait for the horrors of his curse to be enacted.

My vision blurs on the words as I try to focus my mind to concentrate. The way he looked at me outside, like he hates me after he kissed me, burns in my throat.

How is it that he hates *me*? I'm the one who loathes *him*. He took me from my home and is killing everyone I care about.

It isn't his doing.

And yet, I still can't get past it.

Good thing I'm not your mistress. That was the best I could come up with? Obviously, I don't ever want to be his mistress.

I never believed in betrothal anyway, let alone love. If I survive this and go back to my mother's estate, I will find a way not to marry. I'll take care of my crops and be my own source of business. Just like Mother wished of me.

My fingers start to ache from how hard I'm gripping the corner of the page, and I relax my hand.

I hate the way he makes me feel when he's around, not speaking to me. It doesn't help that I find him so brutally handsome.

Perhaps the horseman's insistence on me learning some spells holds merit after all. It may aid in my escape from him and help me manage on my own in Sleepy Hollow. With magic, I could tend to my farm in secret, proving to everyone that I need no one.

If I ever get out of here alive.

What was he even so angry about? That I cleaned his dusty old cottage? I didn't do it for him. If I'm to sleep on the floor, I don't want to do it in filth.

I ball my fists. I hate him. He's going to make my life miserable at any attempt I do to feel the least bit comfortable.

He's right about one thing. The only way out of this horrid place is to break his curse. But I have flipped through most of the spell books he owns already, and none of them allude to breaking the curse of a headless horseman.

My gaze lands on a brown leather book at the far end of the table with a title so worn I can't make out its words. I pick it up and flip through its pages.

This one isn't a spell book, so I haven't bothered, but it doesn't hurt to read it anyway.

I flip to a heading that reads *The Hessians of Germany,* and I pause on the page.

"German soldiers from Hesse-Kassel fought on the side of the British Army during the Revolutionary War. The majority of these men were former slaves who escaped from their masters to become Hessians. Some, though, were captured and bought by the Hessians and forced to serve."

My lips part.

Hessian.

Don't call me that.

Was Fallon forced to serve with the Hessians? But why? How did an Irishman end up among the slaves forced to fight in the war?

The front door opens, and a cold draft comes in.

I still, my fingers clutching the page tightly. His footsteps echo on the wooden floor, and he pauses over my shoulder. He doesn't say a word to me and keeps walking into his bedroom. When the door closes, I stand and decide to leave the cottage once again.

The gray skies remind me of Sleepy Hollow, and I wonder how my nana is doing.

Instead of walking toward Vengeance, I decide to take the route toward the Andre tree to see if I can gather any more fruit. I spend the rest of the day out here, and the horseman doesn't bother to come find me this time.

Or perhaps he will be on his way the moment he realizes I'm not with Vengeance.

"Katalina!"

My mother's voice spins me around, and I find her at the base of the Andre tree.

"Mother!" I run up to her, knowing I won't be able to touch her. "Where have you been? I've been looking for you."

"Are you well?" She goes to touch my face with both hands, but all I feel is the cold she usually brings.

Oh, how I miss her warm embrace so much.

"I've been so worried. Did he hurt you?" She darts her gaze around. "Are you escaping?"

Her voice lowers to a whisper, although I'm not sure he could see her if he were here. The last time I saw my mother, he dragged me back to the cottage and didn't acknowledge her. I'm not sure if the undead can see a spirit.

"I'm fine, Mother. Your charm works. He can't kill me."

She breathes a sigh of relief as she stares at my pendant. "Good. Never take it off." She looks over my shoulder as though she's worried about him appearing. "This isn't what I wanted for you, Kat. I am truly sorry."

"It's okay, Mother. None of this was your fault. He knows I'm out here. I couldn't escape even if I tried." I point up to the gray swirls the tree limbs disappear into. "I need his curse to be enacted to be able to ride with him out of here."

My mother's brows furrow. "No, I don't believe that's true." She looks down at the fruits on the ground. "If those have fallen down the portal, I'm sure you can leave if you can make it up there."

I blink at her. I hadn't considered that. "But his horse... Vengeance is also under the curse. I can't ride him out of this place. It would be physically impossible for him to leave."

"Did the Hessian tell you that?"

I wince at her calling him a Hessian. "Yes."

"And you believe him?"

I regard her words. "I have grown to know the horse... Perhaps if he lets me ride on his back, we can try to leave..."

If we do make it out of the portal, it wouldn't necessarily leave Fallon stranded here. The moment his curse gets enacted, Vengeance will be back to retrieve him, and after the horseman is killed, he'll come looking for me.

But perhaps it would give me the time I need to get me and Nana away from Sleepy Hollow.

I swallow.

Or perhaps the best course of action is finding a way to free him from his curse. Otherwise, I'd always be on the run. What if he could leave Sleepy Hollow to find me? I am his charge, after all.

"He won't stop until he kills me, Mother. It's best I do what he says and try to break his curse."

"Break his curse? Is that what he's after?"

"Yes." I touch my pendant. "Mother...is...there anything you could tell me about the headless horseman? Anything that could help me stop the curse from enacting?"

"Enacting?"

Right. She doesn't know.

"His head comes back after he's killed. Whenever the curse gets enacted, he relives the way he dies...over and over until he's killed whoever he's been charged to kill. He's stuck in this domain until he's called again. And the only reason he hasn't killed me is because of this." I lift my necklace off my chest. "Which means the only reason he's been trying to kill me is because someone in Sleepy Hollow wants *me* dead."

My mother's ghostly face pales even more than usual.

"Do you have any inclination who among our peers could want me dead?" I ask.

She chews the inside of her cheek and stares down at the ground. "Someone in Sleepy Hollow wants you dead?

And they wanted your father dead as well? It must be someone after your farm, daughter."

My lips part. "Is that what this is about? Land?"

"It usually is. The last time he was summoned, my stepmother wanted the farm for herself. Greed is usually the culprit of sorcery."

Cecilia. Although I know of her, Mother never spoke of her.

"And how did you come across a book of spells?"

Shock plasters her face.

"Don't tell me you didn't. How else would you have known what would have protected me from him?" I touch the pendant once more, letting her know I'm all the wiser now.

"It was a spell book, yes. I stole it from my stepmother, but then I buried it. If someone found it, then they are the ones who summoned him back to life. The question remains as to whom. No one could just kill you or your father to take the land. They would have to have claim to it." She nibbles on her ghostly thumb. "You do have some relatives..."

"Who?"

"Agnes, for one."

"The baker's wife?" I gape at her. "Why have you never told me that? She dropped a dead crow on my lap the day of my father's funeral. I knew she practiced magic."

My mother's eyes widen. "She's my aunt... We were never close." She starts to pace. "It would have to be her, wouldn't it? I've known your father since childhood...and we had been together for a long time. There was no one else..."

"What are you talking about?"

She spins to look at me. "Nothing. I regret to say this, but it must be Agnes. If she followed me into the forest that night, and she could have...that sneaky, beady-eyed widow... She would have seen me bury the book. She's always been jealous that my father gave the farm to me. It only makes sense that she would make a move after I died."

A cool breeze passes over me, and I wrap my arms around myself. It will likely rain soon in Sleepy Hollow, which means rain down here too.

"I should go back," I say.

"I'll go spy on her. When can I see you again?"

"I'll try to come back to this same spot tomorrow. But Mother?"

"Yes?"

"Can you try and find out why Hessian soldiers would buy an Irishman and force him to fight for them in the war?"

Her brows furrow. "I'll see what I can find out."

"Thank you."

Thunder claps above the tree, sending vibrations through the air.

"Go now. And be careful," I tell her.

"I will."

I slowly creek the cottage door open to find the horseman isn't here, but his bedroom door is still shut. I quietly let the door close behind me, lifting the latch and letting it down slowly so that it doesn't make a sound.

If he's asleep or reading in his room, I don't want to let him know I'm here so that he can come out and question me about what I've learned.

I walk over to the kitchen counter to empty the apples and walnuts from my pocket, when I pause at the hearth, the cast-iron stove already lit and warming the area. A thick blanket and a pillow lie neatly folded in front of it.

Are my eyes deceiving me? I go to the makeshift bed and place my hands on the fabric. A thin layer of a soft sheet over cotton acts as a mattress below it. It's not much, but it's better than the hardwood floor and no blanket at all. On top of the pillow lies the book of Shakespearean sonnets he took away from me.

I look over my shoulder at his shut door. What came over him to return this to me?

I contemplate knocking to thank him but decide it's best to leave him undisturbed. I'll get my chance to thank him soon enough.

Instead, I brew another cider on the stove and open the book to read by the fire. It doesn't take me long before I drift off to sleep.

I wake to the cottage door crashing open and Vengeance standing at the entrance. The headless horseman mounts his steed, and I nearly stumble over myself to stand.

I don't bother rubbing the sleep out of my eyes. My heart hammering in my chest is doing that for me.

The smell of gunfire lingers in the air. I grab the horseman's brick-like back and lift myself over Vengeance. Reluctantly, I seat myself as close as I can to the horseman, taking in the brimstone scent of him.

The horse takes off through the dead of night, and I grip the horseman's torso as hard as I can as we lift up above the Andre tree and through the portal.

Chapter Nineteen

KAT

PRESSING my face against the horseman's back, I brace myself against the ghostly fingers of gnarled trees reaching out to me.

Vengeance leaps over a hedge and lands with a hard thud, causing my body to jump a little too high. I grip the horseman's body tighter, and I hate how close I have to cling to him.

We cross the bridge, the moonlight casting ripples over the sleepy water. It feels late in the night, so the town will surely be asleep. My heart is in my throat since I don't know who he's after, but I try not to think about it.

This time, I'm going to keep my promise.

The imposing church spire among the dense forest

casts skeletal shadows over the weather-worn tombstones as we pass the cemetery.

When we reach the houses, candlelight beams through the curtains of the windowsills. It mustn't be so late, after all.

Dread lands in my stomach. This isn't good. It'll only make it harder to snoop around for information without being seen.

The horseman pauses at the foot of an alleyway and turns his horse to get ready to charge. I quickly start sliding off, knowing that he has no control over himself right now. I stumble over my footing and fall on my rear as Vengeance stands on his hind legs.

They take off into the dark alleyway, and I force myself to look away from where he's headed for fear that if I figure out who he's about to kill, I'll be tempted to try and stop him. An attempt purely wasted. It's best I stick to the plan.

I climb to my feet and dust myself off. I need to find who's a witch in town, and if my suspicions about Agnes are correct, that will be easy. Then I need to find the spell book. Then break his curse and free Sleepy Hollow.

And then Fallon goes back to hell.

Something twists my stomach at that last thought. Despite how he's tortured me, I can't ignore the fact that he's under someone's command, and he doesn't truly want to kill me.

His horse whinnies in the distance.

Right. Time is of the essence. Best get going. Sticking to the shadows of the trees, I traipse straight to Agnes's home.

Her cottage is pitch dark when I arrive, but even so, I'll have to be careful not to wake her. Inside, I'm hit with the aroma of a chicken roast and potatoes. My stomach has a fit of rumbles.

Focus, Kat.

I sneak in through her foyer and lightly step on the floorboard, holding my breath as if it will help me be quieter.

The coast seems clear. A smoky hearth has just been blown out. To the right, near a slightly open bedroom door, is a large bookcase filled with leather-bound books.

I swallow, take another deep breath, and tiptoe over there.

This is impossible. Without a candle or the hearth lit, I won't be able to see anything, let alone read the titles on these books.

I creep over to the kitchen, hoping to find a candlestick and hoping that Agnes remains asleep during all my walking and rummaging. What would she say to me if she woke to find me sneaking here?

What would I say to her?

Would she be relieved to find me alive? Perhaps I should wake her...and she'll help me.

Wait. What am I thinking? If she's really the witch, then she wants me dead.

I push back my thoughts and focus, feeling around the kitchen for a candle. My fingers stop on something soft and still warm, and I swallow a gasp. Her roast! My stomach roars again, and I lick my cracked lips. I'm so hungry. Would she notice if I had a few bites?

Before I can rationalize with myself any more about it, I'm already breaking a leg off the chicken and taking a bite. Flavors of thyme and rosemary explode on my tastebuds, and I have to stop myself from moaning as I swallow my fill.

Moonlight helps my eyes adjust to the darkness, and something to the bottom right of the cupboard grabs my attention. Flour.

Of course the baker's wife would have loads and loads of flour and cotton bags to fill. If I rush, I can grab just enough to take with me.

A light shines on the other side of the cottage, and my heart stops. Slowly, I turn toward it, expecting to see Agnes standing there with a barrel facing me. But there's no one. Only a lit candlestick on top of the fireplace mantel.

Who lit that candle?

I wipe my hands on a kitchen cloth and make my way over, careful not to make any noise. The flickering of the flame dances over a red leather-bound book with no title. I open it to find handwritten notes. Agnes's diary, perhaps? I carefully flip the thick pages and stop when I catch the words *Fending Away Evil*.

1 part Rue
1/2 parts Wood Betony
1/2 Mugwort
2 parts Juniper Berries
1/2 Yarrow

On the next page are directions on how to cast a magic circle.

A small gasp escapes my throat. So she is a witch.

I stop to read how to cast a circle, and it explains how it's important to do so before casting any spell. I don't know if there's going to be anything specific in this book, but it's better than anything I've read in the horseman's cottage.

I flick my gaze to the ominous candle that lit itself and stick the book inside my trouser pocket. Then I turn around and utter a sharp gasp. My mother's ghostly pale face stops me in my tracks.

"Mother," I whisper.

"Shh."

"Was it you who lit the candle?"

"Never mind that. Come here."

My brows furrow as I follow her back toward the kitchen of the small cottage. She stands in front of the last drawer of the counter and points to it. I open it and cringe when its hinges squeak.

When I don't hear movement coming from Agnes's room, I take a look inside to find letters of some kind. I take them out and start skimming through them. Some of them seem to be old letters between the baker, Henry, and his wife. I stare back at my mother, but she nods back to the letters in my hand.

"I don't understand."

Her eyes widen at me as she purses her lips.

"Fine, all right." I keep flipping through the letters, but I don't see anything suspicious or out of the ordinary...

Hold on. What's this? One of the letters is addressed to my father.

My good friend,
I would felicitate thee on these tidings, but it doth not seem seemly. Know that our amity hath ever held great import for me, and I shall carry thy secret unto mine grave.
Henry

My lips part with a gasp. A secret?

The sounds of galloping make me pause, and both my mother and I stare toward the window. The horseman.

I quickly put the letters back in the drawer and close it. Then I start heading out the door, when the sack of flour catches my eye.

Maybe just a little.

I rush over, grab a small cotton pouch, and start scooping flour into it, careful not to pour too much or I won't be able to carry it. Once I'm done, I stand to leave as quickly as possible.

Vengeance's shoes clap on the cobblestone road, and I hurry to tie the sack together.

Finished.

I stand, but when I turn, I meet face-to-face with a middle-aged woman, her skin pale. The blood drains from my head.

"Agnes...I..." My throat dries. I've forgotten how to speak.

She grabs my arms, and my lips tremble. I stare her square in the face, and her large eyes grow wide as she seems to peer right through me.

The witch has finally caught me. How stupid a plan was this? To come to the witch's home, expecting to steal her spell book and get away with it?

"Beware the Dullahan."

I blink. "W-what?"

"Leave now, child, and beware the Dullahan." She starts to push me out of her house, and I'm quick to oblige.

"Beware!" she calls after me as I step out into the cold night.

I stumble backward but quickly catch my footing.

Vengeance turns the corner, and I run toward him. He slows for me to climb on, and the horseman grabs my arm, helping to pull me up. At first, shock surfaces, but then I remember how he fought me after he beheaded Percival's father.

The town may be waking now if he caused a ruckus by killing whomever he just killed. The horseman nudges Vengeance, and we take off down the moonlit alley.

Unease settles in my stomach.

I'm still alive. She didn't kill me.

But she is a witch. Perhaps just not *the* witch we're after.

What did she mean, beware the Dullahan? What's a Dullahan? And what was that letter addressed to my father about? What secret?

We make our way back toward the cemetery. The horseman seems...more relaxed. I have my arms around him as before, but he's less rigid, and his shoulders seem more slumped, like he's coming back to himself after killing his charge.

I swallow the dry lump in my throat. I'm going to end up asking him who he killed, and he's not going to willingly give me the information. It's a matter of whether I'm prepared for the answer.

We make a right turn at the bridge, and I tense.

"Where are we going?" I ask, unsure why I bothered as his head is still missing.

That's also something I haven't understood yet. If he's coming to and regaining control over himself after obliging the curse, how long does it take for his head to come back? And until then, is he still partly under the guise of the curse?

I'll have to make a note of asking him how he can see as well.

The dirt path becomes grassy and covered with small wildflowers. A grove of moss-covered trees canopies our heads. I've never been down this path before. Who lives out here?

Vengeance speeds up, and it catches me off guard. I grab the horseman to prevent myself from falling off. My periphery become a blur as the cold wind snaps my hair behind my head, as now we're in a full gallop.

I press my face against his back, opening my eyes only when we slow down at the long entryway of a large white manor with beautiful oaks on either side.

My heart starts to beat rapidly in my chest. Why are we here?

Does he have another charge? Is it possible for him to have two in one night?

Unsure whether I should get off Vengeance while he's slowed, I shift positions to get ready to swing my leg off the horse, but I almost fall backward when he rears back on his hind legs.

Must he do this every time?

His loud whinny alerts whoever his charge is that he's here. I suppose it wouldn't be right to give them a silent kill without any warning to defend themselves. Not that it would do them any good.

When Vengeance lands, he takes off at full speed. I shut my eyes tight, pressing my face against the horseman's back, waiting for it to be over.

A gunshot makes my eyelids fly open, and I yelp.

Whoever this is must have been ready the moment he heard Vengeance's call.

Another gunshot, and I yelp again, bringing my hand in slightly, not wanting to get my arm blown off, but also not wanting to fall off the horse.

Perhaps I should jump off, but we're still going at full speed.

Another shot, and this time it's at close range. The horseman's shoulder snaps back and hits me hard on the cheek. I hold my ground and look over his shoulder.

A lean older man, with gray hair and stubble, stands holding his rifle, pointed directly at us. The horseman doesn't slow as we near the entrance to his manor.

The man takes a step back, fear surely making him reconsider his stance on shooting down the mythical headless horseman. The look on his face tells me all the legendary horrors of his nightmares have come to life.

He drops the rifle to the ground with a loud clatter, and the man falls to his knees with his hands close to his lips as he begins to pray.

The horseman unleashes his ax from its sheath around his hip and spins it around in one hand, preparing his grip.

I hold my breath, wanting to plead with him to stop. Wanting to beg him to spare this man's life, but before I can mutter a word, Fallon swings his arm next to the praying man and takes his head clean off with one single blow.

Blood splatters on the white walls of his manor, and a scream rips from my throat.

The horseman hooks his ax and takes out his longsword as he turns Vengeance around. I look away to not witness the cracking sound that's made when the sword pierces through the head when he scoops it into his sack.

Now there'll be two heads in there. Two heads from two men I don't know, but at least one of them I know prayed for his life before his final moments.

And I can't help but wonder what was going through my father's head when the same fate happened to him?

Chapter Twenty

KAT

FALLON IS in his bedroom with the door shut, and I'm glad for it. I can't bear to look at his headless body right now.

I don't like it when he doesn't have a head.

And when he does have his head, he's infuriating. I'm happy to be alone with my thoughts now. Even though my thoughts are a plethora of confusion and confliction with all I learned in one night.

After we jumped through the portal, the horseman climbed down Vengeance and stuck one of the heads on a pike in the long hollow that leads to the Andre tree.

I remember it from the first time he took me. I woke up and glimpsed the heads all along either side of the dirt road. I thought he'd stick them there as trophies each time, but it appears not all the heads go up for decoration. No, these seem to be different. Trophies maybe.

The other head remained in his sack, and I'm not sure where it goes, but when I peered into it, the head was gone. Disappeared. I didn't see him do anything with it, so I keep replaying it all in my mind, wondering if I missed anything.

After sticking the praying man's head on the stick, he climbed up behind me and pressed himself close to me to steer Vengeance.

It felt oddly intimate. But when he nudged the horse to walk, it was almost as if he...

I swallow.

It was almost as if he purposely moved his arm high enough to force my gaze away. I managed to catch what he was blocking my view from—my father's head. His tongue hung out from the way the horseman propped his head on that pike.

My eyes well with tears. I want to cry for my father. I do. But I've never felt so much confusion in my life. I should be more devastated from seeing him up there. Instead, my devastation comes from memories of a life I used to have.

Pity for myself.

My stomach twists, and I move the blanket above my eyes and try to force myself to sleep in front of the hearth.

～

Time passes, and I still haven't fallen asleep. My mind is a whirlwind of frustrations.

Footsteps fall behind me, and I take a deep breath. Usually, he stays in his room till morning. The sound of a chair dragging and then set down says he's still stable and aware. And not in a crazed frenzy to kill me.

Hoping his head is where it should be, I turn around in my blanket to find him sitting on the chair beside me and staring into the fire. He wears a pensive look on his face. Wisps of his hair touch his cheekbone as he sits back.

I study his features. He seems calm. Collected. Not like he just came back from murdering two people. Innocent or not, I feel like if it were me, I would be haunted by something like that. Maybe he's just been doing this for far too long.

Reaching under my blanket, I pull out the spell book I took from Agnes's house. His gaze follows my movements, and I don't waste time handing it to him, lest he thinks I was keeping secrets from him that would cause him to think I was scheming with a witch.

His brows rise as he opens the book and flips through the pages.

"You did good today," he finally says after a few minutes of reading. "However, this is not the right spell book."

"Not the right one? How many spell books do you suppose are hidden in Sleepy Hollow?" I sigh, resting my head back to stare at the lights from the flickering flames on the ceiling.

"Nevertheless, it's a good book for you to study."

"You're going to end up turning me into a witch," I say flatly.

He quirks a brow. "Am I to believe that would bother you?"

I turn my gaze over to him, and I'm surprised to find him smiling. I'm too tired to muster any wit, but I also don't believe either one of us is convinced we'd turn down magic if offered to us.

I've not exactly been the most pious person. And evidently, neither has my mother. I've never been honest about that with myself. If I ever get out of here, I'll have to keep it a secret.

"I suppose you're wondering why I killed the second person." His deep voice is devoid of emotion.

I swallow. I had been wondering about that. "The curse gave you a second charge?"

"No."

My eyes widen, but I fight to steady my breathing. He did it out of his own volition. It had crossed my mind, but I was still deciding on how much agency he had regained.

"Why did you kill that man?" I sit up, not wanting to feel so vulnerable to him. "He prayed for his life."

He cocks his head back with a silent chuckle. "I'm no god to grant him his prayers."

"Have you no sympathy at all?" My voice comes out weak.

He turns to face me. "I'm not even sure I still have a soul."

"So that's all, then? You killed him just because?"

"No."

I stare at him expectantly. After a few silent beats, he finally opens his mouth to speak.

"His name is Bill Pepperwell. Despite the abolition, he was a persistent slave owner. I have a deep loathing for slave owners, and I happen to know he was still keeping one in his basement."

My mouth drops open, and I gape at him, speechless.

"I have been going down my own personal kill list each chance I get. After each charge I receive, I take advantage of being on Vengeance without my head. Me only regret is that they cannot look me in the eye when I kill them. But knowing they feared me until the very end is solace enough. May they rot in hell."

I close my mouth and swallow. "H-how do you know this?"

"I've kept a close eye on specific people all this time. I remember surnames from when I was here before. I make my rounds and watch."

"How do you watch without a head?"

"I don't know," he answers in an inquisitive tone. "It's a knowing I can't describe. As if my spirit sees it and remembers."

He glues his gaze back to the fire. "Are you still afraid of me?"

I inch myself closer to him and stare into his blue eyes, forcing him to look at me. He answered a question that burned within me. He can kill out of his own volition.

I don't know how I feel about that, except I hate slavery too. My mother's family never owned slaves.

I know the horseman must have been through some horrible things when he lived, and after too. I can forgive him for wanting to kill previous slave owners.

"What do you think will happen to the one trapped in his basement?" I ask.

"I'll see to it that she escapes."

I bite my bottom lip. "I'm afraid of your curse."

He looks at me questioningly.

"I mean I'm not afraid of *you*. But I am afraid of your curse."

His eyes slightly soften. "As you should be."

"Thank you, by the way. For this." I touch the thick blanket.

He clears his throat in response and begins to get up.

"Wait," I say. "Don't go just yet."

I don't know why I say it, nor why I want him to stay longer, but the thought of him leaving me alone to my thoughts doesn't bring me comfort.

He swallows but leans back in his seat and stares at me.

"I...almost didn't get out of there."

His head tilts in question.

"She caught me but then let me go."

His brows furrow, and he gazes away. "Did she say anything to you?"

"Beware the Dullahan, she said. Any idea what that could mean?"

He chuckles and then sighs, running his hand through his hair. "Nothing you don't already know," he says. "She means me. According to Irish lore, I am the Dullahan—a headless horseman sent to collect souls of those who expect it."

"Except not all expect it."

"Lore is just lore. It doesn't need to be exact."

Right. I'm sure she doesn't know I've been living here with the horseman this whole time. Or she's cracked.

"I was thinking…" I shift my position to my side. "Perhaps you've been looking at this all wrong."

"Oh?"

"Instead of narrowing down who may have the spell book, try thinking of what people in the town could desire."

His eyes widen, and he smiles at me. "And this is the smartest thing out of her mouth yet."

I frown at him. "Are you being condescending? I'm only trying to help."

"You're only trying to stay alive." He leans in. "But I can respect that. Tell you what, since you know your townsfolk so well, help me come up with things people of Sleepy Hollow desire enough to summon a Dullahan." He smirks. "What do you think it could be? A great harvest? Property? Riches?"

"Fair." I fold my arms in front of me. "I suppose it was dumb of me to ask."

"No." he says, and I flick my gaze to him. "It wasn't dumb. I give you thanks for trying to help. I apologize for my short temper. I..." He clears his throat and looks up at the ceiling. "I'm tired of it all."

"I understand."

I can't imagine what it's like to be trapped here in a desolate dimension, only to be allowed out by having to relive how I died, over and over again. To be released back after killing someone I had no intention of killing.

"It must be awful," I say just above a whisper.

After a beat, he speaks again. "My wife's name was Noreen."

I stay silent and rest my head on my arm, facing him. Wanting him to continue and not change his mind about speaking to me.

"Back in Ireland, we had no money. Famine had taken upon our farm. Our cows were dead."

I swallow.

"We had to steal to survive. But as long as she and I stayed together, we knew we'd be okay. Then, under British rule, staying together became difficult. We were caught for our crimes—which, to be fair, I made worse for putting up a fight or two."

His eyes become a dark blue as he talks. The flames flicker shadows over his features. He stares at the ceiling and sighs a heavy breath before continuing his story.

"We begged for our lives and finally agreed to come to America to enter a life of indentured servitude. Many others were doing it, and besides, what could be worse than what already was?"

I don't know why he's decided to tell me all this, but I dare not disturb him.

"Our masters were vile." His throat bobs. "They had been violating her." He shuts his eyes and swallows hard before looking back up to the ceiling. "I didn't know until the end."

My mouth runs dry. "That's awful, Fallon. I—"

"It's been years since I've spoken of this to anybody. The only reason I'm telling you this, witchy, is so that you understand why I do what I do when I'm not under the curse."

I nod.

"I planned to save her. Save us. But it didn't work. We were caught, and they broke my arms and legs before tying me to a tree while they violated her right there in front of me. Her screams still haunt my memories. And then they killed her."

I haven't any words except for, "I'm so sorry, Fallon. How horrible."

"It was half a century ago now. After that, I was sold to

the Hessians, where I became a slave for the British. And you know the rest."

"That's why you hate being called Hessian."

His gaze falls from the ceiling and settles on me. We stare at each other for a few moments. A cold draft passes through me, and I shiver.

"Are you cold?" He stands and walks to the hearth to move the wood around, causing the fire to blaze.

It's odd, having him suddenly be this nice. The pillow, sheet, and blanket. The fire. I want to ask what's changed, but I'm afraid it'll cause him to turn back to torture. Could he have seen that I've been telling the truth? That I'm not a witch?

"I'm sorry for shooting you with a silver bullet and burning you alive," I blurt in one breath, then I suck in a gasp and hold it.

His back straightens, and he slowly turns toward me. "Are you truly?"

"Yes."

"Why?"

I blink up at him and swallow. "I didn't know you weren't a...demon. I didn't know you had a life before this. A past. I didn't know you were being made to kill against your will, to relive the time of your death..."

His features soften, but he quickly remedies it with a stoic gaze. "I suppose I ought to thank you."

"For what?"

"You could have shot me and then cut my body limb from limb into tiny pieces."

I grimace.

"Then burnt me."

"Would that have worked?"

"No, but it would have been grossly painful to be put back together."

God.

He flicks me a look as he walks back to the chair. "Are you not tired?"

I lie with my hand under my cheek, facing the chair as he takes a seat on it again. "Are you?"

"I don't need to sleep. But I enjoy the notion of not existing."

That sends an emptiness down into the pit of my stomach.

"I'll help you stop this curse," I say. "I promise."

He lifts his eyebrows and just stares at me.

Having him here, talking to me like this, in a normal conversation, feels funny. I never could have imagined a night like tonight.

I want to ask him a question. Something that's been in the back of my mind since tonight, but...I'm afraid of the answer.

"What is it?" His eyes narrow.

It's almost like he can read my mind.

"I don't know..."

"You might as well ask, witchy."

"Are you still going to call me a witch?"

He grins. "Absolutely. It suits you."

I lie on my back and stare at the ceiling, trying to find the words to ask him about what's on my mind. About... my father...

But instead, I ask, "If you're not able to know who has the spell book, how will you reach them?"

He narrows his eyes at me. "By process of elimination. I'm hoping that once I've gone down my kill list, the one I can't reach is the one who has the spell book. My fear is, if by then they've gotten what they've wanted, will they send me back to hell?"

I linger on that for a few moments. It isn't enough for this to be over, or he'll end up going to hell. We have to break the curse to set him free.

"You have a burning question in your eyes. I can see it."

I stare at him.

"The answer is yes, Katalina. I saw what he did to you that night when returning from a charge, and I saw the whole thing from the window."

My heart lunges into my throat. I rub at my eyes. "Are you...?"

Is he referring to my...

"The man you called Father. Aye, I mean him."

My heart begins to race. That night surfaces in my memory all over again. And then skips to the night the headless horseman—he, Fallon—took his head in front of me. I ball my fists to keep them from shaking.

"Do you hate me more because of this?" he asks.

My bottom lip trembles, and I stare at him as I sit up. This entire time, I've felt conflicted. I've always known my father was not a good man. And then he...

"No..."

No, not anymore.

"It isn't uncommon for a stepfather to make an advance at his stepdaughter to keep the farm under his name. After being widowed. But I still couldn't bear the thought of it."

I bite my bottom lip in quiet contemplation. He stares at me, a serious look on his face.

I loathed him for killing Brom. I planned his murder and would have succeeded had he not been immortal. And this whole time, he had saved me.

Fallon lets out a sharp grunt, and I sit up.

"Are you all right?" I ask.

His eyes widen, and his chair falls from under him as he stands, grabbing his head. "Th...c..."

The curse.

I stand, awaiting the gunfire, but when it doesn't come, I realize what he means...

The cycle of the curse has run its course. He needs to kill me.

I feel the blood drain from my face as I back up into the wall next to the fireplace, searching for a weapon. He spins around, a fierce yet dazed look on his face as he approaches me.

I grab the fire poker and point it at him. He takes it from me and throws it behind him. I gasp as it lands on the table with a crash, causing other weapons to fall off with loud clatters.

"Oh no." I place my hands on his chest as he presses himself against me, his hand reaching for my neck.

His fingers squeeze around my throat, cutting off my air. Tears well in my eyes.

I now know he can't kill me because of my necklace. But he'll cause me great pain for an unlimited amount of time.

Somewhere between the last few days, he's gone from wanting to starve me out to release him from his curse, to being nicer and keeping me alive to help him break his curse.

The image of his lips on mine flashes across my memory.

His eyes dip to my lips. And then to my neck.

He lifts me up against the wall with impossible strength so that my face is close to his. I grab at his arms, my nails digging into his skin. Then I arch my back, causing my groin to rub against him.

His nostrils flare, and he breathes deeply.

I move my hand to his fingers around my neck and tug down as I reach for a kiss.

Chapter Twenty-One

KAT

His lips are firm on mine. He lets out a strained breath, and then he groans as his tight grip loosens on my throat. He glides his hand to the back of my neck, pulling me closer to him.

Every muscle in my body weakens. His tongue slides between my lips, and I moan into his mouth.

His hand finds my breast, and he gently rubs my nipple, sending a spike of goose bumps all over my body. He squeezes enough to rip a groan from my lips. My eyes flutter open to see his gaze feral at my outburst.

"You like a bit of pain, don't you, witchy?" His warm breath tickles my neck as he speaks into my ear.

I part my lips to answer, but I'm at a loss for words. Then he squeezes my nipple again. I let out a cry, and this makes him wild, like he's discovered a new way of torture. One mixed with pleasure.

His grip tightens around my throat, and my airway closes enough to make breathing difficult but not enough to completely choke me. Heat spreads down to my core, and my yearning for him increases.

His grasp of my breast intensifies, and I dig my fingers into the inside of his trousers, drawing him as close as I can. The length of him hardens over my core, and I let out a gasp.

His eyes widen, and he lets me go.

My chest heaves, and I struggle to hold myself up, my knees weak from what just happened. I stare at him, and confusion swarms his gaze.

"It's stopped," he rasps.

"What's stopped?"

"Me urge to kill you. Momentarily, at least."

"Oh…" I had almost forgotten why I kissed him in the first place.

I rub my chest.

"This is wrong," he states. "We shouldn't do this."

I stare at him, knowing he's right. We absolutely shouldn't… I mean, he's the headless horseman. A dangerous demon from hell.

I bite my lip. Call me a heathen, but is it so bad that…I enjoyed it?

He must catch the look in my eyes because something voracious passes through his. And then he's on me again.

I welcome it. My entire body tingles with the need for him to touch me again.

His thumb touches my bottom lip, and his gaze intensifies when he drops it down to my lips before he kisses me again.

"You wicked thing," he says. "You've cast a spell on me."

"I've done no such thing," I breathe out.

His hand goes under the shirt I wear—*his* shirt—and moves up to feel my breast. The feel of his skin on mine sends an explosion of need through my body. His teeth bite down on my lip, and a moan releases from my throat as he makes his way down to my neck, planting soft kisses on my skin.

I fear the mixture of rough with tender coming from him will create an addiction inside me I'll never be able to replace.

His eyes open, and he lets me down gently, his hands now planted on my hips. He breathes hard with his forehead resting against mine.

"What's wrong?"

He shakes his head. "We mustn't."

I don't say anything. I know he's right. We really mustn't... But I thought we made the decision to continue anyway. Why is he changing his mind?

I don't want to sound needy and beg, so I let my silence fill the room.

He steps away from me, his shirt open at the top,

revealing his chiseled chest. I swallow. He rips his gaze away from me and walks out the door into the drizzling night.

I stare after him. He left me here, needy for him, and wanting more.

He really is a cruel demon.

Chapter Twenty-Two

KAT

THE HAZY MORNING light fills the meadow, but something feels amiss. No birds sing. No sweet scent of life or flowers graces the air—nothing distinct at all.

Once again, I find myself wondering where I am. Is this some barren purgatory where life is neither good nor bad, merely existing? Or perhaps a forgotten plain abandoned by fair folk and fae? This place feels like a memory—everything in its place yet not quite right. Or could it be that this world is a moment frozen, like a painting?

It's brighter in Sleepy Hollow; the sun touches everything there. Here, the sun's kiss seems to hardly reach the sky itself.

Watching this little pocket of the world through the

window's panes seems surreal. The view itself is pleasing enough, but it still looks amiss.

This world has no heartbeat, no life. There isn't even a wind to rustle the leaves of the trees that are frozen in time.

A slight movement by the apple tree catches my attention, and under the gnarled branches stands my mother. I can't see her face, not clearly. She is too far away, and her head is bowed.

But I can clearly see her hands, her long fingers twisting and turning together as she pulls and bends them. She is worrying her hands like she did when she was alive, waiting for my father to come home, not knowing if he was drunk or not. In a foul or fair mood.

She only ever twists her fingers when she is anxious or something is scaring her. Something is wrong.

Father. I cannot bear to ask her about him. About what she had begun to tell me the other day when I ran out, and she told me she was ashamed.

I believe what Fallon told me to be true. Why else would he lie? There are more pressing matters, and though I want to know who my real father is, it is not a conversation I want to have with her right now.

Fallon has gone somewhere for a walk or a killing spree. I have no idea where he likes to wander when he tires of my company, but still. I trust him some, but still not enough to tell him my mother visits me.

I don't know if he can see her if he wants to or if he has any kind of power that would be useful against a ghost. Still, it seems better to keep her a secret, at least for now.

In case he returns, I take one of his heavy leather-bound tomes full of spells and incantations and tuck it under my arm. If he comes back, he'll assume that I'm working on spell work, trying to figure out if I have any power and can be useful.

Which, in truth, is what I should be doing.

If not for the sake of his soul, then for the sake of mine. There's only so long I can survive down here, even with the apples and walnuts fallen from the Andre tree.

More than that, I want to return to my life. My nana is all alone. I want to be there to care for her.

More than anything, I want to put the kiss I shared with Fallon far from my mind. I am a lady. Even if a tainted one. A lady does not kiss men who hold her captive and torment her.

"Mother," I greet as I sit in the long, too-rough grass and fold the lengths of the horseman's trousers around my ankles to keep the blades from pricking at my skin.

Even the grass is hostile in this valley.

"Oh, thank the heavens." My mother sighs as I make myself comfortable with my back to the cabin, lest Fallon look out to see me talking to myself.

I open the book on my lap and turn to a page with a spell for a bountiful harvest. A handwritten note scrawled in the margins of the page catches my attention.

This spell can be cast over crops and pregnant livestock.

It is not advised to use on expectant mothers, as twins and triplets can cause complications with the birth. It is only to be used on women if the family can afford and obtain an experienced midwife. The spell on page 135 is much more suitable.

Intriguing.

The handwriting is well-faded sepia, and I am only just able to make out the words. Other notes have been scribbled in the books, with different-colored inks and different handwritings. How many witches have used this book to help their communities? How many people unknowingly prospered from the efforts of a woman they would have burned at the stake?

"Kat," my mother says, stomping her foot.

It doesn't make a sound or a percussion in the dirt, but the movement is still enough to pull me from my thoughts.

"I'm sorry," I say, closing the book. "I just saw a note, and it got me thinking—"

"Never mind that for now," she says with her hands on her hips. "You are in danger. I thought the horseman had already..."

Her hand goes to her throat like the words are stuck there, and she doesn't want to let them free in case she may give life to her thoughts.

"I'm fine. Fallon is—"

"Fallon? You know the demon's name?"

"He is not a demon." Heat flares in my blood, and the blush spreads on my skin. "He is a man who is cursed."

Why am I defending him? He has tortured me and killed my father and so many more. He killed Daniel. Is one kiss all it takes to make me a silly little girl who would look beyond such significant acts of terror?

Technically, there has been more than one kiss...

"Is that why you are still here? It isn't safe. You have to leave." She wrings her hands again, then shakes out her fingers like she is getting rid of an ache.

Is it habitual, or can she feel her hands?

"I don't know how to leave," I answer simply. It's the truth. "Just because Fallon can go through the tree doesn't mean I can."

"I thought we had already agreed you'd steal the horse," she says, like it's nothing.

She paces in front of me, her ghostly footsteps not disturbing the spiky grass beneath her.

I don't want to steal the horse. I don't want to leave him here to suffer alone, waiting until the next time he is called to do that witch's evil bidding.

He may not have a choice in who the witch demands he kill, but he has admitted to taking lives on his own. Am I certain they all deserved it?

Why is this so confusing? Why am I defending him so readily to my own mother?

"Fallon seems sure that won't work. He allows me to come outside and wander because he knows there is no escape for me. I am trapped." I shrug, guilt eating at me for not telling her the whole truth.

She hangs her head for a moment then nods.

"Then we must find another way. You must leave this place. That demon will be the death of you, and I will not stand for it."

"He isn't a demon." I can hear the childish whine in my voice.

That isn't going to help me, so I sit up, pushing my shoulders back, and try to speak to my mother with an air of authority in my voice. Maybe then she will see me not as the little girl she left behind but as the woman I'm growing into.

"Fallon is a man who led a hard, tragic life. He watched his wife die at the hands of men who violated her. He tried to protect her and was sold into slavery and forced to fight for a cause he didn't believe in. Now, even in death, he is being used as a tool for someone else's vendetta. None of that is his fault."

Am I defending him because I can still feel the press of his lips against mine? Am I defending the man who did all these terrible things, or am I defending my choice to kiss him back?

"I don't care if he is a saint," she yells, throwing her hands in the air in frustration.

I startle at her sudden outburst. It isn't common for her to react this way.

"Mother, it matters. Who he is and how he treats me is important, and he won't hurt me."

Never mind that he had me bound to a garotte for what felt like days and threatened me nearly constantly at first. That was before when he thought I was one of the witches who would use him. Now, things are different.

He is different.

More than that, he never really hurt me. He had more than enough opportunity to cause me endless pain, to cripple or hobble me, and he didn't. He was so positive I was, at least in part, responsible for his suffering. Still, he did not bring me any harm.

"It doesn't matter how sweet he is to you when he isn't under that witch's control. She will call on him again. She will demand your head, and he will be spellbound, forced to act against his own will." She folds her legs under her, and she kneels in front of me, taking my hands with her own.

It's strange; I can feel the icy touch of her hands, but they don't feel like hands at all. They feel like cold vapor, like wind billowing through a winter storm.

"The necklace—"

"The necklace's charms won't last forever. The witch's power is growing. She is studying her craft well and learning quickly. Soon her strength may overwhelm the necklace, and then it will be separated from your body with your head. The demon may mourn you, but that doesn't mean he will be able to save you."

"No." I can't listen to what she is saying. I can't believe that Fallon would ever allow that to happen.

But she is right. The witch's power has overwhelmed him before. He has laid his hands on my person in anger, ready to swing his ax.

"You must escape," she says again. "Please, daughter. Leave this place. Leave this cursed place, and leave Sleepy Hollow. There is nothing there for you other than death."

"I can't leave," I say, wrapping my fingers in the blades of grass at my side.

Even they feel wrong. Their color is pale green, but they feel dry, dead like hay.

"Even if I want to go, he will come for me before I can even leave this valley. If I try to climb the tree or steal the horse, he will chase me down."

"There is a way to trap the demon. It will buy you enough time to get out of here and Sleepy Hollow. If you leave this village behind, the curse will not follow you."

"How can you be sure?" I ask, staring at the horizon.

My stomach twists. Whatever she is about to tell me is going to be horrible. I just know it will further curse Fallon, and then I will be no better than the others who have used him. But what choice do I have?

"Because our family's curses didn't follow us before. It wasn't until we came back that everything turned pear-shaped."

"How do I do it?" Even asking feels like a betrayal.

"You need to find a way to trap him in an iron maiden," she says, and my heart sinks.

"I tried that before he took me and brought me here. I trapped him in a wooden maiden, and we burned it. Daniel and I burned the house we dragged him into. It only served to make him angry and put me in his path."

"No, there is an iron maiden. It is covered with enchantments and symbols. The witch who created him, the one who took his body and dragged his soul back to the land of the living, used it to work the spell."

"What?" Had I had the right plan but the wrong box to put him in?

"The spell to create a demon such as this is in the same book that houses the spell to bind his will to the spell caster. The witch who made him took his body, fresh from the grave, and put it in an iron maiden to trap him and hold his body while his soul was returned to it. Any tool used to craft a spell can be used to break it. The tools used to make the demon are the only ones that can trap him or unmake him."

I swallow hard. I know the iron maiden she speaks of. I have seen it many times—the old, rusted thing in the corner of the cottage with all the symbols. I hadn't dared to look at it for too long, not wanting him to catch me and decide his revenge would be best served in kind.

"I can't," I tell her, my eyes brimming.

"You must." Her icy hands cup my cheeks and brush away my hot tears. "It's the only way to protect yourself and the people of Sleepy Hollow from the witch and from him."

"What will happen to him in there?"

"Nothing." Her shoulders lift in a shrug. "The trap is down here where no living being can get to it. He will be trapped for all eternity."

"That is horrible," I cry, more tears freely flowing down my cheeks. "How do we even know it will work? What if he comes out the second the witch calls him again?"

"He won't," she says and then presses her lips into a firm line.

She always did that when she grew tired of my endless questions as a child. Even after her death, my mother can make me feel so small.

"The iron maiden will hold him, even through the curse. No one will be able to reach him to release him. I'm afraid it's the closest thing to peace he will ever know."

"It's cruel."

"If he is the kind soul you seem to believe, wouldn't he prefer to be trapped than to hurt innocent people?"

She doesn't know Fallon. I can't tell her about the heads he decided to take himself. No one ever sent him after half the people he's killed. No one ever sent him after Father. Fallon's ax still fell on his head.

"It's the only way to protect the people of Sleepy Hollow from him. It won't end his curse, but it will end everyone else's.

Her words make sense. I understand what she's saying, but I can't do it.

Can I?

It would mean that no one else can use him again.

"There has to be another way." I wipe the tears from my face, tighten my stomach, and try to sound as determined as I wish I felt.

Her eyes soften for a moment, and she cups my cheek again. I miss the warmth she had when she was living. Her touch was soothing then. Now, it is a cold reminder that she was taken from me.

"Right now, every death is on the hands of the witch who summons him. If you can stop him and don't, then every new death is a stain on your soul," she says. "Can you sit by and let more people of Sleepy Hollow die?"

Chapter Twenty-Three

FALLON

It has been so long since I felt my heart hammer in my chest with anything other than anger or despair that I didn't recognize the feelings of hope, longing, or desire.

Have I finally allowed this witch to cast a spell on me? The mere notion of me wanting more of her is... I clench my fist. Pure insanity.

Climbing to the highest point by the cottage, I take a seat, overlooking the rolling hills and the early morning mist that covers the roof. Still, hours later, all I can think about is her sweet, full lips pressed to my cold, cursed mouth.

Christ.

She kissed me to spare herself the pain of my torture.

There can be no other explanation. Nor should there be. I cannot hold the will to live against her. I won't.

The question is, how is a curse, one that is intended for me to take off somebody's head, momentarily quenched by acting on lust?

Her kiss culled the curse, at least momentarily.

Like the time I kissed her before last, the curse subsided.

How is that possible?

The first time, perhaps she didn't want it. And by my doing so, I was still torturing her. But this time, she kissed me because she remembered it saved her from the pain of being choked.

That I understood, but I didn't expect that after my pain from the curse subsided and I pulled away from her, she still wanted it... The look she gave me made my cock stir to life and ache with need. That hadn't happened since I succumbed to the curse so very long ago.

I shouldn't be happy about that.

My lust needs to be ignored. I could never make her happy.

If I were to give in to my desire, I would owe her my life. Even if she could break the curse and give me my life back, I have nothing to offer her.

If I'd be so lucky for the curse to finally be broken, I'll leave this plane, which is what I want. It has been all I have wanted for what feels like eons. Now, there is something more in my heart, some other desire. I haven't wanted to be with anyone since...

I clench my fist. "Since Noreen."

For the longest time, I couldn't bring myself to say her name. Yet for the first time last night, I spoke her name out loud.

It's been so long since I allowed myself to think of her. I let her die. She is gone, and I am cursed because I failed her.

I don't deserve to be with anyone else. Kat does not deserve to have the same terrible fate bestowed upon her that Noreen did. If I claim her as my own, my failings as a husband would return, and Kat may suffer something far worse than Noreen.

I refuse to be that selfish.

No, not again.

I can be nothing more to Katalina than her torturer and executioner. I wish there were a middle ground, but what would that even be? Torture the pleasure out of her? Bend her body to my will so I can act out my depraved desires on her innocent, delicate body? Hope that will be enough to fend off my curse to kill her until we break it?

While that sounds like fun, it's never how I intended to take advantage. That isn't me.

That selfish depravity is saved for the men who take life and freedom without consideration. I may be a demon cursed to kill, but I will not be the kind of man who takes what a woman isn't freely giving.

But will I be able to deny her the next time she kisses me to save her life? What if, when she banishes my curse for only a moment, I cannot stop?

Movement coming from my cottage catches my eye. I can just make out the shape of her rounded hips and pert behind in the trousers I lent her. For a moment, I curse my chivalry, missing how she looked in the thin transparent nightdress she wore.

The way her hips sway as she walks makes my cock stir again. The temptation to go to her and find out if she would help me ease the ache is there, but I could never.

I will never.

She goes to the field and sits in the grass, her back to me as she looks at another spell book. I should be grateful she works so hard to hone skills she clearly doesn't possess, hoping to break my curse and freeing me.

Even if it is only to save her own life.

With her content in the field, I slip back inside my cottage. For some inexplicable reason, I do not want her to see how I watch her. So, for a moment, I watch her from the window, her shoulders twitching with every movement she makes.

Each movement is so delicate and precise that I can't help but wonder how the soft skin of her back would feel bare under my fingertips. Already, I have touched far more of her than I should have, but I ache for more.

The aroma of cinnamon and apples pulls me from my enamored staring as I stare down at the pot sitting by the fire. She has made her cider concoction again, but something more too. Inside the cast-iron stove, something besides peat heats inside. I open it and take a look.

It's no wonder it smells so strongly of apple today. A pie sits on top of a few blocks of peat, almost burnt at the edges. I pull it out carefully and let it cool on the counter by the window.

In the corner is a small sack of flour she must have stolen from our last outing. A smile tugs at my lips. Clever girl, isn't she?

My mind drifts me back when I was alive, out in the brisk air, chopping wood and tending to the garden and animals. I would come in with frost coating my skin, and my wife would hand me a mug filled with her apple cider. She made hers spiked with the sweetest whisky, adding a pleasant burn to my gut.

I had pushed those memories out of my mind.

Before realizing I'm moving, I fill a mug with the alluring elixir and take a deep drink. The flavors burst over my tongue, and I almost groan with pleasure.

When was the last time I did something simply because I enjoy it? Even the last years of my life were so wrought with despair and strife. I can't remember eating or drinking anything that I took some enjoyment from.

The more I think about it, the more I realize I have done nothing for the simple pleasure of it since Noreen passed. The last time I felt anything was when she died.

From that point on, I was numb to anything but pain and rage.

A chuckle leaves my lips. And to think, all this is are some apples and hot water. Given nothing else grows here, she's only privy to what she can find under the Andre tree.

This is a dangerous game I'm playing. If I decide to take pleasure in what Kat is offering—taste, physical touch, and maybe even passion—what would that mean for me when she left?

She would leave me. Because we broke the curse, and I will finally be laid to rest. Or because she found a way to be rid of me and to continue to live her life on the surface where she belongs. By saving me or damning me even further, she will be leaving.

Of course, there is a third option. The third option that twists my stomach and shatters my black heart. The witch could win.

There is always the possibility that Katalina will leave me in death. If her kisses lose their merit and become no longer enough to subside the curse, the next time the witch calls on me to take her head, then she would leave me with only her corpse in my hands.

The sweet drink turns sour in my mouth, and I have to force myself to swallow.

Suddenly, I can feel her flesh under my fingers, not in a soft caress but in violence. I try to shake the thought from my head, but it just won't leave. My skin seems to crawl, and anxiety slithers up the back of my spine.

It makes me realize just how numb I have been. Somehow, Katalina has awakened the memories of pleasure...of life, but also the suffering that only the living deal with.

I need to do something, to move to...something. How did I deal with this feeling as a living man? The most obvious answer was off of the table. Anxiety, worrying, and fear could often be curbed by having my wife under me. Katalina would be just as effective.

Feeling her skin pressed against my body, warm and supple. Her chest moving with each breath, and her pulse fluttering with each heartbeat. Sure signs that she is alive and well.

Christ. I am a damned man.

That would definitely ease my distress, but it couldn't happen.

Not now, not ever.

Her father may have ruined her, but I refused to do it further.

No, I need something else to occupy my time. I drag a chair and sit next to the window, telling myself it is for the light, not so I can watch Katalina.

I pick up a small block of wood and a knife I left on the table with other various instruments that I have been tortured with. Looking at the grizzly assortment, I realize I should put them away somewhere where they're not a constant reminder of the threat that I am to her.

Then again, maybe it's best that she doesn't forget who and what I am.

The knife I hold is a larger pocketknife meant for cleaning small game. Its blade is made of pure steel and sharpened to a wicked edge. The hilt is a beautiful, polished mahogany. Whoever made it took great pride in their craft. It is almost a shame to be in my possession.

Some years ago, further back than I care to count, a boy no older than fifteen tried to stop me with this blade. I had been ordered to take his father's head, and he tried to defend his father by plunging this blade into my heart.

His aim was true, but the curse was more potent. I then took the knife and added it to my collection.

As I hold the well-balanced blade in my palm, the curves of the handle fitting so perfectly, I am transported to another long-forgotten memory. As a young man, I spent hours sitting by the fire, entertaining my mother, siblings, and anyone else who was at our home by telling stories and whittling figures from spare pieces of firewood.

That was so long ago that I didn't think I'd remember how to hold the knife, but somehow, my hands know. The memories themselves may be well faded, but the muscle memory is still intact.

With one eye outside on my witch, I carve into the small block, pulling curl after curl away until the wood starts to give shape.

Whittling away at the wood gives my hands the outlet they need, while I let myself drift into contemplation.

Slowly, the shape of a hare forms, and I stop to refill my mug with the cider. I lose myself in the repetitive motions, so much so that I don't notice Kat returning to the cabin until she is almost at the front door.

I jump up, pouring my cider back into the pot, and run to the other side of the room to sit in a dust-covered, stuffed armchair to continue carving.

I don't want her to know I was watching her or enjoying the sustenance she created. Lest I give her the wrong impression about our situation.

As she walks through the door, I can't help but notice the vertical line between her eyes is more pronounced. Something's got her bothered.

"Something on your mind, witchy?" I ask, unable to stop worrying about her.

If something's happened, if there's something that hurt or scared her, I'll handle it immediately.

"Nothing." She waves off my concern, but I know there's something there.

Just like how last night there was something on her mind, and she quickly changed her question. I couldn't let that go. She deserved to know the truth, and I wanted to know if she'd be honest about her feelings.

I knew deep down she hated Brom, but the relationship between someone and the person who raised them is a complicated one. It was confusing for her, and in some way, I hoped my admittance to me freely killing her father and why would help her come to terms with her emotions on the matter.

I think about asking again, and then I realize that my

little captive can't hold her tongue for anything. Most would see that as a flaw, but in this instance, maybe I can use it as a benefit.

"As you wish." I lift my shoulders in what I hope looks like a bored, unafflicted shrug.

She won't stay silent; she can't. It goes against her nature.

"It's just that..." She drops the tome on top of many of the tools still lying on the table. "What if I can't do this?"

I quirk a brow. "What do you mean?"

"What if I can't make magic work? I tried so many of these spells, and I can't get any of them to work." Her bottom lip trembles as her arms wrap around her body.

I want to be the one to hold her, not the man forcing her to hold herself.

I refocus on the wood before me, carving the knife to create a more defined line of the rabbit's leg.

"What were you trying to do?"

"I wanted to grow the grass around the tree, just something small so I know I can do magic—"

"The grass doesn't grow here. Nothing grows here," I interrupt.

She knows this. Why does she think a beginner spell would make any difference?

"Then how am I supposed to practice?" she all but screams as she paces around the room, her hands on her hips.

Even her beautifully pale cheeks glow with her anger.

Instantly, I see her like that under me, her cheeks just as flushed with passion and pleasure instead of frustration.

"You'll figure it out," I say and go back to my wood, carving long, smooth shavings off the back of the hare, trying to even out the curve of its spine.

"Maybe," she says under her breath. "But not while I am this frustrated. I need you to distract me."

"Excuse me?" My eyes narrow.

She's still upset, but something tells me there's more to it than being unable to make grass grow.

"I need to take my mind off of all this for a moment. Can you distract me? Tell me a story or..."

Has she lost her mind?

"I am not here to entertain you. What you are or are not fretting over is of no consequence to me." I give her a dismissive look before going back to the hare, hoping she doesn't see the way my hands tremble.

I can sense her standing there, frowning. When I glance up, she's staring at the pie cooling by the window.

"It almost burnt down the cottage," I tell her before she can ask me about it. "Be thankful I moved it for you."

Instead of responding, she goes rummaging through my cabinets. She stands on the tips of her toes, reaching for a plate.

I keep carving the hare out of wood, trying to stop noticing her, when she walks over to me.

"What do you think you're doing?" I ask without looking up.

"Won't you at least try a bit of this pie I made?"

"How many times do I have to tell you? I don't eat."

"But you can." She cuts a forkful and puts it above the wooden hare for me to look at.

I glance up at her and sigh. "If I try it, will you leave me alone?"

"If I must," she says.

I want to laugh at that, but I hold it in, taking the fork from her.

I stick the piece of apple in my mouth, and my taste-buds erupt with the mixture of flavors. It has been ages since I have had something this good.

I close my eyes, and my mind drifts me back to when I was a child playing in the cold, damp Irish autumn and then coming inside only when the chill got too much. My mother would have something similar waiting for me. It always tasted sweet and soothing as it warmed me from the inside out.

My chest tightens, and I have to hold back a groan as I swallow.

When I open my eyes, Katalina is still standing there, holding the plate of pie. She has a smug smile on her face as she stares at me.

"Would you like some more?" She holds out the pie.

As badly as I want to take it, I can't let myself keep indulging in these pleasures. This will all be gone soon enough.

"That's enough. Now go away. Leave me to me thoughts."

She's trying to get to me and succeeding. I can't let her.

After a few moments, I glance up, and she's still standing there. I'm about to tell her something snarky and crude when she speaks first.

"What does it feel like to be in love?" she asks, coming over to where I sit.

My muscles tense. Clearly, what happened last night has her distracted. Perhaps me opening up to her has led her to believe we are now friends.

Again, I cannot let this happen.

"I haven't the slightest. I feel nothing, or have you already forgotten?" I answer, not daring to meet her eyes.

"No, you were married before. From what you told me, it sounded like you loved her, didn't you?"

"I did," I say, refusing to sully Noreen's memory with a lie. "But that was—"

"I don't care." She pulls up a seat and drags it to sit in front of me. "Tell me what it felt like."

She takes the fork I forgot I'm holding and takes a bite out of her pie.

My eyes slightly widen, but I try to hide the shock on my face. "Quite a question for a prisoner to ask her captive."

She quiets as she chews, and I tilt my head to study her features. I'm more surprised she isn't asking about her father or who her real one is. Or she's in need to be distracted from that as well.

A blonde wave touches the side of her face, her green eyes pleading.

I let out a sigh. "Fine. You aren't going to drop this, are you? If I answer you, you'll go back to being a good little witchy and helping me break me curse."

It wasn't a question.

She nods, a sly smile crossing her face, and oh, how badly I want to bite into those plump lips...

Focus.

Do I remember? I think back, trying hard to remember the look on Noreen's face, and it's there—just beyond my reach.

"Love is...both wistful and damning. It makes you believe in a God that doesn't exist, and it lies to you, telling you that life can be more than pain and suffering. There is no fiercely cruel feeling in this or any other world." I bow my head. "I would not wish it on anyone."

Chapter Twenty-Four

KAT

"No," I say, crossing my arms over my chest. "I refuse to believe that's what true love feels like."

"Perhaps, then, witchy, stop asking me irrelevant questions you don't wish to know me answers to," he says dismissively.

Something is different about him, an air of uncertainty maybe. It makes me wonder if he is being untruthful intentionally or if he has been locked in his own torment for so long that he doesn't remember.

My mother spent the afternoon convincing me to lock Fallon away. If she were right, he would be stuck in a fate much worse than hell. He would be in his own private purgatory forever. Alone. Unbothered by the witch's curse but knowing nothing but solitude and pain.

How she thinks I have the strength or cunning skill to lure him into that iron maiden is beyond me, and something else I need to consider entirely. For a brief moment, my gaze falls to the maiden at the far end of the cottage, tucked behind the breaking wheel. Its sigils decorate the entire face of it, and I wonder what they mean.

He eyes me suspiciously, and I swallow the piece of apple in my mouth. Perhaps I should stop looking for a distraction and asking him irrelevant questions like he says. Perhaps I should stop buying time. Or perhaps I... I want to know more about him. Learn about the humanity in him.

Despite the cruel nature of what he's done to me and my family, I understand now that he did me a service.

"How did you meet her?" I ask.

The idea of him thinking of another woman, even his wife, makes a kernel of jealousy writhe in my gut, but I ignore it, pushing it down where it can't show its ugly head. I cut into another slice of apple pie with the fork, but this time I hold it out in front of him.

"Why does it matter?" he asks, his shoulders stiffening as he continues to carve at a piece of wood.

"Because I want to know."

"What if I don't want to remember?" he says harshly.

I swallow. Maybe all my musings are just that. A naive mistake.

He looks down at the fork and then at me. "Are you trying to bribe me for answers, witchy? It won't work."

But then he takes the fork from my hand and sticks it into his mouth. His eyes flutter closed for a moment as he chews, and I can't help the satisfaction I feel.

I know the horseman hasn't had a bite to eat, or anything pleasurable, in half a century. I wasn't sure if he'd take it from me, but I'm so glad he did. The look of bliss on his face while he eats my pie... It's as if the humanity in him is coming alive, and all I had to do was feed him something sweet.

He is silent for a long moment, but then he sets the fork down on my plate and speaks. "It was when I was barely a man, and I had not yet seen my nineteenth winter. There was a traveling group coming through town, gypsies going to each pub to entertain and amuse for their supper and then dancing and singing in the square for a few extra coins. She was with them."

He stops speaking, and the cottage is silent except for the quiet scraping of his knife shaping the wood. I am about to ask him a question when he starts again.

"She was a singer. I had a long day in the fields. I was still living with me mother, helping her tend to the land after my father passed, but she had gone to visit someone. A relative, I think. It was a hot day. I was exhausted and thought I had earned a pint and a hot meal made with someone else's hands. I was at the bar when she walked in with her group. Most of them were dark-haired and exotic-looking, but she was local. Her hair was bright red, like the sunset, and her skin was fair, but the tops of her cheeks were pinkened with a kiss from the sun."

The way he speaks in his soft timbre and the awe in his voice relaxes my entire body. It occurs to me to be jealous again, but I dismiss it, wanting to hear the story more than anything.

"There were several acts, a juggler and a man telling jokes. All were entertaining enough, I think. I don't really remember them, but I don't think I remembered the other acts as they were happening. I was too busy staring at her. After a while, she took her place on the stage. By then, several of the patrons were drunk and loud. A few yelled at her to remove her clothing, and she stared them down with a glare so cold they apologized." He chuckles.

Fallon's eyes are hazy, and he seems lost in thought, as if he is reliving the moment, unaware he is even speaking. A soft smile appears on his lips, and I am struck by how beautiful this man really is. Years of cruelty have made him a monster, but under it all, there is still a man, lovely and sweet like the boy I imagine he used to be.

"Then she sang a jaunty tune that was surprisingly scandalous. She sang a classic drinking song called 'Wild Rover,' but she changed the lyrics, and it was quite funny. That wasn't what held my attention. It was the way she shone on that little stage. Her hair seemed to glisten, and her bright-green eyes sparkled. I could see them from across the room. When she was done, the entire bar stood and cheered. She came to the bar next, needing a drink, and I spent me last coin on her whisky."

He is truly lost in his story, and I am lost in him. I want him to talk about me with such devotion in his eyes and honeyed words dripping from his lips.

"We talked for hours, and that night, I brought her back to me cottage, and she made a man of me the way only a woman of worth like her could. It was her first time, too. She never told me that, but there were signs. It was a night of bliss and love. I gave her everything, as she gave me, just to leave the next morning with her group." A rugged smile quirks his lips, and I know that isn't the end of his story.

"I followed her, chased her down, and confessed me love for her. She called me a silly little boy and told me that me infatuation would wear off. It never did. Then one night, they were in a particularly rowdy bar where some men got a little too drunk and a fight broke out. I pushed me way in, taking several hits for me trouble, but I went in and fished her out. We were wed the next week, and I took her back home to meet my mother."

"What does it feel like to be in love?" I ask again.

He stares at me, leans in, and takes a piece of the apple pie himself before responding. "Light fills your soul, and you will do anything to protect the person you love. You want to lift them to the greatest heights they can ever strive to and do anything in your power to make them happy. Suddenly, your needs are not your most important priority. And you know, if it's true love, you will be happy and safe, because while you are lifting them up, protecting them, and making them happy, they are doing the same for you."

His gaze moves to mine. "It's like what you wanted before isn't as important as what you want together. You are still you, but now you are part of something far greater. It strengthens you and feels like as long as they are by your side, there is nothing you can't do."

My lips part as I take in everything he says. I've never known the feelings he speaks of. I've certainly never wanted to.

But as of the past couple of days, those feelings have raced through my veins. Defending a cruel, cursed demon to my mother. Me wanting to save him instead of trap him inside an iron maiden in order to save myself and the innocents of Sleepy Hollow.

My mind drifts back to my father. Ever since finding out he isn't my biological father, I've been more confused than ever. He still raised me, but he was so horrible to my mother. I never want to feel like she felt when she was alive. She died young and never experienced true love.

I clench my fists, and my eyes start to well, despite me trying hard to keep in the tears. I set the plate down on the floor.

"Witchy?" he says with an odd sense of concern in his voice. "Did you not find my story distracting enough?"

My breathing shallows, and I close my eyes, turning

away. I stand and walk to the window. I can feel his stare on me, and my cheeks redden from embarrassment.

Don't cry now, Kat. I'm being ridiculous.

The chair moves as he stands and makes his way over to me.

"Are you going to tell me what's the matter?" His voice is deep and soothing.

From the corner of my eye, his hand moves up, and just when I think he's about to place it on my shoulder, he brings it back down.

I swallow. "I never want to marry." I wait for him to come up with some witty remark, but when he doesn't, I say, "My mother never wanted me to either. Strange, isn't it? Improper. What sort of mother would encourage her daughter to pursue a career in artistry instead of marrying to carry on a legacy, or if anything, for wealth?"

"It sounds like she wanted you to be happy."

"Unlike how she was, you mean?"

Silence fills the room. I stare out at the dead blades of grass and fruitless trees. A grey shadow sweeps over them like a blanket at night.

"Is that the only reason you never wanted to marry? Because of what your mother wanted for you?"

I dig my nails deep into my skin and try my hardest not to look at him, keeping my gaze fixed on the trees. I know what he's alluding to. And I don't want to discuss it.

But he's right. I never wanted to believe in love. But if

a man such as him was killed for trying to protect his wife, then true love must exist. Does it not?

He reaches for my face, but I pull away. He drops his hand, but I take it and bring it to my face, turning to him now. His eyes grow soft as he thumbs my chin. I blink at him, unsure of what he's about to do.

"Listen to what I am about to tell you, Katalina."

I swallow, my heart beating rapidly at him calling me by my real name instead of "witchy."

He stares at me with great intensity as his fingers continue to gently hold my chin so I look up at him.

"He betrayed your trust," he says, as if having read my thoughts moments before. "You are allowed to hate him and feel hatred for what happened to you. But you are also allowed to love him for being your father. However, that does not mean you stay with someone out of obligation. You do not owe him your loyalty just because he raised you. Stop judging yourself for how you think you should be feeling and forgive yourself, for you did no wrong."

A tear betrays me and falls down my cheek. The soft light from the dying sun twinkles in his eyes as he catches my tear with his thumb.

I scoff, pulling away from him. "You're one to talk."

"I died long ago, so love is dead for me because the only place I belong is back in the ground. But you... you're still alive."

Chapter Twenty-Five

Kat

My eyes flutter open, and I find myself warm by the fire. The air remains cold and unnervingly still, much like everything in this strange place. Yet somehow, it feels different.

I no longer fear for my life, even knowing Fallon's curse could wake him at any moment. When it does, I'll face what's to come. The compulsion to kill me may resurface, but oddly, I'm not afraid.

A warmth rises in my cheeks as our shared kiss resurfaces in my memories.

The fire has been carefully tended through the night. A quiet sense of peace settles in me—something I never thought possible here, alone with the Horseman.

His door is still shut, so I rise quietly and make my way to the basin to splash water on my face.

The rest of yesterday we passed in near silence, with me practicing simple spells while he read. We exchanged a few glances, but neither of us pursued our earlier conversation. Perhaps we were both afraid of where it might lead—or perhaps that's just my imagination.

We were sure the curse would return, but it didn't. The unease of waiting left us both tense, until I finally drifted off, and he retired to his room.

My thoughts wander back to our conversation.

"I died long ago; the only place I belong is back in the ground."

I place the pot of cider near the fire and wait for it to warm. Once heated, I pour it into a tankard and step outside, carrying it along with the spellbook I took from Agnes's house. My eyes sweep the area, seeking my mother's ghost, but when I'm sure she isn't present, I settle beneath the familiar dead walnut tree and open the book.

To attune oneself to the ethereal realms.

Mulled wine or whiskey
1 Part Cinnamon
1 Part Nutmeg
1 Part Oranges or Apples
½ Clove

That's strange. These are the same ingredients my

mother always used. Our home was always filled with the smell of apples, cinnamon, and nutmeg...

"That's what your cider is missing."

I startle, spilling some of my hot drink into my lap. Gasping, I look up at Fallon. His hair is tousled from sleep, and he wears his coat over a half-opened white shirt, revealing his muscular chest. Quickly, I avert my gaze back to the book.

He chuckles. "You seem rather jumpy this morning. I thought you weren't afraid of me anymore, witchy."

"You surprised me." I regard him warily; he appears to be in an unusually cheerful mood.

"Ah, getting an early start on your spellwork. Such a diligent witch you are," he says, bending down to take the book from my hands. "To attune oneself to the ethereal realms?" he scoffs. "The only use for this spell would be to get you drunk."

"Too bad we haven't any," I tell him. "And what do you mean it's what my cider is missing?"

He hands the book back to me, but I catch the sly smirk that dances across his face.

I let out a theatrical gasp. "You had a sip, didn't you? Mr. 'I shall drink none of that from this witch!'" I place my hands on my hips, mockingly.

He rolls his eyes at my antics. "Come with me." He strides away from the stable, moving further from the cottage.

"Where are we headed?" I stand with the book in

hand. He's clearly moving away from his cottage, and it doesn't seem he intends to turn back toward the stable.

"Are you coming, or what?" he calls over his shoulder.

I follow after him. "How far is this place? Isn't it just leading us back to your cottage, in a loop?"

"Then what are you so concerned about? Are you always this cautious? Were you this cautious before you attempted to kill me?"

I stare at him, taken aback. "That was different."

"Was it?"

"Will you at least tell me where we're going?"

He maintains a brisk pace until we arrive at a stone wall, beyond which stands a dilapidated structure. Dry grasses blanket the ground, remnants of the wild, untamed land. A few tombstones emerge from the undergrowth. It cannot be his grave... He perished in Sleepy Hollow as this is a pocket dimension of his homeland in Ireland. "Is your wife interred here?"

He offers no reply, leading me into the rear of the crumbling stone edifice. I halt as he removes his coat, carelessly tossing it atop a stone brick. Rolling up his sleeves, he retrieves a shovel.

"What is this place?" I inquire.

"Long ago, I concealed a bottle of whiskey somewhere back here."

I blink in surprise. "Illegally?"

"How else was I to procure it? Distilleries were forbidden in Ireland, love." He thrusts the shovel into the ground, pressing down with his boot. "And no, to answer your question, Noreen is not buried here. My parents were. This stone structure fell victim to a raid, and the cemetery was closed thereafter. I had no desire to bury my whiskey in my own yard for fear of being discovered."

I watch him as a mound of dirt begins to accumulate, the muscles in his inked arms flexing with each dig. He pauses, looking up at me.

"Are you merely going to stand there?"

"Umm..."

He gestures to another shovel lying among the stones. "If you can chase a man down with a rifle on horseback, you can manage a little digging."

I scoff and seize the shovel. "Where would you like me to dig?"

"Anywhere. It's not like I've got a map."

I gape at him. "I thought you claimed to know where it is."

He wipes his brow, leaving a smudge of dirt. "The general vicinity."

"General?!"

He gives a nonchalant shrug and resumes digging. "Best get to it then, shall we? Unless you can magically discern its location?"

"Not sure I've encountered any spells for that in the spellbook."

He grins knowingly, urging me to start digging. With an eye-roll, I plunge the shovel into the earth.

"Aren't you concerned that the curse might overtake you while you've been drinking?" I ask, creating my own pile of dirt.

"Don't drink too much then, witchy." He winks at me.

I purse my lips, feeling a heat rise in my cheeks.

"I possess no control when the curse takes hold, so what does it matter? It's you who must be wary of how much you consume, witchy."

"I'm certain I can handle it."

He halts his digging, arching an eyebrow at me. "Have you ever had a drink?"

"A little."

"Oh, just a little, is it?" He smirks.

"I have. It tasted dreadful."

"Well, I cannot promise this will be sweet in and of itself. But that is precisely why we shall pour it into your potion."

"Cider."

"Right, right. Cider."

"You've smudged dirt all over your face, you know."

"Have I? Where?"

"Right up there," I indicate, pointing to his forehead.

He wipes at his brow, inadvertently smearing more dirt across his skin. A laugh escapes me.

"You're making it worse!" A laugh escapes me.

"Very well then, why not lend me a hand?"

I walk over to him and wipe it away with my sleeve,

acutely aware at how close we are now. He stares at me as I wipe the dirt away. He licks his lips and I bite my bottom lip.

"All done."

"Now it's your turn."

"Me? Do I have dirt on my face?"

He pokes my nose with his filthy finger. "You do now."

I gasp at him. "Fallon!"

He erupts in laughter, a sound I don't think I've ever heard from him before. An impulsive thrill courses through me, and I bend down, digging my hand into the dirt before playfully smearing it across his face. He stares at me in shock, then retaliates by grabbing a handful of dirt and pouring it over my head.

My eyes shut instinctively as I hold my hands above me, feeling the dirt cascade down. I cry out his name, then playfully seize the shovel as if I intend to strike him with it.

He guffaws at my mock threat but quickly takes off running.

And I begin to chase him.

"Come back here!" I call after him. "No one pours dirt on me and gets away with it!"

"You best catch up then, witchy."

With renewed determination, I sprint toward him, unable to suppress the smile that spreads across my face. A giggle escapes me as I nearly grasp him, but he veers to his left, leading us back around near the portal below the Andre tree.

"You trickster!" I rasp, out of breath.

As we dash back the way we came, the grounds curve back to the cemetery, but this time he's on the opposite side of a creek. I lose my footing, and he leaps over to catch me just as I stumble forward, landing atop him just inches from the water.

"Caught you," I tell him.

"Indeed you have, witchy." He reclines his head back, laughing as he gazes up at me from beneath.

I find myself staring down at him, our noses nearly touching. The awareness of our closeness rushes back, and I feel my cheeks flush as I realize the position of my legs straddling him.

His gaze sends a tingling sensation coursing through me, and I swallow hard as his eyes wander from mine to my lips, making my heart race.

He clears his throat. "How about that whiskey?"

"Yes, sorry." I clamber off him and dust myself off, turning toward the creek as he begins cleaning the dirt from his hands and face. I can only imagine how I must look with dirt smeared all over my face. Yet he had looked at me like that? Was I imagining things? I move next to him and start washing my face.

We return to our shovels and resume digging, but my thoughts keep straying. Every time I feel his gaze on me, I glance over, only to find him focused on his task once more. He's widened his area, and I wonder if we'll ever uncover it—and if it's even still here.

"Why do you think the witch hasn't summoned you yet?" I break the silence.

"I couldn't say. However, I'm not complaining, even with the urgency to lift my curse. Are you?"

My cheeks flush again. "No." I struggle to suppress a smirk, and I could swear I see a spark in his eyes, if only for a fleeting moment, before they return to a more serious demeanor. I wish I knew what he was thinking—perhaps he suddenly recalled that we shouldn't be enjoying ourselves. And maybe we shouldn't be.

"Are you certain your whiskey would even be here in this dimension?"

"Not in the slightest, witchy. I'm just about ready to— Oh—" A clink of metal against glass causes him to drop his shovel, bending down to inspect.

I abandon my shovel and rush over. "Is it—?"

He retrieves the shovel again, using it to loosen the hard soil around the glass until he can reach in and pull it out. With a broad smile, he reveals a dusty bottle containing amber liquid. "Found it." He turns it in his hand, cleaning it off with the bottom of his shirt.

I dust myself off. "I thought we would never find it."

We walk back in contemplative silence, but the mood remains... pleasant. I never would have imagined I'd be digging for whiskey beneath the Andre tree, let alone with the headless horseman—and actually enjoying myself.

Once back inside, I slip off my shoes to spare the floor

from the dirt we've tracked in. After all, I'd be the one to clean it after.

"Why don't you run a bath in my room?"

I blink at him, momentarily taken aback.

"If you'd like, that is..." He glances around, a hint of something like nervousness flickering across his expression. Is the horseman actually nervous? "I'll provide you with clean clothes, and I'll even use the creek to afford you some privacy."

"Umm... Okay." I'm certainly not about to refuse the opportunity for a proper wash, especially after the hours we've just spent digging in the dirt and then frolicking in it.

"Right, then." He turns and steps outside, leaving me to my own devices. He's... permitting me to enter his bedroom, to utilize his bath. Alone.

He's... trusting me.

Well, I suppose there's little I could do to his room anyway.

I warm the hearth with hot water and pour it into the bath to help raise the temperature. Once I indulge in the simple washroom, I dry myself off and step into the chilly bedroom. There, I find a clean pair of black trousers and a crisp white long-sleeved shirt laid out on the bed for me. I quickly dress and make my way out of the bedroom.

The sweet aroma of hot apples wafts toward me, and I spot the pot simmering on the stove.

He's already changed and seated at the table, engrossed

in a book. When he glances up at me, his gaze lingers, as if this were the first time he's seen me donning his attire, or as if I'm clad in some manner of daring gown.

"Is there a problem?" I inquire.

"No." He sets the book aside. "Are you ready to be amazed?" He reaches for the bottle of whiskey resting on the table.

"Haven't you opened it yet?"

"I was waiting for you." He rises, his movements deliberate. "I've begun heating your potion, though."

"Cider."

He huffs a laugh and retrieves two tankards, placing them on the table before filling them with the cider, then adding a drop, followed by a generous pour of whiskey into each. We each lift our drinks and take a sip. At first, the taste of apple bursts upon my palate, releasing spices that weren't there before. Notes of caramel, nuts, and rye dance on my tongue, but as I swallow, it feels as though a fire ignites in my throat, and I erupt into a fit of coughs.

Fallon chuckles, then hands me a glass of water. "This was worth it."

Gasping for breath, I take a sip of water to soothe my throat. Yet, I'm compelled to try the cider again.

"Don't drink it all at once; let it grow on you."

I clear my throat after swallowing, feeling the warmth creep into my cheeks and the nape of my neck. Fallon smiles, shaking his head.

Taking another sip, I feel a rush to my head.

"Whoa, witchy." He's in front of me before I can blink, steadying me by the shoulders and taking my drink, placing it on the table.

I swallow, my gaze locked with his. The room has dimmed, and I can sense that rain is on the way.

"Thank you," I mutter, my voice barely above a whisper.

He maintains his hold on me, and being this close is becoming overwhelming.

"No need to thank me. It wouldn't be gentlemanly of me to allow you to fall."

I chuckle softly. "You weren't always a gentleman with me."

His throat bobs as he considers this. "No, I wasn't. But, I can be. What spell have you cast on me, witchy?"

"I haven't cast any spell."

He cracks a smile, but his eyes grow heavy as he gazes at me, and I can't seem to look away. The sharp angles of his pale face draw my attention, his black hair still damp from his earlier dip in the creek, wisps brushing over his forehead.

"I ought to be thanking you for today, love."

"For what?" I manage to ask.

"I cannot recall the last time I felt wholesome joy. You awakened that in me today. I almost regret it." His grip on my arm lightens as I prove I can keep my balance, yet he doesn't release me. His expression is serious as he says it.

Something in me feels... heavy. Perhaps it's the whiskey, or maybe something else entirely...

"Katalina," he whispers, concern lacing his voice. "Your expression has fallen. What troubles you?"

"When you mentioned that the only place you belong is back in the ground... after we break the curse... is there nothing we could do to make you wish to keep living?"

He exhales slowly, the sound heavy with resignation. "Today you gave me a gift, but that's all it was. "His words churn in my stomach, and I shake my head.

"Wouldn't you want to find a way to live? To be happy?" I ask.

His eyebrows shoot up his forehead, and I know he's thinking the same thing I am—when did things change between us?

His fingers brush my cheek. "That's impossible, witchy," he says just above a whisper.

I close my eyes and find the strength within me before I surge up to press my lips to his in a kiss that conveys everything I am feeling but cannot voice. I pour my soul into that kiss, but he doesn't move.

I feel like I have made a terrible mistake.

Then his tongue presses between my lips, and his fingers tangle into my hair as he takes control. He moves his body into me and kisses me harder, deeper.

A flame lights in my core, and the fire rushes through my veins. My entire body feels like it's alight.

His hands tighten around my shoulders as he pushes

me a few steps back, but I am so absorbed in his kiss that I barely register the movement.

He lets out a guttural sound, and I pause. His eyes are feral, with a mixture of lust but also the curse. He's cycling back again.

Oh no.

I step back as he stands there, panting.

"Witchy..." he breathes.

I can tell he's trying to take back control. The last time this happened, we subdued it with a kiss.

He reaches for my neck, but he pulls himself back, physically trying to stop himself from hurting me. Resisting is hurting him, yet he's trying to stop it. He no longer wants to see me in pain.

With a rush of adrenaline, I walk toward him, letting him grip my neck and allowing our lips to crash together again. His tongue slides into my mouth, and I take all of him in.

It isn't until I feel the hard press of wood against my back that I realize we have gone across the entire room. He has me pressed against the breaking wheel. A cold spike of fear pierces through my body.

"I have done so many things to hurt you, my witch," he says, his voice heavy but steady.

He's controlling the curse—or we are.

"I should have felt nothing. With each one of your pretty cries of pain, with each sweet tear that trailed down your porcelain cheek, I should have felt nothing." He caresses my cheek with the back of his knuckles. "But I wasn't numb. I pretended to be, but I felt...life."

"Life?" I ask.

He nods and stares at his hand on my cheek momentarily, and then his icy-blue eyes flick back to me. "Any witch can bring a dead man back to the land of the living, but do you know what it means to make him feel?"

"No." The word escapes my lips, barely more than a whisper.

"Let me show you." Something dark and sinister flashes in his eyes.

His hands glide up to my shoulders and trace down my arms, leaving a trail of shivers. He takes my wrists and brings them above my head as his body presses to mine, trapping me between him and the breaking wheel.

I gasp. "What are you doing?"

"Showing you what feeling something too deep does to you when you least expect it." Desire laces his voice, and I can't help but feel trepidation about what he's going to do to me. But I remind myself we have come a long way from the garrote.

I want to trust him. I want to believe he won't hurt me, that my mother's wrong about him.

But he just said it himself. He *has* hurt me. He has brought me so much pain, taking me away from everything I know and making me suffer.

Am I being foolish in thinking we're beyond that? I can forgive what he did before. He didn't know who I was.

I was just the girl who put him in a wooden maiden and lit it with a blaze of fire. When I did that, he was just the monster that took my father's head.

He ties my hands to the top of the wheel, stretching them far apart, and this time the fire in my core grows, overtaking me.

"You brought me back from the dead, witchy. And you gave me no choice." His voice is low, seductive.

Confusion flickers through me as I remain acutely aware of every action he does to me. "I told you, I didn't do that. You know I didn't do—"

"I'm not talking about when my body was called from its rest. I am talking about me soul. You brought it back. You made me feel, and I am going to return the favor." He tilts the wheel back so that I am lying at an angle.

My breath shallows as I stare at him in this position, and I dare say "you're right. I didn't. Are you going to punish me for it?" The look he gives me fills me with promise of what he's about to do. And I welcome it.

Moving close to my ear, he whispers, "I have caused you so much pain. Let me make up for that now and show you the other side of that wicked coin." His lips press to mine again in an all-consuming, too-brief kiss.

He reaches for the front of my shirt and rips at the fabric, causing buttons to fly and exposing my breasts to the cool, damp air.

"Gods, has there ever been a sight so beautiful?" he says before covering my body with his.

His warmth sinks into my bare skin as his lips encircle one of my nipples, and then he starts to suck. The soft pull of his lips and the wicked flick of his tongue send shivers of pleasure down my body and gather in my core.

My eyes roll to the back of my head, and a soft moan escapes me. I have never felt anything like this. The more attention he lavishes on my chest, massaging one breast with his long fingers while kissing and sucking the other, the greater the need builds in my body.

"Fallon." I gasp, not recognizing the brazen neediness in my own voice.

"Beg all you want, witchy. You showed me no mercy. I will not give in to your pleas." He looks up at me, a depraved smile on his lips.

This isn't the tortured man I know or the innocent one I caught glimpses of. This is a demon sent to tempt me to hell. He knows what he is doing, and I want it. God help me, I want it all.

I gasp again as his fingers work the laces of my borrowed trousers.

"Tell me, does your body crave the same release I do?" He lets out a dark chuckle as he pulls the trousers from my legs and tosses them away.

"Yes," I pant out before he secures my ankles to the wheel.

"Good. If you beg sweetly enough, maybe I will reward you." He places a kiss on my ankle, making me jump. He puts another on the inside of my calf, his hands gripping my knees and spreading my legs farther apart.

"Fallon, what are you—"

He gently bites the side of my thigh just above my knee.

"I said beg," he growls.

Why do I find that so alluring?

"Please," I beg.

Somehow, my pleas make whatever this is so much more scandalous.

A cold sweat breaks out over my skin, giving my heated body only a moment's relief. "Please."

"Your cries are so sweet, but I wager I can still make them sweeter still." His fingers part the fold of my sex, exposing the hot, damp flesh to the cool air, and then he blows a single stream directly onto the tight little bundle of nerves.

"Fallon, please," I cry.

My legs strain against the ties so hard that my thighs burn as I try to close them.

"No, my witch. I've made up my mind. You're bringing me back to life. This body of yours is now mine, mine to please, to torment, and to feel. More than that, you want it. You can't lie to me, not when you are so completely exposed. I can see how ready you are for me. I can see how this perfect little cunt weeps for me."

My back arches as his thumb draws a small circle over my clit. My arms pull tight, the muscles burning, and somehow that intensifies the pleasure he is giving me. The bite of pain and discomfort makes the delicious torture all the sweeter.

I don't understand how that is possible. I don't understand what he is doing, why he is touching me the way he is, or even why my body aches for him the way it does.

"Please," I cry again, louder this time.

I don't know what I am asking for; I only know that I need it and that he is the only one who can give it to me.

"Again," he growls. "Let me hear that sweet, imploring voice again."

"Please, I need... I..." My voice cracks as he presses his thumb to my clit even harder.

"I know what you need, my witchy, but I decide what you feel. I decide when you feel it. Say it."

"You decide," I repeat, not fully understanding what I am saying, but knowing that I will give him anything right now as long as he makes this torment end.

My calves tense and release over and over, a dull ache burning through the muscles. The evidence of my arousal trails down between my shaking thighs.

In all the nights I spent alone in my bed, exploring the body god gave me and the pleasures of my flesh, I have never felt anything like this. I have never felt this pressure build so intently in my belly, never been so damp that my own juices trickle down my thighs. He must be doing something else to me, something that—

My thoughts stop abruptly when Fallon leans down to

put his sinful lips on my body. I have heard of women—whores—who are paid handsomely to service men with their mouths. I know many wives do it to keep their men from straying, but I had no idea a man could or would so freely put his lips to my...

A guttural cry escapes my lips as he laps at my clit. It feels so good, but I need more. I need him to ease the ache mounting in my body.

"Fallon," I cry out. Not a plea, but a demand.

He stands, placing his finger on my clit and pressing down to give me the most exquisite pressure, but it's still not enough. He leans over the wheel, over my body, now covered in sweat and shaking with desire.

"You do not get to decide when I make your body plunge into the abyss. You are tied to me wheel, witchy. That means your pleasure is mine. I decide if you get to feel that sweet ecstasy and if your release will coat me fingers, me lips, or me cock. Is that understood?"

I nod, not knowing what else to do, praying he will give me the ecstasy he is promising. It seems wrong to pray to God when I am sinning with a demon, but that doesn't stop me.

"Good girl." He kisses me again, and I can taste the salty sweetness that is my pleasure on his lips.

It makes my head spin and my core clench around nothing.

As quickly as he kisses me, he pulls back and disappears from my view. Then his mouth is on me again, this time his tongue pressing into my body, over and over, sliding in and out.

I cry out his name. The pressure swells even higher, and I am afraid I am going to explode until he nuzzles his nose into my clit, giving my body exactly what it needs.

My back arches hard enough to lift my body from the wheel, and Fallon wraps his arms around my waist, pinning me in place while he continues to ravage my body with his mouth.

I scream his name as sparks of light burst behind my eyes, and wave after wave of the most exquisite pleasure overtakes me. There is no way to tell how long it lasts. It could have been but a moment or a century. The entire world stops as he brings me to the most incredible heaven and then eases my body back down to the land of the living.

"Did you enjoy that, witchy?" He lifts a cup of cider to my lips, and I drink deeply.

My throat aches. It feels like my lips may crack, and my head is spinning.

After I drink my fill, Fallon takes the cup from me.

"Yes," I croak out, unsure what to expect of him next.

A devilish grin spreads on his face.. "That's good because I'm going to do it again and again until I am convinced you have nothing left to give me.

<h1 style="text-align:center;font-style:italic">Chapter Twenty-Six</h1>

FALLON

Gods above, save me. I've given in and lost my mind. This is wrong, but I'm not taking it back.

This woman is going to be the death of me. I can taste the crisp autumn wind, sunlight, and rain on her flesh. When I lick between her legs, I can taste life. She is sweeter than honey and softer than Irish moss.

The way her tight little body grips my tongue as I take her with it...almost breaks me. Just imagining these silken walls surrounding my cock with its wet heat and milking it so thoroughly, begging for my seed, nearly brings me to my knees. I am seconds from spilling in my pants like some lovesick boy still so green that a stiff wind could get him off.

But I am only a man, a damned man, a cursed man,

but a man, and how am I to resist the temptation that is this perfectly formed, warm, willing body begging for me to take it? This body with perfectly shaped breasts that taste like fresh dew and this perfectly formed mound that practically drips with honey. This body that belongs to this brave little witch who works so diligently to free me and reunite me with my soul... It isn't fair.

I made promises to myself not to take her. I don't deserve her. She doesn't deserve what I will do to her. I will ruin her.

She isn't just a woman; she is an angel sent to save me, and I am ready to worship her for as long as the fates allow. Then I will die fighting for the honor of doing it again.

"Fallon." She gasps, and my cock surges with need. My name, my real name, is like music on her lips. "Please."

Not even the cruelest of monsters could refuse cries so sugared.

I wrap my arms around her thighs and hold her down as I dive for my second helping of her pleasure. Her body fights against my restraint, but I hold firm as I devour her, licking every drop from her. Then I return to lapping at the little magical button at the peak of her womanhood until she releases a fresh wave of nectar.

The need to release her from the wheel is ever present. I want to lay her out on my bed and claim her, over and over, thrust my cock inside her until she has no desire to leave my cottage.

It will be the greatest love story no one will ever know.

I'll spend all eternity hunting those who would control me by day and every night delighting in the pleasures of Kat's flesh. I want her to be mine, only mine.

Fantasies of her on her knees haunt my mind, soothing the aches of my hunt with her mouth on my cock, until I plunge myself into her heat every night, until the pleasure is so great it outweighs the pain I have suffered at the hands of others.

I believe in her. She can end my torment and make the sacrifices that are demanded of me all worth it.

It is just a fantasy, though. One I will indulge in while pleasuring her. Never taking her with anything more than my fingers and lips.

But why should it be just a fantasy when she wants me to? If she breaks my curse, I will not be here to tell anyone I claimed her. If she doesn't, I simply won't let her go.

With my mouth working her sex, wringing orgasm after orgasm from her body, I move my hand to my cock. I squeeze just hard enough to release the ache.

It isn't enough. I need to come. It has been so long. The aching in my bollocks grows unbearable.

Kat is tied to the wheel. I can thrust into her, but she is still so tight. I refuse to hurt her. Not like that, never like that. I need to keep working with her if she is going to take me.

There is no way I can hold back now. I'm too far gone.

I can spin the wheel, the hammer long since disabled, and turn her, letting her taste what her pleasure does to me. Gods, even the thought of her lips suckling at my cock makes me want to spill.

Though, that would be a waste. I wouldn't last long enough to enjoy the feeling of her lips. No, the first time she sucks me, I will be ready. I won't be so close to the edge. I will savor every moment, commit it to memory, and make it last as long as possible.

That tongue has gotten her into enough trouble. Only when I'm ready will I let it save her.

The demanding need turns painful. It would only take a few quick strokes to end my torment. I could stand over her, admiring the way her body pants for me, making her breasts rise and fall, the way her cheeks turn such a lovely shade of pink, the same shade that colors her lips, her nipples, and her pussy.

I could stand over her, take out my cock, intimidate her, let her be afraid yet curious as I cover her flawless skin with shot after shot of my cum.

With that image in my head, my cock in my hand, her juicy cunt shuddering at my lips, and her cries of pleasure filling my ears, I come for the first time in more than half a century.

The rush of pleasure surges through my back. All at once, the familiar feeling returns as it bends my spine, seizes my heart, and steals all thoughts from my mind.

She comes apart with me. I'm sure she is unaware of my pleasure, but that is fine.

After I tuck my cock back into my pants, licking her

pussy gently to soften her last orgasm, I hide the evidence of my indiscretion. She will know my body soon enough.

Sweat drenches her body, and the strands of her gold hair that frame her face adhere to her skin. Her legs shake, and she looks truly worn out.

With the kind of satisfaction only a man who saw his woman so completely destroyed can feel, I untie her ankles and then her wrists.

She doesn't move. Her eyes are glazed, and if it weren't for the constant rise and fall of her breasts, I'd be worried.

"Come on, witchy. Let's get you clean, and I'll let you rest up before we go again."

"Again?" she asks, her eyes lighting up.

"You are insatiable," I tease as I carry her to the bath.

It takes me a bit to heat the water and adequately fill the tub while she lies there with that dopey, satisfied look in her eyes.

My chest swells with something, another familiar feeling I take a moment to name.

Pride.

I did that; my mouth and hands brought her such satisfaction, and I earned the right to care for her now.

Once the tub is full and she's content leaning against the back while soaking, I trail my fingers across her skin.

Even after making her come over and over, her skin pebbles at my touch, and her nipples harden. Even her lips part so she can take deeper breaths. I would wager if I reached between her legs, she would already be wet for me.

"Tell me something important," she says.

"Like what?"

"Tell me something about you from before."

"Ah." I have to think for a moment. More and more memories are easier to reach, but I still don't have everything. "Ask me something specific."

"What was your favorite meal to eat?"

"I think you just saw it," I say, not trying to hold back my laugh.

The action feels strange and unpracticed, but I have a feeling that'll change.

"That is not what I meant." Her eyes widen, and she covers her mouth with her hand like I have scandalized her.

I laugh even harder.

"Come on, witchy, you're clean. Let's get you dry and in me bed where you belong."

She doesn't argue; she gets to her feet and lets me help her from the tub. I run the towel over her soft skin, which I crave to explore.

With a mental note to steal better towels, I wrap her in my shirt, wanting her to smell like me, and pull her into my bed. A sense of calm washes over me, a kind of peace that I have longed for and thought only the grave could give me. Maybe she is my salvation.

"What are you doing?" she asks, her body stiffening under my touch.

"Nothing yet. We are going to lie here together and

talk about nothing at all. Then, if you so desire, you will have free rein to explore me body the way I have yours."

"You're going to let me tie you to the wheel?" she asks, batting her pretty little eyes at me.

"No, but if you wish to be in control, I will happily let you ride me like a thoroughbred steed," I taunt.

Her blush deepens, and I find I enjoy making her blush. I press my lips to the base of her jaw to feel the way her pulse flutters. Her heart races, making my cock stir. She likes it, too.

"I bet you would look so pretty sitting on my cock, your tits bouncing with every rise of your hips. You would take me so good. Maybe I should get you to ride me face first, give me another taste of your cunt, while your lips wrap around my manhood. Then you suck me until I am hard enough for you. Does that sound good to you, witchy?"

Her eyes cast down to her feet, and then she moves her head to my chest. My witch doesn't want me to see the pleasure in her eyes, it seems, but she needs to be near me. She needs that skin-on-skin contact.

I lift her off of me long enough for me to sit up and strip off my shirt. When I lie next to her again, I pull her into my arms and lay her head on my bare skin.

The second her face touches my chest, her entire body relaxes.

"Rest now, witchy." I run my fingers through her locks.

Her soft, perfect little ringlets curl around me, like even her hair needs to touch as much of me as possible.

"Tell me something about you," I say, parroting her earlier question.

She goes silent for a moment. Did she not hear me?

"I hate radishes. They are vile little things and aren't good enough to be fed to the pigs, but I love apples."

A chuckle escapes me. "I'd have thought you'd grow tired of apples by now."

She glances up at me through her lashes. "I thought so too, but now they remind me of you."

"What else do you love?" I ask.

"Drawing." Her eyes grow distant, and I catch how her voice becomes almost whimsical. "I miss my sketchpad. I've spent my entire life keeping to myself or hiding when my parents fought. My mother gifted me a sketchpad to keep me company, and I've kept one ever since."

I brush her cheek with my thumb as she talks, taking note of every muscle movement her face makes. I find myself wishing I could take away the suffering from her childhood. "What do you draw?"

"Everything. And anything that scares me, or things that bring me comfort. My mother, spirits, the Andre tree. Thoughts of you, what I thought you'd looked like before I met you..."

"Where is your sketchpad now? I ask.

"In my bedroom."

Her gaze deepens, determination hardening the

corners of her eyes. "I love the way you made me feel on the wheel. I love what you did to me."

"Is that so?" My witch not only brought my soul back but also feeds my ego. "Did you want me to do it again?"

"No... Well, yes, but not now. Now I want..." She casts her gaze down again then flicks it back to me, like she refuses not to say what's on her mind. "I want more."

With a primal growl, I pull her closer to me, taking her lips in another kiss and holding her hands to my skin, urging her to indulge her curiosity.

I'm so fucking glad I stopped denying myself of her. Even if this is all temporary. Even though I know it will all go away after my curse is broken. For now, we can both enjoy it.

Her fingers are so gentle it's almost as if she's barely touching me as she traces the lines of my chest and abdomen. The life I led may have been hard, but the strenuous work kept my body in top form. The curse froze my body at the time of my death, so my youthful physique and vigor are still intact.

Kat's plump lips part again as her hands trace my muscles slowly, as if memorizing my body. I took similar care to commit her form to memory, so I will not rush her. Even if I burn to roll us over so I can bury myself inside her, claiming her as mine forever.

Her fingers trail lower, brushing the top of the trail of hair that disappears under the top of my pants. Barely a dusting of hair, but she seems fascinated by it, her fingers gliding over it, going lower with each pass.

My witchy is nervous. She wants to explore further but is afraid. I could undo the ties, giving her permission, but where is the fun in that?

When it's just us in this bed, I want her to be bold, to tell me what she wants, or even just to take it. If I want her at my mercy, unable to do anything but follow my commands or be helpless to my will, then I'll tie her up again. She likes that enough.

Her fingers dip lower, tracing the edge of my pants and then slipping under a bit. My cock jumps, and she gasps.

"Are you just going to tease me?" I taunt. "I know you've heard the maids whispering, maybe even your little friends giggling about what men and women do when they are alone. I know you understand how to please a man in theory, if not in practice."

She doesn't look up, too nervous to meet my gaze, but as I put my hand on the back of her thin neck, my fingers resting against her pulse, her heart pounds against my touch.

"Can I..." Her words are quiet, and her voice trembles.

"You can do whatever you wish," I answer, silently adding, *until my patience breaks, and I must have you.*

I expect her hand to trail under my pants so she can feel my flesh, but she grazes over the top, not to the lacing of my pants but down farther to caress my cock through the fabric. Her touch is still so light, and if I weren't so hard for her, so ready, I would barely feel it.

She gives a little firmer pressure, making a groan escape my lips and making my cock twitch.

She gasps and moves her body down a little. Her head now rests on my ribs as her hand becomes bolder, touching me, learning the feel of my cloth-covered manhood.

I grip my hand into a tight fist as I try holding myself back. I know that if I can pet her cunt right now, she'll be wet again. She'll still be relaxed from the pleasure I pulled from her body, but it won't be enough, not yet.

She needs to know my body to want what will happen. I know she may not be innocent, but I want to treat her as if she is. This may not be her first experience with a man, but it will be with a man who knows how to treat a woman.

In my mind, this night will wipe away any traces of any other she's had. This night will be as if it were her first. This will be the memory she will hold on to.

So, with strength I did not know a man could possess, I hold myself back. I let her explore, allowing her desire to grow until she isn't afraid or nervous. I want her desperate.

Even then, even when she's begging to feel me, to know what it's like to be mine, I'll bring her to the edge of oblivion again with my fingers, with my mouth, anything. There is no doubt in my mind that even after having so recently spilled, her tight body will make quick work of me.

She's going to fall apart on my cock. I'm going to do anything and everything I can to make that happen.

After tonight, she will crave my body with the same fierceness that I so foolishly denied to my little witch.

All thoughts of being a good man and leaving her as untouched as I found her, thinking she deserves someone better or that I wouldn't be here to take care of her, have vanished. She made me feel and brought my soul back to me. She reminded me of what it is like to be a man and not just a monster.

So now I'll be the man she deserves. The demanding, covetous man who will treat her like the goddess she is, worship her body, provide for her, and kill anyone who dares to even dream about harming her or touching her.

She is mine. At least until my end.

And I'm going to make her adore every minute we spend together.

Her hand presses down on my cock firmly as she runs her palm up and down my length. Her fingers even venture to my bollocks for a moment, making lights burst behind my eyes and a drop of pre-cum soak through my trousers.

She touches the damp spot, massaging the tip of my cock with her fingers, and I have to grit my teeth to keep from coming in my breeches like an inexperienced boy.

I clench my fist harder, and I can't help but tighten my fingers on the nape of her neck, too.

"Did I hurt you?" she asks.

I shake my head, unable to look at her or speak. The struggle to control myself is far more challenging than I expected.

"Fallon?" she asks.

"I am well. You did not hurt me. I just need a moment to collect myself."

"Oh," she says, looking up at me with that little line of confusion forming between her eyebrows.

Has that always been so becoming on her? Have I simply not noticed?

I lean up and press a kiss to her lips, taking her hands in my own and then pressing them to my body.

"I only need a moment. Then we may continue," I promise, kissing her again.

She relaxes against me and melts into my kiss, which is pure bliss. I am almost completely lost in the feeling of her lips when her body goes rigid, and she sits up.

"What is it?"

"We have been going about it all wrong," she says, pulling away from me.

"I assure you we have not, and I intend to show you exactly how right this is." I reach for her, but she crawls off the bed and runs to the table.

"Not that," she says, already flipping through the

damn spell book. "That was amazing, but I'm talking about the curse. I thought I didn't want this night to end and wished every night could be as incredible. You have shown me so much that I didn't know was possible and made me feel things I didn't..."

Her words trail off as she flips through more pages.

"Anyway, it made me think about how there are so many ways to do something, and some are better than others. Some have completely different results—"

"Please, get to the point so I can get you back in the bed."

I don't even try to hide my annoyance. I went from rock hard, about to spill, to aching bollocks I am sure will turn blue if I don't get her back into bed immediately.

"We are trying to figure out who the most likely witch is based on who we think it could be. We are looking at the townspeople as suspects."

"Aye, that is how you—"

"No, we need to look at the people the witch has had you kill. We need to look at what those poor souls have in common." She twirls around naked, pressing that damn book to her chest while her eyes light up with excitement.

I would much prefer that excitement to come from the first time she feels me thrust deep inside of her, but as much as I loathe the timing, she is onto something.

I stand, adjusting my cock to a more comfortable position, move to the table, and pull out a quill and a piece of parchment. "Right, then, let's see if we can figure this out. Then, when we have the witch's name, I am going to celebrate by feasting on your pleasure before claiming you as mine."

The tops of her cheeks pinken, and she moves the book a little lower to cover more of her body.

"Put my shirt back on so I can concentrate," I say as I dip the quill into the ink.

When she finds it and puts it on, it's thin enough to give me a hint of the shape of her hips as they swing with each movement. Each time she moves her arms, I can just see the silky pale skin of her firm breasts in the gaps between the shirt buttons.

It is maddening, but I can't have her again, not until this task is complete.

Finally, we have our list:

Henry, the baker

The notary

The midwife

The magistrate

Daniel

Burgomaster, the mayor.

The mayor was the last head I claimed.

"Who could want all these people dead?" She chews on her bottom lip.

"Anyone who doesn't have power," I answer easily. "These men are the most respected in the town. They are the ones who can decide the fates of others. They are also terrible men who abuse their power. So the question is, who has felt the ire of all of them?"

She thinks for a moment, and I can't take it anymore. With a quick tug, I pull her onto my lap then position her so she faces me while straddling one of my thighs.

"Who do you think it could be?" I take her hands and put them on my shoulders then grab her hips and tilt them at the right angle.

"I don't know. I..."

I kiss her throat and press her hips into my thigh, rocking her slowly, letting the rough cotton of my trousers provide the friction that will give her pleasure.

"Oh..." She gasps as she presses down harder and keeps rocking without my encouragement.

"I think we have done enough for tonight," I whisper, undoing the buttons that keep me from her breasts.

"Yes," she says, riding my thigh faster.

Her moist heat builds. This is how I am going to get her ready for me. She will come apart riding my thigh like a wanton whore. Then I will lay her out like a goddess among the soft blankets and pillows and take her.

"Good girl," I pant out, my cock rock hard.

I take one of her hands and bring it down my body. This time, she doesn't pet me through my pants but unties my trousers. She wants me, all of me, and that is what she will get.

I am so lost in her that it takes me a moment to realize

the tingling sensation climbing my spine isn't arousal. It's magic.

I grab her hands to stop her. My heart stops beating as I look into her shocked eyes.

"The curse." I gasp as the tingling becomes a searing pain. "*Run.*"

Chapter Twenty-Seven

KAT

I WILL NOT STAND by and watch him endure this torment.

The curse will continue until the witch is stopped and the curse is broken. But now I have a lead, a small kernel of a clue that should aid me in narrowing down the list of suspects. I am determined to follow this trail, no matter where it leads.

As quickly as I can, I run across the room, looking for the thicker shirt I wore earlier. When I find it, I throw it on and button it.

The loud shot makes my stomach clench. I know Fallon is suffering, and I cannot help him, at least not yet, not until the witch is dead.

I throw on my borrowed trousers and tie them, making myself more presentable.

Just as I hear the horse neigh, I turn, ready to leave. Fallon, now the headless horseman, climbs on top of his steed, and I quickly follow him.

I don't know if he knows I am here or if the curse's grip is too firm. It doesn't matter.

He rides hard and fast to the Andre tree, and I have to hold on to his waist with everything I have, using his back to shield my face from the branches and the icy wind. It isn't until we are closer to town that I loosen my grip.

When he slows, I get off the horse and start my hunt. While here, I also want to steal a few more spices to improve my cider.

But first, the investigation. The notary was one of his first kills.

Most of the other kills were in a position of power. They could make someone's life pleasant or hellish. The notary wasn't a kind man, but he wasn't someone who harmed others; he did not possess the power the others abused.

The only reason I can see that someone would kill him was if he witnessed something the witch wants to hide. So the first place I want to look is in his ledger.

It takes too long to get to his house on the far side of town while sneaking through bushes and being careful not to be seen. The thick, stormy clouds cover the tiny sliver of the moon, making my path dark and treacherous. It makes it far easier to avoid detection, but it is harder to safely make it to my destination.

When I get there, I am covered in dirt, and the thorns of a rosebush have left a deep scratch on my arm that is bleeding.

This is important, and I don't mind shedding a little blood if it means Fallon doesn't have to suffer. I cover the cut with the sleeve of the shirt and move on.

The house looks empty and cold. For a moment, I wonder if anyone has been here. The tiny amount of light the moon gives does not reach inside the small cottage. The windows, though bare, are covered in a thick layer of dirt and dust.

I'm forced to feel my way around the cottage, tripping over a chair and other things I can't identify. Once I'm inside, I'm able to find a candle and light it.

The cottage is, in fact, empty, but someone has been here. Someone has ransacked the entire place, looking for, I assume, the same thing I am.

Taking a deep breath, I set to work and riffle through the items from the knocked-over table, looking for any of his notary supplies. There's nothing in the main room, but a small door off to the side gives me hope.

The door takes more effort to open than I expect, so much that I am forced to throw my shoulder into it several times, ignoring the pain as I push inside.

I find a wooden chair wedged to block the door, which probably sat in front of the desk at one time. The desk lies on its side, papers littering the floor, and several bottles of ink have spilled out, making the pages completely illegible.

I go inside, looking at the few pages that are not entirely distorted by the spilled ink. There is nothing of use. A few land sales, some to my father, others to the mayor. Even a few death certificates, one for my mother.

I know her death was not involved in this. It happened so long ago, well before the horseman was raised from the dead.

My father was considering claiming her inheritance or making a match for me. He probably needed her death certificate for that, or maybe he needed it to obtain another marriage license.

I swallow a hard lump in my throat.

It's nothing I have to worry about now. Thanks to my horseman.

I drop the paper to the ground and let it flutter into the still-wet puddle of ink.

There are no other doors, no other rooms, and not even a trapdoor leading to a cellar or a crawl space under the home. If the door was blocked by the chair from the inside, how did the thief who ransacked this office leave?

My question is answered when a high-pitched screech fills the room.

I freeze, terrified that whoever did this is still in the cottage. It isn't until the wind howls and the screech sounds again that I can see the cause. It's coming from a small window on the other side of the room, too small for a grown man to fit through.

The little bit of light that may have come through the window is blocked by the barren branches of a tree. The noise is from its branches scratching the glass.

This window confirms the only observation I allowed myself to make about the witch. The witch is, in fact, a she. I have never really considered that it could be a man, though I suppose she could be acting at the behest of a man. Something about that doesn't feel right, though.

But the person who tore through this home, wrecking it while looking for something, was a petite female.

If I tried, I could probably wriggle my way through that window, but it would be difficult to fit my larger breasts and my fuller hips through that small opening.

Whoever did it is likely quite agile, as it is several feet above the ground.

With one last look around the room, I give up hope of finding anything actually useful here and head back to the main room.

A crack of lightning lights up the sky and fills the room, giving me a better view of the damage done. Whoever was here earlier was very thorough. They left no stone unturned.

The high-pitched whinny of Fallon's steed catches my attention. Outside the window, I see him rear up, one head hanging from the bag attached to the saddle.

I think he is calling to me, telling me it is time to go back, but they take off towards the Van Brunt estate.

"No, not Nana. Anyone but her," I cry, frozen in my spot.

When another crack of lightning flashes, I come to my senses and run with everything I have. I don't care who sees me. I don't care if I trip and fall. I *run*.

The cottage isn't too far from the estate, but by the time I get there, he'll have already—

No. I can't give up.

Cutting through the forest, I leap over brambles and sprint into the thicket.

My lungs ache. My thighs, already sore from being bound to the wheel, feel like they're on fire. It doesn't matter. Nothing matters but Nana. I need to get to her.

When I finally near the door, Vengeance is standing outside, waiting for his master to return with his bounty. I run inside, not sure how to stop what is happening when I see him.

Fallon, still headless, calmly walks out of my bedroom. My sketchpad is under his arm, and my drawing charcoals are in his hand. He passes me, making no move to suggest he senses me. I stare at him, dumbstruck.

He only has a few moments of his own free will under the spell, and instead of killing someone who may be the witch or who has done something he finds distasteful, he retrieved something he must have suspected I missed.

A warm, comforting sensation pulses in my chest.

Tears threaten to spill over my cheeks, but I hold them back.

I know enough about the world to understand that a man can give his physical affection to a woman without feeling anything at all. I even know that the sweet nothings a man may whisper in the ear of a woman mean very little. They're words often used to lure women into their beds, but as soon as they've achieved their goal, it's as if those women never existed.

But this tells me he cares for me, not just as a body to warm his bed. He listens to me and cares for me, and maybe he's as lost for me as I am for him. It didn't even occur to me he could return the feelings of admiration and devotion that have been growing in me.

The more time I spend with him, the more I learn of his story, the more I want to be his.

Without a word, my mind still reeling and my heart overflowing, I follow Fallon back to Vengeance.

Despite not wanting him to suffer any longer, I know breaking the curse will end his life. I will have to live with the loss while knowing he will finally be at peace.

Part of me wants to be selfish, but there is no prolonging this. Lest I let him kill all of Sleepy Hollow to be with him, but that would include my nana, Claudia, and Tilly... And then the only ones left are me, him, and the witch. My heart aches, but we both know how this ends.

After we return to the cottage and his head is back

where it belongs, I will give voice to the emotions swelling inside me and tell him I care about him deeply.

We mount Vengeance and head back to the Andre tree at a comfortable trot. There is no rush. There are no more people to kill—not tonight—and no more clues to find. We will take our time and pick up where we left off when we return.

I press my body against his, my arms wrapped tightly around his torso, and close my eyes, taking him in. It's odd, being this close to him when he's headless. But I know he's in there in spirit, and I can trust him now.

Vengeance comes to an abrupt stop, and I open my eyes.

Someone is on the road ahead. I can't see around Fallon, but Vengeance takes a few nervous steps back.

A shot rings loud, piercing through the quiet night. Fallon jerks back and then falls off to the ground.

A vicious scream tears from my throat.

Someone shot him. He lies on his back, red spreading on his shirt, and he isn't getting up. He was shot with silver. Whoever came after him knew what to do.

Panic beats at the back of my throat.

Jumping down, I go to him, trying to figure out how to help him. Do I dig out the bullet? Do I try to stop the bleeding? How long will this leave him incapacitated?

It isn't until the horse rears up again that I remember we aren't alone.

Rough hands grab me and pull me away. I try to fight

to stay with Fallon, but I can't break the crushing hold on my arms.

"Stop fighting," my captor growls, and his voice sounds familiar. "I am going to take you far away from this monster."

Percival.

He doesn't think he is my captor. He thinks he is my savior. How do I explain to my would-be hero that I want to be with this monster?

"No, please," I beg as I try to come up with some excuse to go back to tend to Fallon. "I need to..."

My words die in my throat as several men in thick black coats surround Fallon.

The Nightward.

I watch in horror as they link a chain under Fallon's arms. His body makes a screaming whine as the metal touches him. The chains must be cursed or blessed or something.

I try to pull away again, but Percival hauls me up and throws me over his shoulder.

"You might not want to waste your time worrying about his fate," he sneers.

The cruelty in his tone makes my blood run cold.

"Your concerns should be centered on your fate. You have a lot to answer for, witch."

Chapter Twenty-Eight

KAT

"I AM *NOT* A WITCH," I say, beating my fists into his broad back.

How many times do I have to explain to some brute that I am not a witch?

Though, I guess I have spent the last several days—or has it been weeks?—studying witchcraft, learning spells, and speaking to the dead. Maybe that is sufficient to accurately label me as a witch. Still, I am not a very good one.

"That's exactly the type of thing a witch would say," he says, tightening his grip on my thighs. "But everyone knows a woman who wears pants, disappears without a trace for an entire fortnight, and then suddenly reappears on the back of the horse of the headless rider must be a witch or his whore."

"Unhand me!" I scream, kicking my feet and banging my fists harder against his back.

He tilts his head back and laughs, the shaking pushing his shoulder painfully into my gut.

"So, which is it? Whore or witch?"

"I am neither." I try to push myself up and away from his shoulder, but I only end up with his shoulder digging into my ribs, which is even worse than before.

"See, I think you are both. A woman with no parents, no husband, and hardly any family might be forgiven—shamed, but forgiven—for selling her body. But the second a little wench like you sells her soul to the devil for power she doesn't even know how to wield properly... Well, we have ways to take care of you."

"I am neither a witch nor a whore," I say through clenched teeth.

The dirt paths of the forest disappear, and we head down streets paved with cobblestones deeper into town toward the center. No one should be awake.

But my home is in the opposite direction, as is his. Where is he taking me?

"There are so many ways the town may decide to deal with you. Drowning is possible, but your evil may infect the drinking water. Perhaps they are going to stone you to death. Brutal, but effective."

"I am a lady, not a witch. Unhand me!" I yell, still struggling to kick against his tight hold.

His shoulder presses harder into my body, making it difficult to breathe.

"That is true. Not the witch part, but you are also a lady. So there will be some consideration for your station. If you were a maid, you would be stoned, but your family name garners respect, even if *you* don't. We aren't unreasonable."

I relax a little at his words and look around, praying to find someone who can help. But there is no one. With only the faintest sliver of the moon, the superstitious people of Sleepy Hollow are locked inside the walls of their homes to keep the headless horseman at bay. Like a door could save them if he is called to take them.

"So, no stoning, but a hanging would be fun to watch. Usually, they are fast and dignified unless you die poorly. If God has forsaken you, like the rest of us, your neck may not break. If that happens, you will struggle, your eyes will pop out, and your tongue will turn purple as you try in vain to breathe. You look like you have a sturdy neck, but I will make sure we have a thin rope handy."

This sick cad is enjoying this.

He keeps talking. "Of course, if you had a better standing in the town, like your mother, there may have been more people to speak on your behalf. We would still kill you, though. Of course, thou must not suffer a witch to live.

"But if you were well liked and not so odd, maybe someone would have fought for your soul to be cleansed in the fires. Then, at least, the sin of witchcraft would be cleaned from your body and soul, and you would be laid to rest in a manner fitting for your family.

"As it stands, I would put money on hanged by the neck until dead and then dumped in an unmarked grave."

"Put me down," I demand, still searching the empty streets for someone to help me.

"Of course," he says.

A metal-on-metal screech behind me sounds before he drops me on the hay- and dirt-covered floor of a cell. Then he slams the door closed and locks it.

"You can't do this," I say, scrambling to stand and then grabbing the iron bars. "I am not a witch. You have no proof against me because there is no proof."

Percival rolls his eyes. "We can find proof. If not, we'll make it. No one is going to believe the weird girl who talks to herself isn't a witch. You would have done much better to make friends in this town. Even better, you should have agreed to a match the moment you crossed into our county. Now, I'm afraid you are under arrest."

"What are the charges?" I bite out, ready to defend myself from whatever they concoct. "And I demand a lawyer."

"You are charged with the crimes of witchcraft, sorcery, raising a spirit from the dead, conjuring the horseman, and murder."

"You cannot seriously think that I conjured the horseman or that I am capable of having people killed. I know we aren't close, but you know me well enough to know that I could never—"

"Never what?" He steps toward the bars, towering over me.

I fight my instinct to shirk away from the hatred in his eyes.

"Never what, Katalina? You say we aren't close, and I guess that is right. I asked your father for your hand. He came back saying that you had your heart set on another. He laughed at me.

"I told myself no, that couldn't be true. I am the best match in this town, and you are the only lady pretty enough to bear my children. We would have had powerful sons and beautiful daughters. I would have taken care of you! Instead, you embarrassed me. *Me*!"

By the end, he is yelling, spittle gathering at the corners of his mouth, and his eyes grow wide and crazy.

"I didn't—"

"You did!" he practically screams. "I was going to go back and reason with your father. There was a plan where I would lay out how good I would treat you.

"Only the children you bore would have a claim on my estate. I wouldn't be like other men and claim my bastards. I would save you that indignation. You would never worry about our children's inheritance.

"I would have provided for you. I wouldn't have beaten you unnecessarily, only when it was provoked. I would have even been considerate enough to look elsewhere for my pleasure while you were with child."

I stood staring at him, amazed by how low this man set the bar for other suitors to rise to.

"I was never told you asked for my hand," I say calmly.

I would never marry this blighter, even before I met Fallon. My father never came to me with Percival's proposal, but I would have rejected it without a second thought.

He shakes his head. "Lies. Then to make matters worse, when I went to persuade your father, I found his body lying on the road in front of your house, missing his head. I thought, what luck! Katalina is going to be terrified. She will need a vigorous man to take care of her and her grandmother.

"It would be a great inconvenience, but I would have happily, without complaint, had us wed within the week and then have your father's property signed to me so I could properly take care of you. I would have even moved into your family home to make you more comfortable."

He has to be jesting.

Fire lights up my veins. "That *is* considerate of you. To offer to marry a grieving girl, forcing yourself into her bed before she even laid her father's body to rest. To move into a home several times larger and statelier than your own and take over the oversight and profits of my father's land without a single complaint."

I regret the words as soon as they leave my lips, even though each one is nothing but God's honest truth. But the second I spoke them, I knew they would rile up Percival.

"How dare you!" he screams. "I went looking for you. Do you really think I want to tie myself to the town loon?"

"Isn't that exactly what you said?" I shoot back.

He scowls. "I was doing you a favor. More than that, when I realized you were missing, I tried to find you to protect you."

Hunt me down is the more appropriate term for what he wants.

"So imagine my surprise after I spent an entire fortnight searching for you, searching for any sign of your body or where you went, when suddenly, in the tavern, I heard rumors about you riding with the horseman.

"I thought you'd been taken captive, and I was ready to chop down every tree some drunk said he saw the horseman ride into. I was ready to burn the entire forest down and kill anyone who suggested you were not being held against your will."

His eyes are bloodshot. His knuckles whiten where he grips the bars.

I wrap my arms around myself to keep from trembling and step back.

The bars between us will hold, but what does that matter when he has the key?

The words to apologize tip my tongue to pacify his rage. "I—"

"No. Witches and whores do not speak unless I allow it."

I clamp my lips shut, not wanting to anger him further or provoke him. The stench of ale is pungent on his breath, so it would be far more productive to wait for someone more level-headed to plea my case.

He huffs and narrows his eyes. "Do you know the shame I felt when I saw you tonight, the smile on your face as you climbed on the horse and rested your cheek on his back? Do you know the shame I feel for ever claiming you publicly as my wife?"

"But I'm *not* your wife."

"Whose fault is that? If you were more reasonable, none of this would be happening. You could be in my bed right now, serving me the way a wife should with her body, and I would gift you with children. You stole that future from us."

The idea of spending any time, let alone the rest of my life, in Percival's bed while servicing him makes me queasy.

I stay quiet, unwilling to make a peep or look him in his crazy eyes. Instead, I stare at the ground.

He keeps ranting, repeating the same things over and over about how I could have been his wife. How I am a witch and a whore. Soon, I stop listening, and my mind goes to Fallon. Where is he? Is he okay?

What's going to happen to him?

Logically, I know those men can't kill him. They can hurt him, but the second his body dies, he'll wake up back in his cottage, awaiting the witch's next order. Still, they can hurt him. Like I did.

I'm not sure if it's part of his curse or just an accident of the magic, but Fallon feels everything when people capture and torture him. He remembers the pain.

Tonight was not supposed to be more pain. Tonight was supposed to be about pleasure and love, and that was taken from us.

Stolen by a pig-headed man who arrested me for witchcraft, but it seems to him my crimes are far more severe. I, a woman, had the audacity to reject him. That I didn't reject him is completely inconsequential. I would have. I was just never awarded the opportunity.

What pushed him over the edge was seeing me riding a horse in the arms of another man.

So because this big man had his frail ego wounded, I'm forced to sit in a cell and listen to him rant and rave while awaiting trial for witchcraft.

Percival has a reputation for doing truly terrible things, sometimes to small, defenseless animals, sometimes to people he sees beneath them. Regardless, I hope *this* is the sin that guarantees his entrance to hell for all eternity.

He wants me punished by death because I didn't fall at his feet to worship him.

My head pounds, and my jaw aches from clenching

my teeth so hard that I worry they will crack. Still, I stay quiet. There is nothing I can say in this situation that won't make matters worse. The temper tantrum he's throwing would have made even the fussiest of toddlers proud.

So, I do what every other mother I have ever known does when her child throws a fit. I take a seat on the floor and cross my legs, and I wait for it to be over. Eventually, this man, like every other screaming two-year-old, will tire himself out.

"Are you listening to me?" he screams.

I blink up at him and say nothing.

He calls me a few words that men with his pedigree should never use, not even in a bar.

I still say nothing.

"Fine!" He throws up his hands in annoyance. "Tell me, then, if you are not a witch or a whore, why were you on the monster's horse?"

I tell him about how I saw my father cut down, how I had been taken that night. I keep my voice low, calm, and soothing. Like my mother did when she read me a bedtime story.

"I was at Daniel's house because we made a plan to trap and kill the horseman," I explain.

"You should have come to me," he says.

"You're right," I lie, trying to placate him. "Truly, my father never told me of your proposal. I had no idea that you saw me as someone who could be under your care. If I had, perhaps I would have made a much different choice, but I didn't think you would have any reason to help someone like me."

Lying like this makes my skin itch, but I wounded his ego, and the only way I can get him to see the reason is to repair and re-inflate his sense of worth.

"We burned the horseman," I say, then I continue with how I came to be Fallon's prisoner. "I got to know him."

Percival scoffs.

"That is why I was helping him. I wasn't helping him kill people. I was trying to find the actual witch."

"You *are* a real witch," he shouts, spittle flying.

"We were trying to find the witch who raised him from the dead and controls him," I clarify.

I recite the entire story, skipping any mentions of my mother or any non-ladylike feelings or activities I indulged in. I don't mention the books on witchcraft because I don't want to condemn myself further.

But I do tell him about the torture devices Fallon has in his cabin, and I tell him how I was held in an immovable position for days, hoping to garner some sympathy.

He stares at me, his eyes flat, almost dead.

He either doesn't believe me, or worse, he knows I am speaking the truth and doesn't care.

"I am done with you. Simply done. A man of my standing cannot be seen consorting with a witch, no matter how fetching she once was." He staggers back from the bars and turns on his heel to walk away.

But then he stops and turns once more before he leaves. "Your trial is tomorrow. You will most likely be sentenced to death. I am hoping for a stoning."

Chapter Twenty-Nine

KAT

AN HOUR HAS PASSED since Percival grew tired of his own voice and left.

I press my fingers firmly against the bars of this cage as I peer through them. I've tried pushing and pulling at the door, but it's futile. Nothing can pry these bars open without a key.

I've paced back and forth in this tiny cage, set in the middle of our town square. Every time I hear a horse, my heart skips a beat, thinking it may be Fallon.

What could they be doing to him?

I never thought I would be in the position to hope for the horseman's quick death. At least a quick death would see him back in his bed in his cottage tonight instead of something truly horrific, like the burning I put him through.

Someone walks briskly by, and I tense, trying to make out who it is. They disappear into the churchyard, and my shoulders relax.

From the rumors I have heard, when there is someone new in the cell in the town square, the other townspeople like to come and mock. For them, seeing someone dragged down, justly or not, is entertainment. There is a sick joy that many people get in piling on other's grief and embarrassment.

It's only a matter of time before people start to gather around me.

I'm perhaps lucky this all happened at night, when it's dark. They're too afraid of the horseman. If only they knew what I know, and if they knew he isn't the threat but merely the tool. The real danger is the person controlling him.

Letting go of the bars, I pace the cage again, taking a small corner of my borrowed shirt and twisting it between my fingers. I can't believe this is happening to me. I never thought I'd be the one to await trial for witchcraft.

Small towns, even quaint ones, are not known for their fair court systems. Worse, towns plagued by curses like the horseman seem to suffer a touch of "superstitious hysteria," as a newspaper in Providence called it.

Regardless of my involvement, Sleepy Hollow has a history of witches—genuine witches who cursed Fallon and who used him as a weapon to torment and murder. Sleepy Hollow isn't like Salem, a small town gripped with fear of rumors and vile girls who were too obsessed with gossip and the power it gave them.

They hanged women because of false rumors. After they killed those innocent girls, the town was wracked with guilt.

For Sleepy Hollow, witchcraft is not a rumor. It's a reality. They know women can practice witchcraft. Regardless of if I am guilty, they will see me and see a dark hope. They will hope that by killing me, they will break the curse Sleepy Hollow has been under.

There will be no guilt in my death, just relief until Fallon's return. Then more fear until the new dark hope. No one will mourn me. Not a single soul will call for justice for my death.

No, I can't think like that. I can't give in. I can't accept that I am going to let these people murder me. Nothing good can come from those thoughts.

I may be a woman without a family, but I am educated. I am still an American, which affords me certain rights—mostly the right to a trial. It is one of the few rights afforded to single women. I will have my moment, make my case, and show that I am not the monster.

There is no getting around the townspeople's fear, but surely there cannot be any witnesses against me, no evidence, because I have done nothing. Maybe if I can appeal to the judge's sense of justice and civic responsibility, I can show that I am a victim. I can make my case, and there may be hope of me surviving this ordeal.

I wish my mother were here. I don't understand where else she could be right now. How can she not be at my side while this is happening?

The sky grows lighter as the sun rises, and townspeople move about their mornings. It won't be long until the mocking begins, and what little of my reputation remains is already in tatters.

The first jeer comes from a child. He points and laughs, but his mother grabs his hand quickly, forcing it to his side, and hurries him along.

The other townspeople who pass the cell don't look at me. They keep their eyes on the ground, and I realize my situation is far worse than I thought possible. The entire town has already decided that I am guilty and dangerous.

When the town is fully bustling, two guards with swords on their hips, muskets strapped on their backs, and iron chains in their hands come to get me.

"If you attempt anything, we are authorized to use deadly force," the first guard says.

"Sirs," I say sweetly. "I have been wrongfully accused, and I anticipate clearing my name. You shall have no trouble with me."

They snicker and open the door. I step out and obediently lift my wrists for the chains. They clip them on and escort me to the courthouse several yards away.

I say nothing; I keep my head down and act modestly, the way a lady, afraid but hopeful, would behave.

"Wait here," one of them says as he shoves me into a small, windowless room.

I crack my ankle on the doorframe, but I refuse to cry out.

"Change into this." The other throws a dress at me. "This is a respectable court. Even witches and harlots must be dressed accordingly."

"Thank you," I say, not looking up.

Tears fill my eyes, but I ignore the pain in my ankle.

I change as quickly as I can and secure the lacings on the back of the dress myself. The fabric is cheap and rough, and it makes my skin itch. It's also too short, showing my ankles, and far too tight on the bodice, pushing up my breasts.

Perhaps if the judge can see me as a beauty or even find me mildly attractive, he'll be more willing to be lenient. That's what I hope as I try to adjust the dress to cover as much of my body as possible. It's hardly modest, but it's better than a man's shirt and trousers.

I sit with my ankles crossed under the chair and my hands folded delicately in my lap, and I wait. I lick my parched lips, my thirst and hunger sending a wave of nausea into my stomach.

Finally, the guards return and clasp my wrists back in the irons. They say nothing as they drag me, not into the courtroom as I suspected, but outside.

A stage has been erected in the middle of the town square. On it is a large podium where the judge sits, and an iron cage to the side. Several townspeople have gathered to watch the spectacle they are turning my trial into.

This isn't right. This isn't how it's supposed to be done, but I have no choice.

These people won't listen to a woman tell them they are wrong, let alone a woman accused of witchcraft.

The guards toss me into the cage. No one bothered to set a chair inside. It's too short for me to stand up straight, so I'm forced to crouch, which makes my back ache and my hunger pains more intense.

"Hear you, hear you," a man calls before the podium.

He introduces the judge and recites the charges brought against me. My heart races at the list: witchcraft, conjuring, sorcery, and murder. The same charges Percival promised.

The world around me slows as the man continues my list of charges.

"Adultery, seducing her stepfather, seduction of married and/or taken men, heresy, antisocial behavior, communicating with the dead, thievery, and public indecency."

My mouth hangs open, and my heart stops beating.

"Kill the witch! Kill the whore!" the crowd chants, their scrutinizing glares aimed at me with hatred and disgust.

My bottom lip trembles. None of that is true, but...

Seducing my stepfather? Rage boils inside me, and I have to stop myself from hitting the iron bars.

The chanting continues, and suddenly, my body feels numb.

Stepfather. Who else knew Brom wasn't my biological father? Did everyone know but me? Did Nana know? The knot in my stomach tightens.

When the town crier raises his hand, the crowd silences, and he continues. "The punishment for these charges, if found guilty, is death by hanging, followed by dismemberment of the corpse, and the pieces shall be burned and then buried in separate unmarked graves— separated by no less than five miles."

That seems like overkill. Dead is dead. What do they think is going to happen? Do they believe I am going to rise from my grave and seek vengeance on everyone here?

One look at the crowd cheering for my death and dese- cration of my body, and I know immediately they believe I will rise after death to come for them.

Isn't that what they believe Fallon has done? He was dead, then he rose and removed heads left and right. It's not like he can argue with a mob, calmly explain that he doesn't want to kill people, and that he's being controlled by someone else.

These people are scared. They wouldn't listen anyway.

Just like I doubt they will listen to me.

"Do we have representation for the accused?" the judge asks.

"No, Your Honor." Another man in a black suit with a string bowtie steps forward. "I am Mr. Fielder, representing the town of Sleepy Hollow."

A cheer rises from the crowd.

Once it dies down, Mr. Fielder continues. "I'm afraid we looked three towns over, and no one will represent the accused on account of if they lose the case, she may hex them. Per town code, we are only required to look *two* towns over."

"Then let's begin." The judge bangs the gavel, and people cheer.

The judge waves to them, and I know if I have any hope of surviving, I need to get the crowd on my side.

The judge turns to me. "Witch, how do you plea?"

"I'm not guilty, Your Honor," I say confidently.

The crowd jeers, screaming insults and chanting the words, "Kill the witch! Kill the whore!" over and over.

"Call your first witness," the judge yells.

The line of witnesses who come forward is truly staggering. One by one, it seems like almost every single person in the town comes forward to tell them stories of what they've seen me do.

Some of them are somewhat accurate... They have a ring of truth, but also of ignorance. Stories about how they saw me get onto the horseman's horse, how he caressed my face, or even how I would speak to people who weren't there.

They *were* there, but clarifying that I was speaking to the dead won't help my case.

One woman I don't recognize speaks about how I'm a bastard, my mother having killed my father before I was born to wed a wealthier man.

My fists clench. That cannot be true. Where are these people getting their information from? I still don't know who my real father is.

People come with stories of hearing me have passionate sex with my father. Some suggest I seduced him while my mother was sick.

Bile rises, threatening to come up all over this cage. I pity those men's wives since they can't tell the difference between passionate lovemaking and rape.

Still, I keep my mouth shut and my eyes dry. I will not let them see the shame of what the man who was supposed to love and protect me did to me.

They will not see me break.

Other witnesses come with stories that are pure fiction. They claim to have seen me dancing naked under the full moon. Conjuring the horseman, offering my body to the headless man in exchange for him to do my bidding.

The tenth "witness" approaches the witness stand. I have never seen her before, and I have grown weary of listening to the baseless accusations.

She lifts her gnarled finger and points at me as her craggy old voice makes her proclamation. "I saw this young woman go to the Andre tree. She lay before it, her breasts bare, and spread her legs for the devil himself. He took her in his beastly goat form for the horseman."

The crowd gasps, and I simply cannot take it anymore.

"Lies!" I yell. "It's all lies!"

My knuckles turn white as I grip the iron bars, desperate to be free.

"Silence!" the judge shouts, his voice booming through the square. "Call your next witness."

When the next woman takes the witness stand, a shred of hope blossoms inside my heart.

Surely Edith will speak and be heard. She's known as a sweet, hard-working, pious girl. Her proclaiming my innocence will surely be my salvation.

"Tell us what you know," the lawyer says, gently patting Edith on her shoulder.

Edith nods, pressing a cloth to her eyes to dry her tears. "She was my friend. We were inseparable when she moved to town."

More tears stream down Edith's face. She looks straight at me, her brown eyes meeting mine. I expect to see pity, some form of assurance or comfort I can cling to. But I don't.

"Then she tried to seduce my Daniel. He refused her because he was a good man, a loyal man, and he was mine. So she used her magic. She called the horseman to take him from me."

I watch in stunned silence as she breaks down in tears.

How can she think I would hurt Daniel? How can she think I would try to seduce him? I saw him as a brother.

I can still see Daniel's face in my mind, slack after his head was removed from his body. His mouth hung open, and his eyes were only half closed.

It's a horrible memory.

My knees collapse from under me, but I don't release the cell bars. My grip is too tight, and I can't let go. The pain of losing him, and now having Edith turn her back on me, is too much.

My chest blazes like the hand of God himself is squeezing my heart, not letting it beat.

If Edith won't fight for me, if she has deserted me, I have no hope. I watch through burning tears as she turns her back on me and disappears into the crowd.

I am truly alone.

My soul aches, and my entire body is in agony as sobs rip through me.

I barely even hear the judge as he bangs his gavel, declaring my guilt and sentencing me to death.

"The witch is to be hanged by the neck until dead in the morning. All shall come to witness the end of her evil."

With one final bang of the gavel, my life is forfeit.

Chapter Thirty

KAT

As soon as the crowd stops cheering for my death, the guards remove me from the cage in this farce of a court and move me to the much larger cage that serves as a jail.

At least this one has three solid walls, and I can stand if I so desire.

I don't though. I can't stand. The weight of everything crushes me, and I don't have the energy to move. I don't even think I walked into this cage. They dragged my limp body to the cell and tossed me in.

What does it say about me that I couldn't put up a fight? My family is all gone, all but my sweet nana, who isn't long for this world anyway. The monster my mother married, Brom, my stepfather, raped me, and I was condemned for it. My mother died, and even though I can still see her and talk to her, she didn't bother appearing at my trial.

The people I chose to be my family are also gone. Daniel was killed by the witch, who so brazenly used a condemned soul as a weapon, and Edith turned her back on me.

The only person who hasn't left or abandoned me is Fallon. My insane horseman is the only person who can save me, and I have no idea where he is.

He may be back in his cabin, readying himself to come and save me, or maybe he's still being held by the Nightward. Perhaps he has turned his back on me like everyone else.

"Daughter, get up." My mother's hushed voice cuts through my misery.

"*Now* you show your face?" I can't help the bitterness in my voice, or maybe I can, but I don't care to.

She steps closer to the bars on my cell. "I was otherwise occupied. Why are you in this jail?"

"Because that is where this town puts the witches before they hang them," I answer.

Instead of reacting with shock or fear, she rolls her eyes and places her hands on her hips. Is it too much to want my mother affected by my execution, even if no one else is?

"I know why they put you in the cage," she says. "I am asking why you are still here. You have power. You are from a powerful line of good witches. A country judge does not have the power to harm you unless you consent.

You should be able to get out of this cage and run. Go back to Providence, or even Boston, and restart your life."

I blink at her, her words only stirring my confusion.

"Who is my father?" I blurt.

After the witnesses brought it up so many times, I have to know.

"Why does that matter now?" she asks carefully.

"Because it does," I insist. "I need to know."

She nods and sighs, seeming to relent. "Your father was a man named Ichabod Crane. I loved him so madly that I was blind to his true intentions."

"And what were his true intentions?" I ask, but I'm not sure I really want to know.

She looks at me for a moment, her hands clasped in front of her, twisting and turning them, a sure sign she doesn't know if she wants to tell me the whole truth or just a part of it.

"Tell me," I demand. "All of it. I deserve to know where I come from."

"He never loved me," she whispers. "I don't even know if he was capable of love, not in any proper way. He wooed me, making promises of grand adventures and how his career as a teacher meant good pay and a steady income, and with Christmas and summers off. He promised we would only stay in one city for a few years before moving to the next."

Her eyes look so sad as she speaks, and I wonder if her

pain still feels fresh. Do spirits not get respite from a broken heart even in death?

"What did he really want?"

"Money, and my family's estate. As you know, I am an only child. There were no sons to inherit my father's fortune—only me and whomever I married. I was set to marry someone else, and Ichabod seduced me and made sure I was ruined in the eyes of the town. He made sure my father had to accept his proposal."

"I see..." My chest aches for her because I understand what she isn't saying.

"When he died, I was left pregnant and with no prospects, let alone a husband, but there was a handsome dowry, and your stepfather accepted."

"Did you kill Ichabod?" I ask.

I know it's painful for her, but I need to know. I need to know if what the people said about my mother is true or just more lies to prove that my wicked ways stem from my family tree.

"I didn't kill anyone. I wanted to, but that is not something I am capable of."

"You could have raised the horseman and..." I stop because I know she didn't kill Brom. That was Fallon's doing, out of his own free will.

"No, I couldn't have," she says. "I am a witch. You have my books, though I have no idea how the horseman got a hold of them. You have seen my notes and the notes of the women in our line.

"Our magic is one of the earth; we heal the land and create abundance in crops. Do you think my family had the largest, most prosperous farm by coincidence? That is the only type of magic we practice. I had the book containing the horseman's spell, but it was never to be used, only hidden."

"Why keep it? Why not destroy it?" I ask.

Fire mounts in my gut. She could have ended Fallon's torment years ago if she destroyed the book. This could have all been prevented.

She wanted me to lock him away forever, leave him living in pain so he couldn't be used as a weapon. More than that, she told me that if I didn't trap him, then the death of people he killed from that point on would stain my hands.

The energy that drained away at the trial returns with a vengeance, and I want to fight.

I leap to my feet, move to the edge of the cell, and wrap my hands around the bars. "How could you put all those people's deaths on *my* hands when *you* could have prevented everything?"

"It's not the same," she says, shaking her head.

"It *is*. It is the same. You could have stopped any of this from happening before it even started. Where did you leave the book?"

A wrinkle forms between her brows. "Why does that matter?"

"Because clearly someone found it, and if I can figure

out who, maybe I can do what you couldn't. I can free him, let him be at peace, and end this small town's torment."

"How can you do that from inside a cell?"

Her words slam into me, and the resentment and anger fueling me fade.

"I don't know," I admit.

Her mouth hardens into a determined line. "Yes, you do! I may not have been able to teach you our family secrets before I died, but that doesn't mean you don't have access to our gifts. Listen closely to these words, daughter: 'What binds can be broken.'"

"What binds can be broken?"

"Place your index finger over and under the middle of the cell lock." She points to where the keyhole is, and I follow her instructions and repeat the words.

Nothing happens.

I stare at my mother blankly.

"Keep practicing." She waves at me to continue.

A sigh leaves my lips, and I relax my shoulders. All the spells I tried in the domain of the Andre tree were in vain. I'm no witch. Or at least not a good one.

I practice on the chain secured around my neck instead. The chain is loose enough to move freely in the cell, but I can't leave with it on me.

Once again, nothing happens, except something bangs farther down the jail hall. Flickering light draws closer.

"It is a simple charm, and you *must* do this," she says,

panic infusing her voice. "The necklace around your throat will only protect you from the horseman. Nothing else. Not whatever they plan to do with you."

I can't help but take comfort in her worry. Someone cares, at least a little.

"Good evening, little witch," Percival sing-songs as he strolls up to the bars with a torch.

My mother gives him a look of disgust and mutters something under her breath. I can't hear what she says, but I never heard her use such a tone before or after her death.

She takes a step back so Percival doesn't walk through her and silently watches him with a disapproving look.

"Go away," I say to Percival.

"No, I think I'll stay. I just want to make sure you know the man you gave your life away for. You know that horseman you dearly love, or at least give yourself to often?"

"What of him?" I don't bother arguing. He won't listen to me anyway.

"Well, since he has plagued this town before, no doubt while bedding a different witch, the old-timers here know who he was when he was alive." He passes me some parchment through the bars. "His name was Fallon Callaghan, a dirty Irishman."

I try to understand the contract I am looking at.

"Turns out he sold his wife into slavery for a few silver, which is illegal in Ireland. When he was caught, they sentenced him to indentured servitude, and the Hessians bought his contract. The records show he was with them, raiding and pillaging, for many years, even rising among their ranks until he cut the wrong man's throat. In retaliation, his crew sold his contract again. This time to the Van Tassel family."

"It's not true," I say, but he doesn't hear or care.

My mother's features are hidden in shadow, but her hands are easy to see, her fingers twisting together.

"They must not have known what kind of man he was. There is no doubt that the Hessians lied to force the sale. He was to pay his debt by working on their land. He was in their employment for less than a month before he had an affair with a married woman, Mrs. Chattaway. She was burned a few years later for being a witch."

That name sounds so familiar. How do I know it?

My mother's knuckles turn an even paler white as she wrings her hands harder.

"See, no one knew what Chattaway was yet, of course. They knew she came from an old family. Her husband was a good man by all accounts and even took good care of his wife and daughter.

"Then, one day, there was some kind of accident that led to a great fire. No one knows what caused it. Just that there was an explosion of some kind, and then trees burst into flames that no one could control. It claimed several homes and a few lives before it finally burned itself out.

"Fallon Callaghan's body was in the center of the blaze. Untouched by the flames, but headless."

My mind spins as I stare at the parchment in my hand, barely able to read it by the pale moonlight and Percival's flickering torch.

"They thought it was odd. Some freak accident, until the first time his body rose from its grave and started collecting heads. That is the man you would rather lie with than marry *me*. You gave up a good life for a monster. I hope that thought brings you comfort in the morning and as your soul burns in hell with the other witches."

"It's not true," I say, but Percival talks over me.

"I was going to be such a good husband to you. I would have taken care of you and provided for you. You gave it all away for a chance to fuck a black-souled demon. The whore of such an evil man gets what she deserves."

He spits at my feet before yanking the parchment out of my hands and walking away.

What have I done?

"Is it true?" I ask my mother.

She doesn't answer.

"Is it true?" I yell, no longer worried about who will hear me.

It's not like they can hang me twice.

"His story is the same that was told to me by my mother," she confirms, reaching out her spectral hand to pat my shoulder.

I back away from the bars, not wanting to be touched.

"Why didn't you tell me? I almost... I wanted to..." I

can't even finish the thought in my heart, let alone give it voice.

How could I believe all the lies Fallon told me, his heartbreaking story of trying to save his wife? It is all a lie. He didn't protect her honor; he sold her like she was cattle. His sentence with the Hessians wasn't for the murder of the man who raped his wife. It was for being the one to sell her.

The world spins too quickly around me. The ground doesn't feel steady, and I fall to my knees and heave into the hay on the floor. With an empty stomach, nothing but a burning pain comes from it.

The truth drowns out the pain, though. He lied to me. He *is* a monster.

No one put him under a curse. He was performing a spell with another witch, Mrs. Chattaway, and it must have backfired.

I was a silly, foolish girl who offered my heart, my body, and my soul to an evil man who was using me.

One look at my mother makes it clear she knows exactly what I feel.

I close my eyes and refocus on the spell.

My mother sacrificed her life and her fortune because she let a man lie to her.

I may have been just as foolish, but I won't go down without a fight.

Chapter Thirty-One

FALLON

OUT OF ALL THE deaths I have suffered—the beheadings, stabbings, gunshots, burnings, and dismemberments—this is by far my worst.

At least I couldn't feel the blunt teeth of the pigs as they gnashed and chewed my body.

The men of the Nightward made quick work of my death—a silver knife to the heart. Painful, but over in an instant.

The second my body dies, my soul leaves it, and then instead of moving on, I am forced to wait. When a normal, non-cursed person dies, the tether that holds its soul to its mortal form snaps, releasing the soul to move on to its resting place.

My soul, however, is still tethered. So I must stay in the

land of the living, completely invisible as a specter until my body heals.

The knife wound they inflicted had not even begun to close when the Night's Watchmen removed my limbs and then tossed my remains into the pigpen with the mud and the shit for those enormous, foul-smelling, grunting beasts to devour my flesh.

Thankfully, with my soul not in my body, I am granted a form of mercy with this death and cannot feel those swine teeth and wet snouts. However, there is some-thing deeply disturbing about watching pigs feast on your own corpse.

Sometimes, when I return to my body, there are signs of my last death. When Kat burned me in that pine box, I could smell the ash and the smoke for a week. The last time I was stabbed through the heart, it left a scar on the next version of my body.

I fear what will linger from this death.

I close my eyes and pray to any deity that is listening. *Please don't let the smell be what lingers.*

"Do you love my daughter?" A woman appears next to me, startling me.

A thin smile spreads on my lips. "Katrina Van Tassel. I see you haven't moved on from the spirit realm."

"I asked you a question, horseman," she says, looking me directly in the eye.

She looks so much like her daughter. The same reddish tint in her blonde hair, the same pale peaches-and-cream skin and wider lips, but where Kat has a softness to her still, a roundness in her face and an innocence in her eyes, her mother is all sharp angles and looks of disappointment.

Her color seems washed out, like she's fading in front of my very eyes. Her clothes, skin, and features are all plain to see, but with a slight transparency.

"Do you intend to keep gawking at me, or will you answer my question?" she barks.

"Aye, I love her. She is an angel who has returned me soul to me and reminded me what it's like to live and lo—"

She holds her pale hand up, stopping me mid-sentence. "Who is Mrs. Chattaway to you?"

I frown. "No one. I know the name only because I know every family in this town. I have no connections with them. Why?"

"Before I died, I was in possession of a book of spells, one that did not belong to my family. It was the Chattaway Grimoire."

"Are you saying a Chattaway witch cursed me? Why?"

"I have no idea. But yes, I believe she was the one who cursed you. Where that book is now, I do not know. She has one living descendant who is senile and mute. She can't be the witch controlling you."

"How do I find the witch who is?" I ask.

"After. For now, I need to know how much you love Kat. Will you kill for her?"

"I already did. The witch did not kill Brom. That was by me choice."

I hate the way this woman looks at me like I was the one who put her child in harm's way. I may be far from a saint, but this woman has done far more harm to Kat than I ever would.

"Are you willing to give up your freedom and any chance to see her again to set her free?" She places her hands firmly on her hips and looks me up and down like the foul smell in the air is coming from me and not the pigs.

"What do you mean? I have no intentions to hold her prisoner."

That is the truth. Things between us have changed, and I hope she will want to spend time with me in my cottage, but I would not force her. If she wants her freedom, it would break me, but I will grant it.

"My daughter was just sentenced to death because she was seen with you."

In an instant, the world shatters around me. This is indeed my doing. I put her in this danger.

The bloody Nightward—the men who shot me. I didn't take them seriously before, but it's clear to me now that I should have. Blasted silver bullets. Where did they even acquire them?

"Where is she?"

"She is where they keep all witches before they hang them. She's in a cage in the town square like an animal.

But I ask again, are you willing to sacrifice your freedom to ensure her safety?"

"Explain." If Kat is locked in a cage, then it's not about my freedom or her safety. It's about her life. There is nothing I won't do to save her.

"Kat can get herself out of that cage. I will make sure she does. She is strong, untrained, but not unskilled. She can save herself from the cage and the noose. But the charm she has around her necklace is almost out of magic. It gets weaker every time you attack her. I can't protect her from the other witch. I can't save her from *you*."

Her words cut like a knife in my chest.

"I would never hurt—"

"Not intentionally, but you have already done far more damage than you know, and if the other witch calls on you when Kat is trying to escape, she won't be able to fight you off, and you won't be able to stop the curse."

"She has stopped it before," I argue.

She shakes her head. "I can feel the other witch's power. She is getting stronger. I've never felt anything like it. It's like she's channeling energy from the other witches in her ancestry."

"Do you know who it is? If I can kill her before she has time to use the curse—"

"I don't." She bows her head and blinks at the ground. "I have been looking, following clues and hunches, but I have no idea who it could be. I had one suspect, and I was sure it was her. The elderly Chattaway woman, the granddaughter of your first...puppet master, but she has been rendered mute for years. There is no way for her to work the spells."

My spine stiffens at her use of "puppet master," though I suppose it is not entirely inaccurate.

"Then what do you expect me to do?"

"The iron maiden, the one you keep that has sigils carved into the shell... The spikes are all pure silver?"

"What about it?" I ask.

I hate that thing with every inch of my soul. The first time I rose from the dead, with my head missing and an unquenchable thirst for the death of a single man, I rose from that iron maiden. It is my prison of the cruelest design, and my casket.

"I need you to lock yourself in it. That was the vessel used to bind your soul and your body to this plane. If you can get into it and lock yourself in, I'm hoping the witch will not be strong enough to pull you from it."

"You're *hoping*?"

"If this witch is stronger than the witch who cast the initial spell, then she might manage it. Maybe. It would take her far longer, though, and I hope that will be enough to buy Kat time to run."

"What makes you think the witch won't have me track Kat down?" I cannot bear the thought of taking my witchy's head.

"You are bound to Sleepy Hollow as much as to that

iron maiden. I don't believe you will be able to leave this town."

What she asks is no simple task. If I were to close myself into that, I won't be able to get myself back out. It's not a matter of sitting in an iron casket and waiting for the world to end or for my curse to finally be broken. It's far worse.

Silver is the only metal that can harm me. It's not the same as knocking me off my horse as if I were shot. That maiden has razor-sharp spikes that will tear through my body, through my organs, and it will burn.

Memories of the last time I was in it, the unbearable pain that never dulled, pummel my head. I never adjusted to it. It only got worse and worse. It burned hotter and hotter, and there was never any relief. As soon as the pain would numb, the spikes would rotate, tearing into new flesh. Over and over, until I was called back to the living.

"There is no guarantee that I would ever be called for by a witch strong enough to pull me from it," I say, sounding defeated.

She's asking me to sacrifice myself, and not to the peace and tranquility of death. She's asking me to sacrifice myself to hell. Constant pain never interrupted and complete solitude. No one will hear my screams. No chance of any kind of reprieve or salvation. I will spend my eternity in torment just so Kat has a chance at *maybe* escaping.

If her life were guaranteed, then it would be a simple

decision. But it's not. I could give myself over to that pain, and Kat could still die at the hangman's noose. Or worse, the witch could call me forth and make me watch as my ax goes to her throat and my hands are stained with the blood of the woman I love.

"Is there another way?" I ask. "A way that guarantees her survival?"

She narrows her eyes. "Guarantee her survival, or lessen *your* pain?"

"I'll deal with the pain," I promise. "But only if I know she is safe."

"No," she says simply. "It's up to her if she fights hard enough to regain control of her life."

I nod, understanding what she is saying, but I know my witch. This will not go the way her mother hopes.

I know Kat is not the damsel in distress who will simply give up. I've seen the fight in her eyes. I have watched the flames of determination blaze inside of her. If all it took was for her to fight, she would make it. But what if she decides I am what is worth fighting for?

"What if she comes looking for me?" I wonder aloud.

I am not about to explain to this woman the things I have done or was going to do to her daughter, but if she knew I love Kat, then surely she must have some idea of the affections that Katalina feels for me as well. Doesn't she?

She shakes her head. "She won't."

"How can you be sure?"

"The man who was wooing her—"

"Harassing her," I correct.

"He told her the story the town concocted to explain your death and resurrection."

"Which story?" I ask, fearing the answer.

Katrina describes in far too much detail the story about how I sold my wife into slavery and then led the Hessians into battles until I betrayed them and they sold me to be a farmhand.

I have no idea who came up with such fiction, but I hope they pursue their talent for lies and make a career out of it—perhaps writing their fiction in penny novels for a local publication or becoming a lawyer. Either profession's tenuous grasp of truth should suffice.

"She believed it?" I close my eyes, not wanting to see the confirmation on her face.

Katalina thinking so poorly of me is painful in a way that I did not expect. It's not the same pain as death or disappointment or any other physical sensation. It is deep, all-consuming agony. Far too similar to what I went through when I found out what those men had done to Noreen.

"She doesn't want to believe it, but Percival had the documents that the town concocted to ease their consciences, and then..."

When she doesn't finish, I open my eyes. "Then?"

She shrugs. "She looked to me, and I led her to believe

it was the truth. I know you won't understand why, but I had to."

The reality of what Katrina tells me overpowers the sounds of the pigs squealing and crunching over my bones.

I nod. "You broke her heart to save her life. I understand."

It seems so wrong that only a few hours ago, she and I were safe in my little pocket of the world, in my bed, naked and indulging in the exploration of each other's bodies. I was in some deluded state where I allowed myself to believe, even if just for a moment, that I could be enough for her. I let myself get lost in the fantasy of a future that was never possible.

The pain of losing that mirage makes the memory bittersweet. Still, I know my past tainted my soul, and I know that I am not good enough for her. I can't give her what she needs, but I promised myself I would become the man she needs.

What she needs is a man who will sacrifice everything for her. I just wish I had voiced my feelings for her the last time I saw her.

Her mother steps closer, studying me carefully. "You really love her, don't you?"

"More than I knew was possible," I admit, "and if what it takes for her to live a full and complete life is for there to be no possibility of me being used against her, so be it. I'm sure after a decade or two, the pain from the silver will become bearable."

Despite her ghostly figure, her frown reaches her eyes, and she rests her hand on my shoulder, offering pity or comfort. Either way, I feel nothing.

"I can't go to the tree until my body is healed, and I have no idea how long it will take the hogs to digest it," I say.

Katrina makes a disgusted face as she glances at the pen full of flesh-eating swine.

"My magic can no longer touch the living, but you are neither living nor dead. You are in between. Maybe I can help." She closes her eyes and raises her hands.

The wind picks up, whipping our hair around. During all the times I have been stuck in the spectral form, I cannot recall a single one where I could feel the air. Even the weather in the middle of a blizzard or the July humidity. None of it has ever touched my skin, let alone a breeze.

Each of the hogs collapses on the ground, their hooves twitching, and one of them starts snoring. Then, slowly, wisps of glowing light flow from the animals into the ground a few yards away from the pen.

Seconds later, red illuminating swirly whisps flow from me. I brace for pain. Everything I've ever been through caused pain. When it doesn't come, I surrender.

It is warm, welcoming, and natural, like the water in the hot spring where I played as a child. I close my eyes and give myself to that magic, and when I open them again, I am back in my body, my clothes intact. Even my head is in its proper place. Best of all, there is no stench of pig manure.

"Go now," Katrina says, pointing toward my tree.

It's an hour, maybe two from here, so I whistle, calling my steed to my side. Then we run.

I focus on reaching the tree and my cottage before the witch calls me again.

The only other thought is a single prayer. If there is a God and his mercy can reach me, may he grant Katalina and me a second chance in the next life.

Chapter Thirty-Two

KAT

ALL NIGHT, I practiced that stupid spell. The chains rattled once.

Just as the night sky lightens, I finally give in to exhaustion. I sleep the deep, dreamless sleep of the damned, without any dreams to keep me company or bring me comfort.

When dawn fully breaks, Percival pulls me up by the chain around my neck and demands I wake.

"You don't want to be late to meet your maker, do you?" he taunts, towering above me inside my cell. "Maybe you will find your headless lover in hell?"

Red clouds my vision when he reaches for me. I claw, scratch, kick, bite—anything I can do to escape this man.

I get one good swipe of my nails across his face.

Percival swears, touches the line of blood beading across his jaw, and then backhands me across the face.

My vision whites out as I land hard on the ground, the metallic taste of blood filling my mouth.

He kicks me in the ribs, causing my body to curl in on itself for protection from his leather boots.

"Get up," he demands.

When I don't, he pulls me up by my hair.

Several people are already crowding around, waiting for the show. Waiting to see the life fade from my eyes. They expect me to go down easy.

"I am not a witch!" I scream.

No one listens to me, but I keep going anyway.

"I have never consorted with the devil. I do not control the horseman. You are killing an innocent woman. Why are you all standing by to watch me be murdered? Haven't you had enough death? Isn't it enough that a horseman is killing people? Do you have to stain *your* hands as well? If you stand idly by and do nothing, then you are guilty as much as the real witch is."

I scream as Percival drags me through the crowd to the Andre tree. It doesn't suffice to hang me at the gallows. No, it has to be the tree where the British army officer, John Andre, was hanged for being a spy. They mean to hang me from the same tree, as a traitor, having worked with the Hessian.

It's nearly a mile, and I scream and fight the entire way.

No one listens. No one cares. All I am doing is making my throat burn.

Percival removes the chains and presses my face against the tree. The rough bark cuts into my cheek. He keeps his hands painfully tangled in my hair as he holds me still while he ties my wrists together behind my back.

Then he hoists me onto someone's dining room table, which is made of dark, polished wood and looks out of place in the grass.

"I hope you understand," Percival sneers. "The wood from the last platform rotted, and we didn't want to wait to build a new one. This will just have to do."

I stand on the table as I look down into the crowd. People cheer for my death, gathering around to watch. A man in the middle of the swarm has his child on his shoulders so the boy can get a better look. It's despicable.

"I am innocent!" I scream.

A few people laugh.

I look every person in the eye. I want them to see me, not a witch, not some effigy they can kill, but *me*. They're not killing an idea, a moral, or even a sinner. They are murdering a woman—a living, breathing person.

Percival sits at the table's edge and starts tying the rope. Watching the same noose take shape that will soon be wrapped around my throat is a special kind of torture.

I refuse to give him the satisfaction of my torment, so I face the crowd again. I don't know many of them, but the few I know stare at me like I am some kind of freak.

"Marcellus Hall," I shout, "you did business with my father. You sat at my table and complimented the food I prepared for you. You called me sweet and told me I would make some lucky man a fine wife and an excellent mother."

Marcellus looks away in shame.

"Carolyne Bradshaw, you used to be my mother's closest friend. What would she say if she knew you were here, ready to let her innocent daughter die?"

Carolyne eyes me up and down. "Your mother would be ashamed of you," she yells back, and the crowd erupts in another cheer.

If only she knew my mother stands beside her, looking at her former friend in disgust.

"And you, Father Spire, preached that only God can judge, yet here you all are ready to pass judgment for crimes I did not commit."

The priest steps forward, an air of authority on his face and his bible clutched to his breast.

He raises a single hand. "I do not pass judgment, nor do I condone when any man commits such an egregious sin. This town does not have the authority to condemn your soul. For that, we are sending you to God himself, and he shall deal with you as he sees fit."

Something wet smacks me in the face, leaving a sticky trail on my face, and the crowd laughs. I stare down at what hit me. A rotten tomato.

My chest tightens. I want to wipe the muck from my face, but my hands are too tightly bound behind me.

I skim through the crowd and recognize several more faces, but thankfully, Nana is not here. I would hate for her to have to see her last living relative die at the hands of an angry mob.

I spot my mother's ghostly figure moving to the back of the crowd and lifting her hands, showing me the motion for the spell again.

I flick my index finger over and under the middle finger, chanting in my head, and hoping, wishing, that the rope around my hands will loosen.

Nothing happens.

The town crier stands before me. His head is about the level of my knee, and I am tempted to kick him just because I can.

He raises both hands in the air to calm the crowd, and instantly, everyone silences. He makes a show of taking out the parchment in his bag and clearing his throat.

I am so glad that my death can give him an opportunity to soak up so much attention.

"Katalina Van Brunt, you have been charged and found guilty of the following crimes: witchcraft, engaging in sexual congress with the devil, fornication in public with a known spectral beast."

Did they add additional charges to the list? I am half tempted to ask him to show me the specific law that says I cannot "fornicate in public with a spectral beast."

I stop listening and look out at the crowd again. There is not a single friendly face. Not one person looks sad or concerned. I have no friends here who can help me, and worse, I have none who would even want to if it were possible.

Even the horseman used me.

The only person here who has any love, care, or concern is my mother, and she is already dead.

The crier stops, and for a moment, I think he is done, but he clears his throat and continues. "Adultery, seduction, conspiracy to commit murder, and murder by headless horseman. For these crimes, you have been sentenced to hang by the neck until dead. May God have mercy on your soul because no one here will."

Another cheer rings from the crowd as Percival jumps up on the table next to me. He throws the long end of the rope over a branch and fits the noose over my head.

It's heavy and itchy.

Maybe this is how it's supposed to end. Perhaps this is for the best. No one will miss me. No one will care. Maybe my death will bring them one step closer to finding the real witch.

In the next life, I will find love and companionship, or at the very least, I won't be abused, raped, kidnapped, and then hanged for crimes I didn't commit.

That is what I want. This cruel, cold, and lonely life to be over and to start somewhere else anew.

I take a deep breath, waiting for the moment the noose tightens and for the world to fade away.

Chapter Thirty-Three

FALLON

THE PAIN IS WORSE than I remember.

The silver sears my flesh, burning it, filling the cramped space with a smell much worse than rancid roasting pork.

I wish I could have lied to myself. I wish I thought that the scent was left over from the hogs that devoured my body. Sadly, I know the truth.

That's what human flesh smells like when it's burning.

Somehow, I have either forgotten or chosen to forget about the worst part of this particular instrument of torture. Once the searing, sizzling sound of my flesh burning stops, the silver spikes rotate, tearing into fresh flesh. The pain starts anew as it burns the new spot, and the previous one heals.

This torment will be eternal, but for her, I will bear it.

For the first several hours that I was trapped in this box, I screamed. With everything I had, I screamed, loud cries of agony, but never begging to be released.

If I were released, then I could hurt Kat. I can't run that risk. Ever.

Katrina was right in saying my curse binds me to Sleepy Hollow, so if Kat moves beyond the town's borders, she will be safe and out of my reach. She even offered to try to open the iron maiden once her daughter was gone. I refused the offer.

It is simply a gamble I cannot take.

There is no telling how long I have endured this pain. The spikes move in even intervals, and there are seven clicks for a full rotation. I have suffered four complete rotations.

For a few hours, I try to sleep through the pain, hoping to find some release, but I can't. I try to bury my mind and lose myself in memories, but every time I can almost see her face, the spikes spin again, and I am pulled back to my current torment.

"It's okay," I whisper to myself. "This is the right choice. She is safe. Kat will escape because of me. She will run far away and start a new life. Maybe she will move to Boston and meet an Irishman who is kind to her, appreciates her, and maybe even supports her art.

"He will love her wholeheartedly and not be a greedy louse like her stepfather or a scoundrel like the man trying to marry her. No, he will be a good man who is respectful and gentle. He will have worth, and he won't come to her with baggage like an ex-wife, a dead heart, or a murderous witch controlling his every move."

I let out another scream as the spikes shift and then grit my teeth when the spikes stop, enduring the pain.

"She will live a long, happy life with many children and grandchildren," I say to myself. "This is me gift to her. If me torment means she gets to live, then so be it."

I repeat the last sentence over and over, chanting it every time the spikes move.

When the spikes are about to shift once again, I brace myself for the pain, but it doesn't come. Instead, a white light shines through the iron. It starts faint, and I can barely see it, but the brighter it becomes, the more I can make out the lines of the sigils. When it becomes too bright, I have to close my eyes against it. Still, all I can see is white light.

The door opens, and I collapse on the cold wooden floor that doesn't have any silver spikes or moving parts.

This time, sleep comes unbidden, and the world fades to black.

I wake to the feeling of cold water on my back, dripping down my spine over where my wounds should be. A rough towel follows, soothing away any residual aches.

The smell of roasting flesh is gone. It's replaced with the sweetest Irish hazelwood and primrose.

"Noreen?" I ask, unwilling to open my eyes and see she isn't there.

"I am here, my sweet," she coos, and her voice is just as melodic as it has always been.

She continues to move the towel down my bare back, washing away whatever marred my skin.

I look around. I'm still in my cabin in my little pocket of the world, and my wife is next to me. Her hair is just as beautiful and bright as always, and her smile is still so sweet.

"How?" My voice comes out rough, painful.

"That isn't important. What's important is the why. I am here because you made a sacrifice, a moment of selflessness so pure that I was sent to free you."

"Free me?"

The iron maiden is still open. The sigils, once neatly carved in crisp, deep lines, look melted and deformed. The door hangs on only one hinge, and my blood covers the spikes.

"No!" I jump up.

The wounds on my chest and back are healed but still tender, and I fall back to the bed.

"Hush now. Calm yourself."

"No, you don't understand. I need to be in there. If I'm free, then—"

"I said hush," she scolds, snapping the towel at me.

Then she wets the towel in the basin next to her and wipes the sweat and dried blood from my chest.

"Noreen, what is happening?"

"Well, as I was sayin', I am here to free you from that evil thing and to bring you a message."

"From whom?"

She gives me a knowing look. "Darlin', I am so sorry for the pain you have endured. It was not yours to bear. This was never the life meant for you, but these witches play with forces they do not understand. They pick and choose who lives, who dies, and who does neither. You have suffered enough. You have paid for the sins of so many others."

Her cool hand brushes my cheek.

"No." I take her wrist and pull her hand away. "I failed you. You were being violated by those men for so long, and I didn't know. Then my foolish actions ended with your death and then the deaths of so many more."

"Oh, sweet Fallon, no. My death was not your fault. It was the fault of the men who hurt me. No one else's. They are paying for their crimes in the afterlife in full. You need to put down their burdens. They are not yours to carry."

"I don't know how," I admit.

"You start by letting that young girl love you the way she wants to, the way you deserve."

Heat races to my cheeks, and I suddenly feel ill. I open my mouth to say something, apologize perhaps, but she places her hand over my lips.

"Our vows were till death do us part. We have both died. You have died several times. I loved you in my life, and part of my soul will always love you, but I am in a better place, one that is not ready for you yet. You are being given a second chance at life, my love. Break the curse, and you will have the life that was taken from you."

"You are the life that was taken from me," I argue.

I swore to love and cherish this woman, but why does my heart say I am betraying Katalina?

"I suppose that is very true, but my time is long past, and you are being offered a gift. That girl loves you. She loves you with an intense fierceness, one that doesn't come around every lifetime. You love her just as deeply, and I couldn't be happier for you.

"Go to her, protect her, and for the love of all that is holy, stop carrying the sins of others. Break the witches' hold over you and start over. Marry her, have children. This area has far too many English descendants. Fix that." She laughs her high-pitched laugh that still sounds like bells, and I laugh with her.

Even in the face of all of this, she is still making jokes at the expense of the English.

"Are you happy?" I ask.

"Aye, I have found peace, and when your time comes, you will too, as long as you break that damned curse. Send that witch to hell so she can pay for her crimes, and you and that girl can let the weight of them go."

"Any tips?"

She rolls her eyes and shoves my shoulder. "Kill the bloody witch, of course. It's not that complex."

Noreen looks up towards the ceiling and smiles. I follow her line of sight, but there is nothing.

"Time is running low. You need to hurry. Save the girl from those who would harm her. Protect her, love her, and break the curse. Go now!"

She stands and throws a shirt at me, then kisses my cheek hard before disappearing. I have so many more questions, but when Vengeance neighs outside, I know I am running out of time.

The sky cracks with lightning, and rain pours down.

I cannot fail her. Not again.

Chapter Thirty-Four

KAT

THE NOOSE CHAFES MY NECK, but still the town crier yammers on about how my death is just, and with my death, the town shall be saved and the horseman will never return to darken their doors ever again.

I'm ready for the end. I understand now that this life has nothing for me but more suffering, more sorrow, and more solitude. That doesn't mean I relish the thought of others pulling the table out from under my feet and feeling this rough rope dig into my flesh.

I want to get it over with. The crier, however, wants to stretch out my torment or his need for attention.

I look up to the pale-blue sky, still with hints of pink dawn in the clouds, and I wonder if it would be better to walk off the table's edge myself so I don't have to hear him keep talking.

I'm considering doing just that when I hear a familiar neigh.

Vengeance.

I look out to see Fallon on his horse at the back of the crowd, his head firmly attached to his shoulders. He is here, without the curse. He came of his own free will.

An airy lightness lifts my heart, and for a moment, I cling to hope. Maybe I'm not alone. Maybe he is here to save...

As quickly as I let that hope lift me up, I come crashing back down to reality. There are the documents. The story Percival told me, which my mother did not deny.

Is he here because there's something else he needs from me? He can't even give me my death in peace?

People scream and scatter as Vengeance lifts his two front hooves. When he lands, he races towards me.

Percival takes a pistol from his jacket, aims it at the horseman, and fires into the already paranoid crowd.

He misses Fallon, but he hits a man trying to flee.

"I do not know how your demon escaped his fate, but I have taken him down once, and I will do it again," Percival growls under his breath as he reloads his pistol with silver bullets.

Everyone is in a full panic, running and screaming. It's complete chaos.

Only one person stands still.

Edith, her eyes closed.

Confusion clouds my mind. Why isn't she running with the rest of them?

Her fingers make a circular motion in front of her, and my eyes widen as shades of purple and blue spiral in front of her. I blink several times. Is what I'm seeing true? She begins speaking under her breath. A spell?

I gasp.

Edith is the witch.

But how?

Chattaway is her grandmother. They may no longer be a noble family. In fact, not only is Edith a bastard, but so is her mother. But their blood is still Chattaway.

She must have found her family's book of spells. She was the one who raised Fallon from the grave. The victims... They were all people who condemned her mother, stripped their family of their wealth and titles.

All of them, save Daniel.

Why kill Daniel? I thought she loved him!

A fire kindles inside my stomach. I refuse to be her scapegoat. I will not willingly add my name to the list of her victims.

So many questions burn through me, and I plan to make her answer every single one of them.

I close my eyes, hoping everyone is too worried about Fallon and Percival to watch me. With a conviction and strength I've never felt before, I chant the words my mother taught me under my breath, my fingers doing the required motions faster and faster, until heat mounts in my fingertips.

The knot behind my back holding my wrists, and the noose around my throat, falls apart.

I'm free.

Fallon dismounts his horse, a blood stain growing on his arm, with a blade in his hand to face off with Percival.

I want to go to him to help, but magic swarms and builds. The wind picks up, cutting through the trees. My mother asked me so many times if I could feel the magic. Before I couldn't, since I had no idea what she meant.

Now I understand.

I turn my attention back to Edith. Her eyes are now open, and her focus is solely on me. Her face twists into a mask of hatred and malice.

I've never seen her so angry, so full of such vile intent, and I realize this is her true face. This isn't the sweet, if not a little simple, girl with a smile she paints on her face for others. This is her true visage.

She will give me answers, even if I have to pull them from her mouth myself. I make my way toward her, and she slips a small leather-bound journal into the pocket hidden in the fold of her skirt.

That is why I could never find the book. She carries it with her, probably never letting it leave her person.

"Why?" I demand, stomping closer to her.

She raises her chin in defiance, pushing her shoulders back and daring me to come at her.

Happily, I oblige.

The fiery rage rising in my gut pushes me forward until I am running toward her. I stretch out my hand, ready to fight her to the ground to pull the book from her and burn it, freeing Fallon from her betrayal.

Once free, he will answer for his crimes if he is guilty or finally be at peace. Either way, the headless horseman will no longer haunt the people of this town.

"You're too late," she sneers. "It's already done, and I have taken what should have always been mine!"

"Why?" I yell.

"You know why." She scoffs. "You have everything that should have been mine!"

"What right did you have to my family's legacy? What right do you have to anything that was mine?" I try to grab her skirts to yank the book away from her.

She pushes me away, hard enough that I land in the dirt, but I jump to my feet again, ready to strike back.

"Why do you get to have him? He was supposed to be *mine*. You were supposed to be nothing to him, but he turned his back on me for *you*."

"You killed so many people, tortured a soul because you thought Daniel loved *me*?" I yell. "There was never anything between us."

"*Daniel*?" She tosses her head back with a high-pitched, wicked-sounding cackle. "This was never about *him.* He was nothing. He wasn't even worth the effort it took to call the horseman to claim his head until he got in my way. You put him in my path. You made him a target. His death is on *your* hands."

"No, his death is on *your* hands," I counter. "You called the horseman. You made him a target, and for what? How did he get in your way? Did he find out who you really are? Was that the problem?"

I reach out again for the book, but she sinks her nails into my shoulder, trying to throw me to the side.

She was never very strong. I lock my hands on her dress, and we push and pull, wrestling each other to the ground.

"No, the problem was that he helped you in trying to steal my greatest power," she says between strained grunts. "He was just a means to an end before you put him on a path that can only lead to his death. This isn't about him. This is about my father."

"What?" I ask, my grip loosening.

Edith pulls her shoulder back and slams her open palm across my face, making my ear ring.

Quickly, she gets to her feet. As I struggle to my hands and knees, my vision whites out while the ringing in my ear grows louder. The sharp, stabbing pain radiating from my inner ear through my head intensifies.

The few times my nana did boxed my ear when I was a child and got into something I shouldn't, it never hurt like this.

The world around me spins as I try to regain my balance so I can stand. Edith's foot rams into the soft part of my abdomen just under my sternum. I cough, trying to get my breath back as she kicks my diaphragm again.

Two kicks, three, then she throws grass in my eyes.

Of course the little bastard witch fights dirty. After all, how else would a hag who calls on a damned soul to do her dirty work fight?

"Brom was my father. Mine," she screams. "He knew my mother was pregnant, and he was going to do the right thing by her. He was going to marry her, and together they were going to rebuild my family's name. I should have been the shining jewel of this entire town. Did that happen? No, it was taken from me. Because your whore mother stole him."

Another kick sends shockwaves of pain through me. The taste of blood fills my mouth, and I try to curl up to protect my organs.

"Your mother, who was already pregnant, did some spell like the witch she was and killed your bastard father, then she bewitched mine! You stole everything that should have been mine! But even that wasn't enough. You are just as much of a whore as your mother."

Her cheap, hard shoe presses into my cheek as she forces my face into the grass and mud.

"I gave her the poison. It was a long journey to Connecticut, and you hadn't been home. I was prepared to meet you then, but you were out drawing in the cemetery. Even then, I knew you were strange. I made my acquaintance and pretended to be part of the help, painful as it was to be near her and near my father. I did this to slip the poison into her tea."

"No. My mother died from typhoid," I mutter into the ground.

She lets out a cruel laugh and shakes her head. "I didn't blame you. Not then. Your whore mother's death was going to fix everything. He would welcome me into his home, claim me as a legitimate heir, and you and I would be sisters. When you opened your legs for him, you ruined everything!"

Her words sound more and more hysterical as she speaks. Her foot presses harder into the side of my face, making my jaw ache and my vision fade.

But then her words slowly sink in, and it strikes me how long she has been harboring such hate, letting it fester and poison her soul. I could have forgiven her for that and helped her heal. If she had just come to me, I would have gladly given her a place in my home and claimed her as family.

But she killed my mother.

With strength I didn't know I possess, I grab her ankle and twist her foot, making her lose her balance and step away from me. I push through the pain, through the disorientation, and spit the blood gathering in my mouth onto the ground. My nana would be disgusted by the unla-dylike act, but what I plan to do is far, far worse.

The world blurs around me. I'm too focused on Edith and the ugliness inside her that I somehow looked past for so long.

"You think my mother spelled that *monster*?" A cruel laugh I have never heard before passes from my lips. "He *trapped her*. She was willing to be ruined when my real father died. He offered his hand, and she was forced to take it. There was no magic involved. He wasn't spelled by her magic. He was lured away by her *money*.

"I didn't seduce him. He took me to ruin me and any prospects I could have had. He wanted to make sure no one could take my mother's estate from him. Brom was greedy, lazy, and blamed everyone else for his problems. Like father, like daughter."

She screams and lunges at me, her hands out and fingers bent like claws hell-bent on my face. I duck under her attack, pushing my shoulder into her corset as she scratches at my back and pulls my hair. I ignore the pain and instead focus on getting my hands on that spell book.

It only takes me a moment to find the pocket while she is still screaming and wailing on my back, but I get my hands on the leather and pull it free, knocking her down to the ground.

"That is *mine*," she screeches.

She reaches for it, but I shove her back into the mud again. She has a red face, wild hair around her head, and bared teeth. She looks like the evil witch she is. She will be dealt with soon enough.

A shot rings out in the air. I look over to see Fallon and Percival still fighting. Fallon grips his ax, and Percival's lays abandoned in the mud not too far from them. Fallon must have been winning the fight when Percival pulled out his pistol.

The first shot misses, but he aims for another.

Edith lunges at me again, and I can barely dodge her. Her fingers tear into my borrowed dress, ripping the too-tight bodice. I am not exposed, but I still show far more skin than is ladylike.

So, I run. I need to destroy the book. Burning it should work. Or tearing out the pages?

Edith sprints after me, chasing me down. Most of the other townspeople have long since fled from Fallon. Some are aiming their rifles from a distance, while others are still scattering.

I run behind the Andre tree, press my back to it, and wait for her to come around the trunk. She never appears.

Where did she go?

It's not until I feel the magic in the air again, and I know why.

"Fallon," I whisper.

I run out, ready to stop her from completing the spell, but it's too late.

Fallon is gone. Percival is panting, covered in sweat, his pistol still pointed and shaking, but not at Fallon. He aims at the horseman.

His head is gone, and he is thoroughly under her spell.

Edith puts a hand on Percival's arm, lowering the gun. He takes her hand and kisses the back of it.

"Horseman, complete your task," she commands.

He turns toward me, and I reach for my necklace, the one that should keep me safe.

But it's gone.

I look up to see Edith holding it in her hands, showing off her prize.

Fallon takes out his ax, spins it, and closes the distance between us.

Chapter Thirty-Five

FALLON

I ALMOST HAVE THE CAD.

He aims his pistol and fires, but he is a lousy shot.

I raise my sword as he pulls the trigger over and over, the firm click of the hammer hitting metal and igniting nothing. No gun powder, no silver bullets.

I press my sword to his throat, but I hesitate. I have never enjoyed killing. The only blood I have ever spilled has been at the will of another forcing my hand, or to end the control of a monster who hurt others. I have killed men who rape, or who think they can own another human.

From what I can tell, this man is arrogant, a coward, a womanizer, and a louse. None of those are crimes that demand death. Then again, he shot me. Surely that justifies the kill?

I am being given a second chance, a clean soul. This man's death would sully it.

"Why should I spare you?" I ask.

He opens and closes his mouth a few times, searching for the answer even I cannot find.

"I can pay you, demon," he finally says.

"What would a demon want with gold?" I press the sword to his throat harder.

"I can give you women, give you slaves, give you—"

"You cannot give me what you do not own." A single drop of blood wells on the tip of my sword and runs down the blade.

"You don't know what I do and do not own." Sweat pours down his face, and the scent of urine fills the air.

"You cannot own people. You are not God. You do not own souls," I say.

I wonder if maybe that is justification enough to end this man's life. The South may still be fighting for what they consider a right, but we are not in the Carolinas or even Georgia. We are in the great state of New York, where slavery is illegal.

"You're right. I-I'm sorry," he stammers.

He throws his hands in the air, the useless pistol hanging from his fingers.

This is a truly pathetic sight. This man thought he was good enough to be with Kat? *My* Kat? He thought he could wed her and provide for her? How can a coward like this, sweating like a pig, crying and pissing himself while begging for his life, be the leader of the Nightward?

No wonder so many craven men get away with murder, and witches openly practice in the square. What is he going to do about it? Piss himself and cry?

I could end his life right now, end not only his suffering, but the suffering of every person's life he touches. But I am no god. It is not my place to judge a man's failings. Not anymore. My soul is clean and intact. If I kill him, then I damn myself all over again.

Before I can make my decision, a familiar feeling crawls up my spine, and magic takes hold of me.

A cry rips from the back of my throat. I drop the sword. The cad stares at me, confusion on his face.

The curse is upon me.

I grip my temples, fighting it with everything I have.

The witch stands across the yard, her eyes closed and her magic wrapping around her. It's Edith, Kat's friend, and it was her intention that aided Kat in her ill-fated attempt to kill me. She is behind this?

I don't understand her motives, but I don't need to. I kick out, hitting Percival in the chest and sending him reeling into the mud.

Then I move toward the witch. Her blood will stain my hands, but not my soul. I am owed her death, and the lord, in his infinite wisdom and mercy, will grant my forgiveness. Maybe he'll even celebrate my accomplishment.

This witch is the last of her line. They have plagued and tormented so many, and I will see it to an end. Once and for all, there will be no other witch who can damn a soul the way her ancestor damned mine.

And then I hear the same gunshot again that claimed my life and now claim my free will.

All it will take just one swing of my ax, and my soul will be free. Her magic crawls up my back, trying to take control, but I refuse to let it. Now that I know who she is, she cannot claim me as before. I push it down with sheer will as I walk across the grass to claim my prize.

As I ready my ax, only a few steps away, she raises her hands in the air. The words she was mumbling under her breath now bellow out.

"Hear me, horseman, and obey my will. You will rise and serve the Chattaway line as our faithful huntsman. Complete your charge: kill Katalina Van Brunt, add her head to your collection, and then rest."

The wind whips around me, and just as I raise my arm to take her head, I hear the shot. Pain erupts throughout my body. It's the same shot I hear in my nightmares. The shot that stole my life so long ago and now steals my free will. I can't control anything anymore.

Agony radiates through me as I stare up at the clouds in the bluish-gray sky, and the magic washes over me. I don't have to raise my hand to my head. I know it's gone, but not my ability to see.

My body moves unbidden. It gets to my feet, grabs my ax again, and turns.

The coward is still there in his piss-soaked trousers, his pistol in his hand, shaking. My body moves toward him, not really caring about him or his pistol. He isn't my charge.

Without stopping to even so much as acknowledge Percival, I stalk past him, my target on the other side of the Andre tree.

I know the moment she sees me, the moment she knows I failed her. Her beautiful green eyes are wide and full of pain and fear. She knows what Edith is; she knows I have no control.

I try to fight the hold, push past the magic, and get control of my body.

She reaches up to clasp her necklace, but it isn't there. The only thing that could have saved her from me is missing.

A sinking suspicion in my gut tells me exactly who has it, but it doesn't matter. It's too late for her to retrieve it, and even if she could, its magic is fading.

"Run!" I scream, but there is no sound.

Still, I scream, begging her to run, to leave and never look back.

I've made it halfway to her when she finally turns on her heel and sprints through the forest.

My legs move faster, chasing her down, hunting her, my blade aching for her blood.

"Run faster, find the border of the city, and cross it," I silently beg.

In my life and my death, I have done many things I did not think I could live through, things I did not want to live through. But watching the light go out of her eyes because I failed another woman I love would be too much. There is no coming back from that.

"Run," I beg again as my body speeds up, getting closer to her.

I demand my legs stop moving and for my hand to drop the ax, but none of it works. The witch has become too powerful. I am gaining on Kat. She is fast, but I am faster, and we are too far from the town lines to make a difference.

She pauses and turns to face me. She raises her hands, not in defense, but something else.

I try to stay my hand, but I have no control. I raise the ax, ready to bring it down on her head.

"Run," I beg.

She screams something, and magic hits me, making me stumble back. She didn't break the curse, but she weakened the witch's hold.

It wasn't a lot, but it is enough. Kat, my beautiful, wonderful Kat, gives me the push I need.

With a scream of frustration, I lower my hand, fighting

every single inch. When the ax slips from my fingers, the witch's hold fractures and then breaks.

I collapse on the cool, soft grass, and Kat kneels beside me, tears brimming in her eyes.

"Fallon?" she asks.

"Aye." The sound of my voice tells me my head has been returned.

"Are you…?"

"Free? No, she can call me again. We need to break the curse."

"Fallon, they told me—"

"Your mother let you believe their stories so you would leave town."

She blinks, and her tears rush down her cheeks. "She—"

"Don't be mad at her, love. She did it to protect you. That's what mothers do," I say, reaching out to pull her into my arms.

I need to feel her, even if it's just for a moment. I need to touch her and know that she is real and alive. Even though bruises mar her skin and a footprint soils her face, she is still the most beautiful thing I have ever seen.

"Fallon?" she asks, pulling back.

"Yeah?"

"They are coming," she says, pointing.

Edith and the coward are heading our way, walking slowly, their eyes on the ground. The witch no doubt felt her control break and assumed it was because I completed my task.

"They are searching for your body," I say, and she nods.

"What do we do?"

"First this." I pull her head down to mine and kiss her with everything I have.

All of my love, my devotion... I pour everything into this kiss.

When I break it, I look into her eyes, brushing a lock of hair from her face and wiping away her tears.

"I love you, and because of your grace and belief in me, I have been given a second chance at life. We are going to end this. Now."

"How? She is powerful, and my magic is nothing against hers."

It is true. Her magic didn't break the spell, and she only pushed it back just enough for me to break it myself. But the curse is still intact.

They draw closer, and soon, the tree we hide behind will not be enough to conceal us. I have a blade, but he has a gun and time to reload.

And this witch is powerful and out for blood.

Chapter Thirty-Six

KAT

"Run," Fallon whispers in my ear. "We are going to make a run for the town square."

I turn to face him. "Why?"

His blue eyes shine fiercely with determination. His head came back quickly, but I don't have time to wonder about that just yet.

"Because it's full of people. If we kill them out here, they will just try to hang you again. I want their deaths witnessed," he says against my ear.

His fingers hold my arm firmly, and I want to relish in his touch. I stare at his features, his chiseled jawline, the way he looks at me. I never thought I'd feel him again.

But we have to move. Edith and Percival are getting closer. She kicks every bush, looking for my body.

"But she already confessed," I argue, wanting to end this now, right here.

"They all fled. There are only a handful of people left by the Andre tree. Their heads were down, and they were too terrified to listen. If we can get them in the town square with braver men—the town judge, the priest, whomever has credibility—they will hear, then you may have a chance at a peaceful life."

"Let's just—"

"No one was listening to her or looking at you. We need to get them to the town square," he insists. "Trust me. Go now. Run."

I don't like it. In fact, I think this is wholeheartedly the stupidest idea anyone has ever had. But I do trust him.

I wait until Edith and Percival are looking the other way, and then I take off, running as fast as I can, carefully watching the ground in front of me so I don't trip.

Fallon sprints right next to me. Shots fire, but nothing hits me, and Falon doesn't stumble. I take that as a good sign.

Edith shrieks with rage. Magic charges around us, but I continue to run, ready to do the breaking spell again if she tries to claim Fallon.

Even though the sky is bright blue, a loud crack of lightning sounds. The lightning hits a tree in front of us, and a large branch falls into our path.

Fallon and I grasp hands, giving and taking strength from each other as we leap over it. Both of us fall to our knees. We say nothing as we get up, hands still clasped. Then we run faster and faster. My thighs burn, my lungs ache, and my head throbs, but I can't stop.

Death will be a sweet release from life when I am old and frail. I still have a life to live, and I will fight for it. For every moment.

I push harder. Soon, we race down the soft, packed earth of the road that will take us into town. It is a long, winding road, but at least there is nothing for us to trip over.

Another shot fires from behind us. Something flies past my head, and I falter and hit the ground hard enough that I can't draw another breath.

"Katalina! Are you hit?" Fallon asks, concern marring his beautiful face.

"No," I croak.

I get to my feet just as another shot fires, this one tearing into my arm. Fallon roars in anger, holding his ax tightly in his hand.

"It's just a graze," I say, grabbing his arm and pulling him toward the square yet. "Let's go."

He grits his teeth but nods, and we turn and run. Edith and Percival have drawn much closer to us during our brief interlude. Our lead is shrinking by the second.

Finally, the square comes into view. Several people stand around talking, clutching their handkerchiefs to their throats, no doubt speaking in hushed whispers about the horseman appearing in the middle of the day.

"Look," a little kid yells as Fallon and I run into the square.

People stop and stare, and several women scream and run into their homes when they see Fallon holding his ax and recognize him for what he really is.

"They're all going inside," I say to Fallon. "This will not work."

"They are watching. Just because you can't see them doesn't mean they can't see you. Look in the windows. Look at the edges of the building and on the roofs."

Sure enough, he's right. We're surrounded by people. Every single window has a face peeking out. A few people lie on the rooftops, watching us from just over the peaks.

Some watch us from the other sides of walls, darting back into hiding as soon as I glare in their direction.

We have a captive audience.

"Coward," Percival yells, pointing his gun at Fallon.

"Said the man who reeks of the piss running down his leg," Fallon shoots back.

"This ends now." Percival levels the gun and fires again.

But it clicks, completely ineffective.

Fallon doesn't hesitate. He rams Percival through, his blade piercing Percival's gut. Percival falls back a few steps, gripping Fallon's blade. He looks at Edith, who stares back with rage in her eyes.

"Fix this, witch," he demands of Edith. "Heal me, or you will get nothing of Van Brunt's inheritance."

Edith rolls her eyes, and with a twist of her fingers and with no one touching the blade, it moves deeper and thrusts upward, slitting Percival open in a gory display that will haunt my nightmares forever.

My immediate reaction would be to look away, to run from the threat of Edith's power. But I resist the urge and hold my ground.

"End this now, Edith," I warn.

"Or what?" she screams. "You have no power. You cannot stop me. I don't know how the horseman broke from my control, but it doesn't matter. I can reactivate the curse and watch him take your head!"

"No," Fallon yells. "I will no longer be controlled by you or the Chattaway family. My head is my own. You will leave me be. I will not be a slave to you or yours ever again."

"You will do as I command," she fires back. "You will behead Katalina Van Brunt. Then you will kill anyone else who stands between me and my rightful inheritance. I will kill every single man, woman, and child in this town with your hands until I get what is mine.

"You do not understand the sacrifices I have made. Killing Katrina Van Brunt, sending you to kill the notary who tried to say I was not entitled to what should be mine... I killed everyone who stood in my way, and now I will kill this pathetic whore and take what should always have been mine."

She just confessed to witchcraft in front of the whole

town. Fallon killed Percival, but Percival fired first. It was clearly self-defense. Even so, if anyone is really paying attention, they saw Edith. She was the one who pushed the blade in farther.

"I will never kill again." Fallon steps back, crossing his arms over his chest.

Edith screams in fury. Her hair is wild, her eyes bloodshot and crazed.

"You never had a choice," she says with wild laughter.

She chants again, pulling him under her spell, when Fallon yells out to the entire town.

"Kill the witch!"

People peek out of their houses, and some dare to venture out.

"She is the one who commands the horseman," someone else yells. "She is the murderer."

More and more people come out of their houses, and Edith backs away, her face paling.

"No." She gasps and points to me. "It's *her*."

No one hears her. She should know no one believes the girl accused of witchcraft.

She turns to run into the forest, but I reach out and grab her wrist, pulling her close to me.

"I would have given you everything had you told me. Now you will get one last thing of mine. The rope meant to hang me." I reach into her pocket, retrieve my necklace, and push her into the angry crowd.

The people yell or cheer.

Fallon and I stay at the back of the crowd. I don't want to celebrate someone's death. Even if they deserve it. But I need to see it happen. I need to witness it to know it's finally over.

They bring her to the Andre tree. Someone grabs the rope and re-ties the noose while the judge stands before everyone, raising his hands and silencing the crowd.

"Today, we have witnessed the true treachery of witchcraft. This woman has proven beyond the shadow of a doubt that she is a witch. We have seen the magic that she has done with our own eyes. We have heard the confession from her own lips that she controlled the horseman. I decree that on this day, she shall hang by the neck until dead. Then her corpse shall be divided and buried in unmarked graves no less than ten miles apart."

I still think desecration is unnecessary, but I'm not about to raise an argument.

Fallon clears his throat loudly, and the judge stares at him and then me.

His face pinches in contemplation before he adds in a reluctant tone, "As this witch has confessed to the crimes that Mrs. Van Brunt was accused, she has been cleared of all wrongdoings, and her inheritance is to be reinstated."

Relief washes through me. "How did you do that?" I ask.

"I have had many run-ins with that judge as the horseman. Though I would not call him a good man, he did nothing to warrant the kiss of my ax. But he doesn't know why I spared him."

"How do you know that?" I ask.

"Apart from the witch cloaking herself from me, I've known and watched everyone else. I've heard their secrets. I've heard more than once how the judge, after he has had far too many pints, likes to tell people how he and the horseman have a bond. He's seen me watch him and witnessed me leaving him unscathed. He believes we have some kind of connection, and he believes it is why he has been spared. But it is because I know deep within, his heart is true."

I lace my fingers with Fallon's as Edith promises to rise and wreak havoc on all who are in attendance if they do not release her.

"She's bluffing," Fallon calls.

That's enough for the judge, and he pushes her off the table.

I close my eyes. I can't bring myself to watch her die, but I hear the distinct snap of her neck and the cheer of the crowd afterward.

"Is it over?" I ask.

"No," Fallon answers. "She is dead, but the curse isn't broken."

Chapter Thirty-Seven

KAT

"Don't cry, me love." Fallon's voice is so sweet and caring as he wipes the tears from my eyes. "There was never any guarantee that the witch's death would break my curse."

He sounds so bittersweet. He would never admit it out loud, but I know he is disappointed, maybe even heartbroken.

"No, we will break this curse."

I look at the other people gathered at the Andre tree. Most of them stare at the corpse, but a few of them give Fallon and me sidelong glances. None of them are brave enough to get too close to us.

"How?" He looks at me with his sad eyes, and I can tell he doesn't believe me.

I pull at his hand. "Let's go before the judge changes his mind, or worse, decides that the horseman, now that he has his head, can be tried."

He shakes his head. "We can't go to my cottage. Not while there are still people around the Andre tree."

"Let's go to my family estate. I am sure Nana is worried sick. I need to let her know I am okay and see that she is being tended to."

We walk arm in arm from the crowd toward my estate, and the world seems much lighter than it was this morning. The air is clean and crisp, and I can't help but admire the bright golds, reds, and oranges of the leaves still on the trees.

The harvest is only a week away, and this is the time of year that was always busiest for my stepfather. He would shamble about, making sure the workers and their supervisors were getting things done in what he considered a timely fashion. I always thought he got more in the way while trying to aid the workers, but what did I know?

Now that I think about it, I guess all that responsibility is mine.

When we're far enough away from the crowd, Fallon lifts his fingers to his lips and whistles for his horse.

Vengeance immediately appears from around the corner. His eyes no longer glow red, but his coat is the same midnight black. It would be a truly terrifying sight if I didn't know him; he is such a sweet creature.

The horse nuzzles me, and I giggle as I wrap my arms

around his neck and hug him. Fallon helps me climb up, this time not behind him but in front of him.

My chest warms as I rest my back against his chest, his arms around me as we ride at a slow trot to my family estate.

There is still so much that needs to be done that may or may not have been handled in my absence, and I still need to figure out how to break this curse.

Still, for a moment, I enjoy the peace. I watch the forest come to life with birds, chipmunks, and squirrels racing through trees and allow myself to believe this could be my life.

This beautiful, sleepy town and my family estate in all of its grandeur could come to life again with the sounds of laughter and love. Maybe one day, I'll hear the sounds of children playing from within my home. It would be so wonderful now that my stepfather and the horrors that came with him will no longer darken its door.

After we climb down from Vengeance, I run inside to look for Nana.

The house feels different; the very air has an oily, sadistic feel to it. Immediately, I open the windows and call for her.

"What are you doing, love?" Fallon asks.

"Airing out the house. It feels wrong in here. Can you open those windows? As soon as I find Nana and ensure she is okay, we will start trying to break the curse."

"How are you going to do that, witchy?" he asks with a

teasing smile. "Invent a new spell all of your own? Or throw that little one at me repeatedly, hoping it will eventually work?"

"I am going to use this." I pull Edith's book from under my corset. "Then I am going to destroy it. But first, we find Nana, and maybe I should change into my own clothes."

Someone has been here, and they left a mess. Food litters the countertops, piles of dishes teeter in the sink, and... there are markings on my kitchen table. I look them over, but I have no idea what they are for. Some symbols seem familiar, and others are entirely foreign.

Sitting down at the table, I study them closer and take out the Chattaway spell book. It only takes me a moment to locate the spell.

Edith was here. She tried working a spell to steal the appearance of the person who spent the most time here. The markings are in front of my seat. This was where I took my meals and spent a fair amount of time working on my drawings.

"Edith was trying to steal my appearance?" I ask.

"Of course she was, dear. That was the only way that horrid man would marry her," Nana says as Fallon carries her into the kitchen and gently sits her on another chair.

"Nana, are you okay?" I get up to tend to her, but she waves me down.

"Do not trouble yourself. I'm just a bit tired. That spiteful girl has always envied you. Blames you for Brom leaving his bed warmer for my Katrina, though I told her not to marry a man like that. Your mother, even with a child, could have fared better. Anyhow, that girl just showed up, claimed it was all hers now, as if I wasn't still a living, breathing Van Tassel, and then had that louse of hers toss me in the basement like unwanted furniture."

Fallon sets a large glass of water in front of her. "Drink this. I will make you some tea, and then we can see what there is to eat."

Nana smiles up at him and pats his shoulder. Then she turns to look back at me. "You, however, have done a mighty fine job of picking a husband."

My face heats. "He... He's not my husband."

Nana clucks her tongue. "So, he is cursed and not quite dead, but he has his head back. Since you returned, I assume the other one is dead, and he doesn't have to do her evil bidding anymore. You have baggage too."

"Nana, you know who—"

"Of course I know. I have lived here my whole life." She rolls her eyes. "I'm old, not stupid. Maybe you should remember that next time and take my advice. Like right now. I am advising you to marry that one." She points at Fallon. "And for the love of all that is holy, stop talking to dead people in public. It makes the normal people uncomfortable."

"You..."

"Can see them too. Of course, child. I speak to my dear Able every night. And your mother comes around when she isn't chasing you. Brom hasn't been back. He won't be. Not in this house, if I can help it."

Fallon passes me a knowing smile, setting down a plate of sliced apples, cheddar cheese, and biscuits for Nana. "All the Van Tassels were witches, love."

"Why didn't you ever tell me, Nana?"

"To try and protect you, dear. And this family will never practice that kind of witchcraft once you break his curse. I want that thing out of my house." She points to the spell book with an apple slice. "The only magic to be practiced here is for the harvest."

I gape at her.

For the rest of the night, we talk to Nana. She was always watching, and I knew there was so much she never said. I just didn't know she wasn't saying it to protect me.

It feels nice to talk to her like this. Once we break Fallon's curse, I will miss him terribly, but at least I won't be alone.

"Ready?" I ask Fallon after Nana goes to bed.

He gives me a solemn nod.

"I wish we had more time together, but with the curse still looming, and my nana in the house..."

"We should make haste, we don't know if or when the curse will take me again," he finishes my words, and I nod.

"Give me your hand," I say, my voice heavy. I reach for the quill on the counter.

Despite my efforts at keeping my voice steady, it cracks at the last word. This has to happen now. If not, the cycle of the curse to kill me may continue, and he'll never be able to rest. Not fully. I can't bear the thought of him in this torture forever.

I take his proffered hand, flipping it over so his palm faces up and I trace the lines of the sigil into his palm with red ink. The lines must be exact, so I am meticulous.

"Not blood?" he asks.

"No, blood will bind a spell. Red ink, however, can break one—simply because it looks like blood but isn't."

He quirks a brow. "Really?"

"Yes. I draw the symbols as if I am performing it, and the new spell will take the place of the old, but since it's not blood, it won't stick."

"So, you are making me your puppet?" he asks, but his words hold no heat.

"Only if you intend on marrying me." I mean it as a joke, but the air grows thick, and when I glance at him, he's staring at me intensely with his blue eyes. "I didn't mean it."

"Never joke about that," he says.

I refocus on my work and place the last sigil.

He cups my face in his hands, and I pause what I'm doing to stare at him. "You gave me life, witchy. Resurrected me like no other ever has before. Even if it was brief, it has meant the world to me. If I could have it me way, we'd stay up all night in my cottage, where the world is still, eat pie, and recite poems to each other."

A smile tugs at his lips.

I swallow hard. "Do you promise me that's true?"

"How could you ever believe otherwise?" He leans down and plants a soft kiss on my lips.

My chest tightens at what I have to do next. I put one hand under his; the other I hold over his, my middle and index fingers and thumb straight, my ring and pinky bent at the first knuckle.

With a deep breath, I close my eyes. I can't help the tear from falling down my cheek, but he brushes it off with his thumb.

"Me witchy," he whispers, and I open my eyes. "Don't cry for me, love. I will always be with you. You know that, don't you?"

I nod, but I have to do this now before I change my mind. "Rise, man, bathed in blood and battles. Serve me in death, and I shall grant you life. Become my slave, my soldier, my executioner."

The power around me swirls and grows with my words, with my own power—my family power from the Van Tassels. It takes hold and surges energy through me, and I can sense that it's coming from below my feet and out through my body.

When I open my eyes, we stand in a cocoon of black and purple light. Then it dissipates.

The new spell is in place, and the old one, gone.

My chest shudders.

"Katalina," he says, his voice hoarse. "What happened?"

"You are mine now," I say simply with a smile.

His eyes widen as he locks his gaze with me. "You tricked me?"

"I would never, my love. I told you this is what would happen. Wait. Trust me and wait."

"Something's wro—" Fallon grabs his chest, anguish straining his face.

I gasp and take his arms.

"What did you do?" he chokes out.

I straighten my spine and stare down at the spell. "I performed the spell, replacing the curse. But with no blood to bind it, it can't stick…"

Did I do it wrong?

"I—" Fallon's body goes rigid, and his eyes grow wider.

Sucking in a sharp gasp, he collapses. I try to hold him up, but I fall on the floor with him, cupping his face.

"What is happening?" I yell, scrambling to my knees next to him. "What do I do? What do I *do*?"

"Nothing," my mother says, touching my shoulder. "All transitions in life are…difficult. Birth and death are rarely easy. Why would this be any different?"

Tears spill down my cheeks as I realize what she's saying—Fallon is dying again. At least this time his soul will be at rest.

I suppose I knew that would happen. I just didn't expect it to hurt.

I bury my face in my hands and weep harder for the

unfairness of the life he led, the death that was taken from him, and the life we could have had. I let out all the sorrow and pain and stress.

"Me love, do not weep," Fallon whispers. "Please, don't cry."

I close my eyes so I don't have to see him as a ghost, forever walking the world and my life, out of reach.

My shoulders shake uncontrollably as I bend over my stomach.

A warm hand touches my back, but I don't look up. The first thought is that it's mother, but her hands are cold. No one else is here, except for Nana, who is upstairs.

"Open your eyes, witchy."

I gasp then let out a sob. Slowly, I open my eyes.

Fallon kneels in front of me. I squint at him, still not fully understanding.

He grins at me. "You did it, my witch. You broke my curse."

"Fallon? I— I don't understand."

He's not just moving and talking. He's alive. His skin feels warm; once pale, his lips look pink with life. He is alive—actually *alive*! Even his hair has a shiny luster, and a faint rosy blush brightens his cheeks.

He is truly alive.

"Yes, me love. The Dullahan curse will go to someone else, but I am finally free. I have been granted a second life. A real life. With you as my wife. If you'll have me?"

I blink at him, disbelief making me afraid to move, lest I'll wake up.

"Yes." I say the word repeatedly until he seals his lips over mine.

The same soft lips, the same passionate kiss, only warm and full of promises of the future.

Chapter Thirty-Eight

KAT

I HAVE BEEN WAITING for this for months.

Excitement buzzes through me as Fallon and I mount Vengeance, who is now an average horse with a beautiful glossy black coat and soulful chestnut-brown eyes. For the first time since everything happened, we head for the Andre tree.

"I don't know if I will be able to enter," he admits, holding me tighter to his chest.

I love riding like this, my back to his front with his arms around me. I feel safe and protected from the world.

I shrug. "If we can't go in because you and Vengeance are mortal, then we can't go in, and all we have done is spend a morning together on a ride."

"I just don't want you to get your hopes up. I had all

of your family's spell books in that cabin, and I am worried they will be lost forever."

"If they are lost, then Nana and I will simply rewrite them. I can talk to the dead; my mother has a lot of it memorized, and Nana will summon whoever we need. It's fine," I assure him.

If I'm being honest, the books are not the only reason I want to go to the cabin with Fallon. We had lain together every night since our wedding, and every night, he made me feel the most wondrous things, but we had to be quiet with Nana sleeping in the next room.

I want to experience time with my husband where we are free to explore what the other likes outside of the confines of our bed with hushed moans and thick quilts to muffle any sound.

The sex is good, fantastic even, and I do go to sleep satisfied in his arms, but I want more. He gave me a taste of what pleasures of the flesh could be like in more adventurous settings.

I want that rush of adrenaline with my passion. I want the hint of danger and fear. And I know just the place where we can go and be undisturbed. He can make me scream and shake with ecstasy, and I do not have to clamp my hands over my mouth or bury my head in a pillow to silence my cries of pleasure.

When we arrive, the tree seems different. It's still huge and intimidating, and it's still stained with the souls of all who have been hanged here, but it looks lighter some-how... Less cursed.

Vengeance doesn't hesitate. He knows right where the break in the bark is and how to use it to go through the portal, and just like that, we're back in the frozen field.

"I told you there was nothing to worry about," I say.

"That you did, love." Fallon places a kiss on the back of my head as we head for the cabin. "Did you want to get your books and head back? I know Nana would love to see them."

"She will get them soon enough," I say as I dismount. "There are some things I would like to explore here."

"What else could you possibly want to see here?" he asks, following me into the cabin.

There, sitting in the corner, is the wheel. The wheel that brought others so much pain and me so much pleasure.

"The first night you touched me when you stripped me bare and tied me to the wheel... Did you enjoy it?" I ask. "Did you enjoy taking my body, forcing so much plea-sure on me until I was a shaking mess? Controlling what I felt and how?"

Fallon bends his head in shame. "Kat, I am so sorry I ever—"

I cover his mouth with my hand.

"Did you enjoy it?" I ask again. "Having me at your mercy? Did it make your lust stir? Did it make your cock hard?"

My hand is still over his mouth, so he nods, still not meeting my gaze.

"Good. I enjoyed it too."

His eyes snap to mine, and he grabs my wrist, his hold firm but not painful.

"Did you like me tying you up?" His voice drops to a sinister tone, and suddenly I'm transported back to when he was the headless horseman. "Was it that you could not move, or did you like me dominating you?"

"I don't know," I breathe, "but I want you to show me so I can figure it out."

He stares at me for a long moment, his eyes flicking over my face to my mouth, like he's trying to read me.

"Show me the breaking spell," he says.

I demonstrate the move with my fingers.

"Do you need to say the words for it to work?"

"Not anymore," I answer.

"Show me again," he says as he takes a piece of rope from the table and binds my wrists behind my back.

I do the finger movements, thinking the chant in my head, and the rope unravels and falls to the ground.

He nods and then kisses me. "If you say stop, we stop. If you can't speak and can reach me, pinch me, and I will know to stop. Use that spell if I bind you, and you need me to stop you. Is that clear?"

I nod, my smile stretching my lips as excitement bubbles in my gut.

"How badly do you want this?" he asks.

I open my mouth to answer, but he shakes his head.

"Don't tell me. Get on your knees like a good little witchy and show me." His eyes darken as his hand tangles in the hair at the back of my head, and he urges me down to my knees.

A dark thrill pulses through my body, and I know this is precisely what I have been missing.

I lower down to my knees on the cold floor, glad that I chose a dress with a lower neckline so he has a good view of my breasts. He is always so attentive to my breasts when we make love, licking them, suckling them, and even biting them. I sometimes wonder if he would derive pleasure from sliding his cock between them. Perhaps that is something else we can explore on what I hope will be frequent trips to this cabin.

"Well, me witchy? What are you waiting for?" he says, tightening his hand in my hair.

I stare at the outline of his hard cock straining against his trousers, and I bite my lip. His other hand cups his cock, and he tilts his head back with a low moan of pleasure before untying the laces.

"You will learn to use your mouth for more than just your spells. I am going to teach you how to please me. Any time we are in this cabin, you will get on your knees, ready to taste me cock while I decide what I am going to do with you. If you do a good job, I will reward you with pleasures you can only imagine. However, if you are lax in your work, I will tie you to the wheel or put you in the garotte and do whatever I please."

His words have my pussy dripping with my own wetness and aching with need. I know he'll never hurt me. He's giving me a way to communicate how I want to play.

When he takes out his cock, I lean forward and run my tongue from the root to the tip, loving the way he sucks in a breath between his teeth. Every time we make love, he makes it about me, about my pleasure. This is the first time I get to serve him.

I take the tip between my lips and suck gently at first, trying to remember what the maids said about this when they whispered in the pantry, not knowing I was listening. I can't remember specifics, so I act on instinct alone.

I suck gently on the tip, then slide down the shaft, using my tongue to massage the underside of his cock while I hollow my cheeks.

"Good gods," he breathes, pressing on my head a little.

I take that as a sign to do it again, so that's what I do, leaving enough moisture so my lips can slide freely down his shaft until he hits the back of my throat. I suppress a cough.

When I draw back slowly, his chest moves, breathing heavily. Knowing that I am affecting him so spurs me on.

With just a few flicks of my tongue, I can have this strong man completely undone, and that is a rush of power I did not expect. I may be the one on my knees, but he's the one lost to my actions.

I push back down, taking him as far as possible, before moving back. To keep me steady, I place my hands on his thighs as I move my entire body back and forth.

"Stop," Fallon growls, pulling me off of him.

"Did I do it wrong?" I ask, worried I am not pleasing him.

"Wrong?" he asks with his eyes wide.

He kneels down to eye level with me and takes my lips in a hard, claiming kiss.

Pride swells in my chest.

"No, love, that was"—he inhales, his eyes burning with desire—"delicious. But if you think I don't recognize your little tricks and don't see how you are trying to make me come undone, you are mistaken and will be punished severely. Stand and strip."

His voice takes on a harshness that thrills me, but there is a playfulness in his eyes that tells me he is playing a part in a game I will enjoy very much.

I do as I am told, but I take my time. Slowly, I unbuckle my shoes and slide them off, then I remove my thick winter stockings one by one. I pull the few pins from my hair and lay them neatly on the table next to his knives and other instruments of horror.

Fallon takes a seat, his cock still out, his hand stroking it slowly while he watches me.

I take off my dress and neatly lay it over an empty chair, and then I start unlacing my corset. Soon, I am completely bare, my nipples peaked in the cold air.

The fresh, icy air in the cabin caresses my fiery skin. Every time Fallon touches or looks at me the way he is now, a flush of heat runs through me.

I don't need a fire or a blanket. All I need for warmth is my husband's intense gaze while staring at me with a mix of wonder and lust.

"What am I going to do to you, witchy?" He stands before me, reaches between my legs, and swirls his fingers over my clit like he is testing how wet I am, then he clicks his tongue in faux disappointment. "I was going to be nice. I was going to eat your tight little quim until you came and then take you in that bed, soft and lovingly. I was going to treat you like a good girl. But then you had to be bad. You had to suck me like a whore desperate for my seed. Do you know what happens to a bad little witchy?"

I shake my head.

"Whatever I want to happen. Stand in front of the wheel and raise your wrists."

Fallon knows me, and he knows what I need. He knows why I wanted to come here, and he is going to give it to me.

With my heart thundering and a fresh wave of excitement flooding my core, I lift my wrists as I am told. He binds them with the same rope I easily untied earlier, then he secures me to the wheel. Next comes my ankles, and then I am trapped. A few flicks of my fingers, and I will be free, but that would defeat the purpose.

He pushes two fingers inside my pussy, and I can't help

the cry of pleasure that escapes my lips. That is okay; there is no reason to hide anything here. There is no one here to spy on us or give us knowing looks that make us uncomfortable in the morning.

He removes his fingers, paints my lips with my juices, and then kisses me again, his kiss tasting of urgency, need, and the sweet tartness that is me.

When he breaks away from my lips, he pulls the lever on the wheel that lays me at an angle. Then he dives between my legs, sealing his mouth over my sex, and feasts.

He is ravenous the way he devours me, licking and sucking, seeming to be everywhere at once. He circles my clit then slips his tongue deep inside of me. Then he licks back to that little bundle of nerves that drives me mad.

The pressure in my core builds almost instantly, promising to pull me apart at the seams in the most exquisite way, but he doesn't let it happen. He holds me there on the precipice of oblivion and lets me suffer there.

My thighs start shaking. Sweat breaks out over my skin, and I need him to let me come.

"Fallon," I beg.

"No, I told you. I do what I like to my bad little witchy. I will not let you come until I decide it's time." He stands again, his fingers pressing into my clit, giving me just enough pressure that I can't come down, but not enough to send me over again. "I want to hear you say it."

I search my mind, but I don't know what he means. All I know is that I need him.

"I don't know what you want me to say," I cry. "Please."

"I think you know," he growls in my ear. He bites down on my shoulder before moving his lips to my breast. "You, my great, powerful witchy, who can enslave any man she wants. I want to hear who you belong to."

"You." I gasp. "I am yours, body and soul."

"Good girl." He thrusts his cock deep inside me.

My back arches off the wheel, my wrists and ankles still pinned, as he takes me in hard, wild thrusts. My vision whites out as wave after wave of the most intense pleasure I have ever known overcomes me.

My cries of passion and pleasure echo between the walls as he fills me over and over.

"That's right, my witchy. You belong to me. I own your body, your soul, and your heart. The only time you will ever come is on me hand, my mouth, or my cock. I own your pleasure, as you own all of me."

Instead of finishing inside of me, he suddenly pulls out and puts his mouth back on my core. He forces my body to obey and come again and again. Each orgasm feels more intense, more incredible, some of them so close together I can't tell when one ends and the next begins.

It's so much, almost too much. I am about to tell him to stop, that I can't take it anymore, when he stands again and thrusts inside of me, giving me the fullness I was missing. His thrusts are forceful and almost violent, and I love it.

When he finishes inside me, he doesn't say a word. He simply unties me and takes me to his bed, where he tends to my every need. Once he is satisfied that I am clean, comfortable, and the ropes did not chafe my skin, he then holds me to his chest and treats me like the cherished wife I am.

"Did I hurt you?" he asks, worry tinging his words.

"No, that was incredible. I want to do that again. I want to keep coming down here where we can be alone... and do things that we wouldn't want Nana to overhear."

"As often as you like, love. All you ever need to do is give the word."

THANK YOU

Thank you so much for reading *Of Headless Hollows!* I hope you enjoyed this Headless Horseman reimagining as much as I loved writing it. I would be grateful if you could leave a review at the store you bought it from. Reviews mean so much to authors as they help to spread the word about our books.

Watch out for the next dark fantasy standalone of The Van Tassel Witches, coming out soon.

If you would like to receive updates on all my new releases, please join my mailing list at http://killianwolf. com/. You will also get access to my books at a discounted launch price when they first come out, along with an exclusive sneak peek or short story just for you.

GET IN TOUCH!

Come say hi in my Facebook Reader group. In there, every day is Halloween!

facebook.com/groups/killianwolf

Please feel free to get in touch with me.

Website: http://killianwolf.com/

facebook.com/killianwolfauthor

instagram.com/killian_wolf_author

pinterest.com/killianwolf22

goodreads.com/killianwolf

amazon.com/Killian-Wolf/e/B07WHFB8FW

bookbub.com/authors/killian-wolf

tiktok.com/@killian_wolf_author

patreon.com/killianwolfauthor

About the Author

Killian Wolf is a Miami, Florida, native who enjoys pirates, rum, and skulls as much as she loves writing about dark magick and sorcerers. She holds a Bachelor of Arts degree in Cultural Anthropology and Sociology and a Master of Science in Environmental Archaeology and Palaeoeconomy.

Killian writes books about obtaining magickal powers and stepping into other dimensions. She lives in Florida with her husband, a tornado of a cat, and the most timid snake you'd ever meet. When she isn't writing, you might find her at an archaeological dig, rock climbing, or sipping on dark spiced rum while working on a painting.